AMERICAN INDIAN LITERATURE
AND
CRITICAL STUDIES SERIES

Gerald Vizenor, General Editor

Bone
Game

ALSO BY LOUIS OWENS

(with Tom Colonnese) *American Indian Novelists: An Annotated Critical Bibliography* (Baltimore, 1985)
Wolfsong (Albuquerque, 1991)
The Sharpest Sight (Norman, 1992)
Other Destinies: Understanding the American Indian Novel (Norman, 1992)

Bone
Game

A Novel

by

Louis Owens

University of
Oklahoma Press
Norman and London

Library of Congress Cataloging-in-Publication Data

Owens, Louis.
    Bone game : a novel / by Louis Owens.
        p.   cm. — (American Indian literature and critical studies
    series ; v. 10.)
        ISBN 0-8061-2664-7 (alk. paper)
        I. Title. II. Series.
    PS3565.W567B66   1994
    813'.54—dc20   94-13882
                                                              CIP

Bone Game: A Novel is Volume 10 in the AMERICAN INDIAN LITERATURE AND
CRITICAL STUDIES SERIES.

The paper in this book meets the guidelines for permanence and durability
of the Committee on Production Guidelines for Book Longevity of the
Council on Library Resources, Inc. ∞

2   3   4   5   6   7   8   9   10

In memory of Ida Brown, who knew dreams

Bone
Game

October 15, 1812. *Government Surgeon Manuel Quijano, accompanied by six armed men, is dispatched from the presidio in Monterey with orders to exhume the body of Padre Andrés Quintana at the mission of Santa Cruz, La Exaltación de la Santa Cruz. The priest is found to have been murdered, tortured in* pudendis, *and hanged.*

November 1, 1993. *The dismembered body of a young woman begins washing ashore on the beaches of Santa Cruz, California.*

Children. *Neófitos.* *Bestes.* And still it is the same sky, the same night arched like a reed house, the stars of their birth.

One

The redwoods are thick with shadow, and an owl calls somewhere in the high canopy. Down the canyon a stream falls. He dreams the deep curve of the bay, the slant of sky.

Black meets white in a line down the forehead, dividing broad nose, lips, wide chin, thick on the long, ropy hair, black and white even to the knot of hair on top and continuing down, dividing bare chest, arms, groin, one leg white, one black, one foot white, one black where he crouches.

The hands are held outright from flexed elbows, fists tight, eyes dark and unblinking.

Around him the redwoods rise straight and hard to the sky. Arms extended, he beckons with lips and begins, head nodding in time to the song, hands weaving, wavering, hawks in flight, woodpecker dive, gut-pulling on the shadows.

And down the steep coast streams dance and sing, the sweep of god in their unspoiled throat.

It is the bone game.

He awakens and dreams again, crouching there.

"*Bestes.*" The orchard is a reek of shadows and he sees them, the Indians. "*Padre Quintana!*" they call, and twice he turns back, but he comes to them, and they hang him there. "*Gente de razón,*" they mock in his foreign tongue and tuck him into bed and kill him once more. *"Los padres eran muy crueles con los indios."* They dance and whirl and copulate through the night, as he knew they would.

The mountains cup the bay in biblical darkness, and he feels the ghosts of ancient forests. The earth frets and cries in her sleep. White men come and murder the great trees, bleeding them into rich men's homes, and Christ walking on water is not enough, never raising the dead sacrificed for such sins. He feels the burden of his lives, the necessary deaths that stretch behind and before him. Otherwise the earth will shake us from her dreams.

Cole McCurtain awakens in the dark room. The wood-paneled walls catch deeper shadows from the open window, and the owl calls from the redwood just outside. He shoves the blankets back and rolls to his feet with a side-wise tilt, reaching a hand to the small of his back and then moving cautiously to the window. The breeze chills the sweat on his face and shoulders, and he shivers and hugs his naked chest. There are mountain lions in the coast range to the south, but it is only the owl that calls.

The dream has come for six nights, the same confusion of voices. He stands in the window and stares at the black shafts of trees beyond the clearing, trying yet again to see, feeling the faint wind that combs rain down the mountains from the north, fingering its way toward the water. The sharp scent of bay leaves rides the damp air, musty madrone and heavy oak, dried grasses and redwoods. The owl calls from the trees, and then it is there in the window, wings spread, white and covering the night. Stunned by the feathered wind and yellow, frozen eyes, he stumbles backward, hearing the awful hammering, and just as quickly it is gone.

Cuarta de hierro. The words of the priest echo from his dreams. "What have I done to you, children, for which you would kill me?"

The young woman stands beside the road where the university campus dips toward the bay and town. She feels the rain stippling the shoulders of her sweatshirt and lying heavy in her long, pale hair. Her jeans darken with rain, and she sees headlights rise and fall from the hill angling downward. In the one streetlamp she steps forward.

His voice when he speaks is low, without offering.

The rain streaks across the light, and the car's tappets shriek a warning at her. *Run, jump, leap to safety now from the edge of this world, tumble into the sea and go home.* When he stops the car at the edge of town, she levers the door open and rises into the night like a star.

He watches her step to the curb, rainlight catching the long hair. The mountains know, the seabirds cry her fate to the winds. He laughs out loud, and he hears the breakers off Lighthouse Point two miles away telling him that it never stops. Tomorrow he will know her.

Venancio sees the water far below, shifting and black, his hatred a creature that swims in his soul, diving into his own depths like the great ocean. What has awakened me to this death, he wonders. Where are the priests? At the crest of the ridge he feels himself rising to full height, the bear in him reaching to embrace this new life and shatter its bones. The strange Indian lies in his house, fearing the dreams Venancio sends. Down there where *they* live, the one who sacrifices hungers for dreams and puts on paint.

Venancio watches from the trees, sending dreams. Why have they wakened him to such hate? Where is his father's world? He holds forth his hands, wondering who will gamble for a world, the blood of the old priest still fresh and sweet in his nostrils. Why am I alone? *Eran muy crueles.* Heavy-footed and slow, he moves toward the house.

Venancio Asisara! A shout, like a clap of thunder that seemed to shake the house, and then Cole rose to consciousness once more, already on his feet, hearing the name clearly.

7

Flipping the light switch, he looked at the clock beside his bed. Four A.M. Running both hands through his long hair, he released his breath and turned in a slow circle, seeing the black square of the window, the chest with limbs of clothing hanging from half-open drawers, and the bed from which he had stumbled exactly the same way at the same time for six mornings. A stray pellet of rain struck below the hem of his boxer shorts, and he went to the window and pulled it closed, pushing the lock down.

"Some kind of *ishkitini* shit here," he said aloud to the reflecting glass.

He walked through the open door into a hallway and went into the bathroom, feeling for the string from the overhead light. "Now you're talking to yourself in a language you don't fucking understand. And dreaming in Spanish, for god's sake. *Gente de razón? Isht ahollo?*" He felt the redwood forest outside, crowding the small house, and he shivered.

When the light came on, his face glimmered into focus in the stained mirror of the medicine cabinet. He flinched and then leaned curiously toward the image. His hazel, almond-shaped eyes were webbed with red, the pouches beneath soft and grayish. Two days' sparse beard cast a shadow down softening cheeks and an incipient double chin. He reminded himself of a frightened animal looking out of a burrow. A winter face awakened from long sleep, furrowed by a season of rain. Dark brown hair, with a sprinkling of gray, hung in a tangle to his shoulders.

He breathed slowly. The shoulders, arms, and chest still showed the effects of years of weight lifting, but his body was shrunken now. His ribs made shadowy lines beneath his diminished chest, and his stomach looked gaunt and pale, greenish in the sixty-watt light. As it had for weeks, nausea lurked at the edges of all his senses.

"You look like shit," he said to the reflection. "Utter and total shit." Opening the tap, he bent to splash warm water over his face, reaching blindly for the ragged hand towel beside the basin.

8

He walked toward the kitchen. "*Shilombish* or *shilup*," he said tentatively, as if afraid to put too much weight on any syllable. "*Shilup* or *shilombish*? Which is which? Which is witch? *Aholhpokunna*? My words flee like rabbits, Grandmother."

He opened the ice-clogged freezer compartment in the ancient refrigerator and removed a bag of coffee beans. When he pushed down on the grinder, the electric whine made him wince and lift his eyes in supplication to a ceramic buffalo on top of the refrigerator. The dull brown buffalo, with its black, doubting eyes, soothed him like medicine.

"Good morning, Bill." He lit the gas stove and nodded to the bull. He imagined it was one of the extinct woodland bison his ancestors had hunted. He liked to think of those enormous, slow-footed beasts threading Mississippi forests, of Choctaw people coming upon the incongruous animals in small, hidden swales, the sudden encounter and recognition. No spotted buffalo runners there, no eagle-feather headdresses and sweeping range of light; just people who loved trees and shadows and went afoot, at home in a world they had found and claimed with the stories and bones of ancestors. He had tried to imagine his own forerunners there, at that time, a great-great-great grandmother and grandfather standing together in the dark perimeter watching the beasts with love and wonder in their eyes. In a world so different it was beyond imagining.

Abby had made the animal in school years before. Abby, the daughter named for Abiquiu, the beautiful canyon of her conception. Asleep now at this hour in their house twelve hundred miles away, across the Mojave Desert and Grand Canyon, beyond Second Mesa, Chaco Canyon, and Acoma, across the Rio Grande, in the New Mexico mountains. Dreaming snowflakes and luminarias. Dreaming snow on rimrock and granite, piñon and juniper. Coyotes drifting through dim arroyos to enliven her dreams, singing into them, chasing the night-rabbits of her adolescent desires and winking when they caught the scruff of a neck. The

Sandia Mountains just north of the Manzano range, watermelons north of apples. The Spaniards had hungered for more than gold when they got that far north, and the fruits of their appetite were everywhere.

As the coffee began to percolate on the stove, he stared at the blue-black pot, listening to the soothing sound and inhaling the fragrance. He'd had the enamel pot for almost twenty years, and its heavy solidity was a comfort. It had ridden in backpacks and horse packs and had sat on campfires and woodstoves. It had been the catalyst for brooding fights with his wife, Mara, who hated the archaic pot. He loved everything about the battered coffeepot, loved most of all the fact that it was, very simply, a coffeepot and nothing more. He had long ago become aware that the pot was a touchstone to something he feared losing. Within a university, the world was magnified through a petulant lens, reflecting distortions and timid fantasies. An enamel pot, the deep surface scarred and dented by things real, was essential in such a world.

A plate smeared with orange pork and beans sat on the counter beside the stove. A black and red beer can, crushed in the middle, lay next to the plate. He looked at the two items with revulsion. For what seemed like months he had been almost unable to eat, had resorted to forcing canned foods into his mouth, tasting nothing. A stranger had burglarized his life, coming in through an unlatched window to violate and outrage, leaving nothing the same.

He picked up a dirt-brown mug from the counter and rinsed it under the tap. As he poured the coffee, he tried to remember which student had given him the ugly mug he liked so much. In a dozen years of teaching, students had given him mugs, posters, candy, whiskey, books, and flowers. Most often young women, they would sit in his office, leaning forward in their chairs, earnest and eager. He would lean back, conscious of his effort to keep a professorial distance, drawn to their youth and desire. With the unbelievable innocence of children they sought corruption like one of the faddish tattoos they hid away on ankle, breast, and buttock, not able to know that all such images would one day moulder in the earth. The flowers would remain in his office, tilted on top of papers on top of a filing cabinet or on the sheer edge of a clotted bookshelf, growing brown and dropping petals for weeks or months until a custodian became disgusted enough to throw them out. The mugs would sit abandoned in the remote terrain of his desk until, moving papers, he would discover a garden of beautiful molds growing in the dregs of coffee.

He loved and hated the students. They brought lovely feathers, presenting them with wonder because he was Indian, as though his mixed blood allowed them access to certain astonishments of the beautiful world. In their own mirrors, they were the explorers, raiding parties, horse thieves of life, and some of them were mad.

He opened a cabinet and pulled out a fifth of Jack Daniels, admiring the hard rectangularity of the black-labeled bottle. He tipped the bottle long over the cup and inverted the pork-and-bean fork to stir with its handle. Glancing at the buffalo, he shrugged. "I'm half Irish, a little Scotch maybe," he said. "What do you know about Gaelic tradition? You're extinct."

He had taken the first sip of Irish coffee when he heard the footsteps. Even with no other sound at that hour before sunrise, in the absolute quiet of the kitchen and small house, he knew he should not have been able to hear the footsteps, but they were distinct, magnified, just outside the kitchen window, unmistakably not animal.

He set the cup on the counter and in four silent paces was in the bedroom and reaching for the twelve-gauge in the closet. He walked across the little living room toward the front door, pumping a shell into the chamber of the shotgun carefully so that the sound was muted. The curtain on the big window was open, showing a dark rectangle. Keeping his face to the window, he flipped the switch to the outside light and stepped back.

11

The gambler from his dream stood beyond the window, the right half of the naked body painted a dull white, the left half black. The hands were outstretched, palms up and open. In each palm lay an object the size of a marble, one pale and one dark. The eyes, black with anger, locked on his own.

The explosion of the shotgun sucked the air from the little house and sent the large window flying like slivers of rain into the night. He didn't remember closing his eyes, but he was aware of forcing them open. He stood for a moment trying to breathe, and then stepped close to the window and looked out. He pumped another shell and opened the door.

A few minutes later, he was sitting at the oak table in the kitchen, drinking the pungent coffee, watching his hands shake, the warm shotgun leaning against his leg. Cool, damp air, laced with the acrid flavor of gunpowder, flowed into the house through the shattered window, reaching him across the bar separating the two rooms. You move a thousand miles to hide from people, he thought, and you get dreams. What if there was a seventh night, a seventh dream?

Two

From the road to the cabin a straight path, obscured at night. Within the trees the dark is like angled steel, him beneath and within, and no sound when the door opens. From the town to the road is a web of asphalt and gravel, dozens of turns not taken, then soft earth and trees. From the stopping place a hundred yards of quiet road and then

the path. Ascending toward remembered daylight, a dove's

wings whistle, and he pauses, looks up. He doesn't want to go, struggles against this thing. The mother is in the kitchen, the two boys sleeping.

From the road a straight path, ascending toward daylight.

You can even run at night, into the deepest part of the woods, squat naked behind a black waterfall in the blackest creek in the blackest canyon, and the voices will find you. Like Jonah, who couldn't get away even in the belly of the ocean but had to come back and do what he was told. A voice reaches in and yanks you out from that waterfall all naked and wet like you were just born and says now it's time to sing the die song. And you know you have to or the earth. . . . He gave his only begotten son so how can we say we won't give someone, anyone? Without commitment how will she know? Without sacrifice how will she be reborn in the spring? The awful daring of life, and the dreams come to show you how. It can't stop. It never has.

When he dipped the cloth into the stream a fingerling trout darted into the shadows. Water striders dimpled the small, dark pool, and he heard the whisper of waterfalls up and down the narrow canyon. He wiped away the paint, first white and then black, rinsing the cloth in the once-clear pool.

Three

Cole sat at a sticky table in a student-run coffee shop on the Santa Cruz campus, stirring the morning's third cup of coffee. Rap music tattooed its way vaguely from the kitchen behind the sandwich counter. A boy with blond dredlocks stood nearby, talking to a girl with three circular rings in one nostril and a blond crewcut. The boy leaned close and spoke intense words, gesticulating with chapped hands. The girl shook her head in a good representation of amazement and said, "Fuck, man."

There had been no footprints outside the house. Beneath and around the thousand slivers of glass refracting damp morning light, the earth was unmarked. He'd walked into the grass, searching for a swath through the rain-soaked oats, but there was no sign. He'd stopped at the edge of the trees, resting a hand on the slick bark of a madrone and feeling moisture from the grass creep up his pant legs. On the sixth night he had fired a twelve-gauge shotgun at a dream.

"She was chopped up," the blond rastafarian was saying breathlessly. "A cop found her arms on a cliff by Carmel, a guy surfing off the point found one of her hands with two fingers missing, and her head washed up by the yacht harbor."

The girl shook her head and drew back, emphasizing her horror with a round, open mouth. Cole saw a golden ring in the end of her tongue. "She was from campus? Fuck, man." Another ring hung from one eyebrow, and several climbed up each ear like the motherlode itself.

Cole focused on the cup in front of him, wondering what the students were talking about. He felt as if he should know, as though it were something just at the edge of his memory, ready to come into focus. He raised his eyes to look away from the young couple. Along one wall were large photographs of erections, wide-angle closeups of cocks in gleaming black and white. Every couple of weeks the cafe displayed a different art student's senior thesis. He tried to imagine the way such a thesis prospectus would be worded.

A poster on the wall closest to his table advertised a performance piece by a student. "Ricedick," the poster proclaimed. "Selling my Asian body." The poster showed a black-and-white photo of a skinny, naked boy with the genitals whited out. Next to the poster was a university flier warning of mountain lion sightings on campus. "STOP! DO NOT RUN FROM A LION," one of the lines of the flier read, and he imagined hordes of prematurely jaded, be-ringed and illustrated students, genitals whited out, fleeing from leaping yellow cats. Next to the lion warning was another flier advertising an association for students interested in sado-masochism and/or group sex. At a table beneath the fliers, an enormous young man in a military fatigue jacket sat hunched over a newspaper and coffee. As Cole's eyes trailed past, the man looked up and smiled.

He recognized the student from his modernism class—Paul Kantner, the one who sat near the front and seemed to listen intently without ever speaking. Older than most of his classmates by a dozen years or more, Kantner hulked over the room, at least six foot six or seven, putting out a strange animosity with his bright eyes and short, wild red hair. The chairs on either side of him were always empty, as though students suspected he might cast them into the sea.

"Good morning, Professor McCurtain," Kantner said in an oddly soft voice, the smile holding on his broad face and lighting up the pale blue of his eyes.

Cole tried to smile in return as he said "Good morning," but he felt his own face contort painfully in the attempt. Pushing the cup to the center of the small table, he stood up and left the cafe, crossing a small courtyard between dormitories, past a pond swarming with gold and spotted carp where a student in white spread bread crumbs from a saucer. The student wore a white, belted tunic, white turban, white leggings, and white shoes. The flesh of the face and hands was powdered white. As though sowing seeds, the student bent at the waist and raised a long arm in a graceful arc, raining bread on the bloated fish.

Cole climbed two flights of stairs to his office and paused to read a new, alarmingly red paper pinned to the bulletin board beside the door. "When possible," the announcement warned, "girls especially, stay in dorms after midnight with

15

doors locked. If you must be out at night—walk in pairs. DON'T HITCH A RIDE, PLEASE! If you feel you must hitch a ride—do it with a friend, but NOT ALONE. Try to choose cars with University parking decals (A, B, C, or R)."

As he contemplated the absurd ambiguity of the warning—*Don't! But if you must*—a voice from behind said, "This is a dangerous place."

He turned the key in the lock and spoke without looking around. "Hello, Robert."

"Good morning, Doctor McCurtain."

Inside the office, he lowered himself into the wheeled swivel chair and spun slowly to face his teaching assistant, who stood with one foot inside the door.

"Why do you call me that?"

"What?" Malin looked confused, ambushed.

"Never mind." He let out a deep breath. "What's going on here, Robert?"

"I finished the exams." Robert Malin held out a stack of papers like an offering.

Cole studied the young man's tired, thin face with rising sympathy. Malin's shoulder-length brown hair had slipped partly out of its ponytail and hung in loose strands on one side, the large gold ring in one ear showing through. His dark eyes and gaunt cheeks seemed to hold permanent shadows. The face reminded Cole of the faces of Vietnam vets from twenty years before, his own brother's face, and he wondered what this young man could have in common with those others. Malin was an exception on the campus, a serious student who seemed to approach learning with a kind of reverence, like a man back from war and intent on understanding what had sent him there. Cole doubted that the teaching assistant even knew what a stir he caused among the female students. He had watched the turning heads when Robert passed out papers in class, had felt with slight jealousy the mass quickening of pulses that followed the TA's movements in the big lecture hall. Robert's dark, haunted self was what MTV performers tried unsuccess-

16

fully to mimic, and the students must have recognized at once that here was the real thing. He had tried to make a joke of it, saying, "They're creaming their drawers for you, Robert," but Robert had looked at him as though he were both distasteful and at the moment entirely irrelevant.

I am losing my mind, he thought, watching his teaching assistant. Owls attack me and ghosts taint my dreams. I am guilty of sins I cannot fathom, and my life has tumbled like a scree slope. Nightmares paint themselves and seek me out. I teach amidst madness.

"Sit down, Robert. I hope you didn't stay up all night doing these. You look tired." He took the tests and laid them on top of the four-inch clutter of papers covering his desk, noticing two unopened envelopes from the dean's office as he did so. He shoved the pile a few inches toward a filing cabinet at one end of the desk and uncovered part of a computer keyboard he had not seen for weeks. Someday, he thought, a Santa Cruz anthropologist could chart the collapse of his personal microculture by conducting a stratigraphic dig of his desk. *As you can see, coincidental with this October level is a rather obvious decline in the mixedblood's socially acceptable behavioral characteristics. Notice the Mexican beer stains on the unopened envelopes, indicative of low survival quotient, intense liminality, possible homophobia.*

Robert Malin eased into the room and sat in one of the two extra chairs, glancing at the wall of books over his head, shelves of vertical books topped by collapsing layers of horizontal books. "Just a little trouble sleeping last night. I've been having dreams." He looked at Cole as if the words were a code.

"Dreams? What did you mean by *dangerous*, Robert? What's going on?"

The teaching assistant leaned forward, his eyes damp and feverish looking. "Haven't you heard? Several students are missing. Parts of a woman washed up on three different beaches in the last couple of days." After a silence, he added, "It's terrible, isn't it?"

17

Cole studied Robert's face. Was it terrible that a young woman, perhaps one of his students, had been murdered and strewn in pieces upon the sea?

"Beyond terrible." Cole tried to shut out the images, and a picture of his shattered window came to him. "Do you remember your dreams, Robert?"

"Always. I remember each one. Edgar Cayce said that in every man there exists a vast expanse, unfamiliar and unexplored, which sometimes appears in the guise of an angel, other times a monster. This is man's unconscious mind, and the language we call dreams. But I wonder sometimes how we know which is speaking to us, which voice we obey."

"Edgar Cayce?" Cole thought inexplicably of a graffito he'd seen outside the History of Consciousness office the day before: "I am not a *woman*. I am not a *female*. I am a gyno-american."

"They called him the sleeping prophet. He said that the earth speaks to us in dreams."

Cole nodded. "What are we doing today, Robert?"

"Excuse me?"

"In class. What are we doing in class today?"

"We're starting *Black Elk Speaks,* according to your syllabus."

Cole ran his hands through his hair and looked at the bulletin board over his desk. That was where he pinned the pieces of paper that could not possibly be ignored. Invariably, he forgot to look at the board until the papers no longer mattered. Now he saw a powwow schedule for all of northern California, two carefully printed phone numbers with no names attached, and several announcements of campus meetings he hadn't attended. He didn't go to meetings, and he hadn't been to a powwow in two years. Small white phone messages from the college office were scattered like snow over his desk. He wondered fleetingly what it was so many people were trying to tell him. Rubbing the back of his hand across his chin, he realized that once again he had forgotten to shave.

He sighed. "You know why I assigned *Black Elk Speaks*?" Robert shook his head, keeping his eyes fixed on Cole.

"How much do you know about *Black Elk*, Robert?"

"It's my favorite book. I've read it a dozen times. And I've studied Lakota spiritualism. I thought I told you that."

Cole pushed his hair back again, trying to remember how Robert Malin had come to be his teaching assistant. The Literature Board had made the assignment. "That's right, now I remember. *The Good Red Road*. You want to lecture on *Black Elk*?"

Robert's eyes narrowed. "What do you mean?"

"You want to do the lecture?"

"Why?"

"Because it'll be good experience for you, and I'm not feeling too well this morning. I think I'm coming down with something." *Because I shot at a spirit conjured from my dreams. Because of angels and monsters.* Because you will give them the Black Elk they want and need, Robert, the tragic visionary of doom. "You'll dazzle them."

"When?"

"Right now, today."

Robert looked around the room, focusing for a moment on a framed poster of an Indian in sunglasses holding a melting ice-cream cone. The face behind the sunglasses glared defiantly from the wall, daring definition.

Cole tried to smile, to back away from his error as gracefully as possible. "No. That's okay, Robert. I was just joking. Everybody needs time to prepare a lecture. I think I'd better deconstruct *Black Elk*. Yes, it's a terrible thing."

"*Black Elk*?"

"Those young women."

When the teaching assistant was gone, Cole spun in the chair and looked at the framed dust jackets from three of his own books, hanging on the back wall of the little office. The covers, each by a different Indian artist, were beautiful, and he'd been proud of the books. Now they struck him as someone else's words. For the first time in years, in his mind he saw an image of Onatima in Uncle Luther's cabin as she had been when he met her, pulling a paperback from the pocket of her apron and smiling at his youth and helplessness, already ancient and so beautiful the memory made his heart ache. "That's how they make the world," she had said that day, and for twenty years he'd tried to make his own world with words, like they did, always remembering Onatima.

He thought of the old woman, and his father and great uncle the last time he'd been back in Mississippi, just five years ago. The moist air of the Yazoo River had lain heavily upon them all, and the old man, Uncle Luther, had looked about him as though lost in shadow. Now Cole found himself here in this farthest point of the world where something, finally, had sought him out.

He closed and locked the door and sat back down in the chair, giving it a half-twist with his foot. With the toe of a scuffed cowboy boot he pulled a desk drawer open. Inside were a dozen red and black cans of Tecate beer in a loose jumble, a plastic lime, and a pint of Jack Daniels. With a rebate, Tecate was seven bucks a case at the Price Club in Albuquerque. He'd filled half of the pickup bed for the drive to California, prepared for a long season of self-pity.

From the office next door a voice rose through the wall. "I need, I need, I need," the voice shrilled. The words dissolved into sobs, and then another voice came in, a melodious murmuring of obscure sounds, and the sobbing fell until speaking and crying formed a single, barely audible thread. He imagined the heavyset Latina counselor in there, her arms around a frothing student, murmuring those words that were just sound. The student would have her face buried in the counselor's shoulder now, her need neutralized for a moment. Did the counselor ever have the urge to yell back, he wondered, to shake them and scream, "Shut the fuck up"? Did she go home at night and scream at her own mirror, "What about me?"

20   The voices fell silent, and he picked a can from the drawer

and levered the tab open, thinking of the girl they'd found in the sea, imagining a story that could end that way. Somewhere in that story was a moment of shrieking horror so great it struck at his soul. And again, he felt the strange sense of responsibility, a terrible weight. He tipped the bottle and then lifted the can, waiting for the combination to wash away the image of the painted man.

Someone knocked on the door, and he screwed the cap on the bottle and placed bottle and can back in the file drawer, wedging the can upright in a corner with papers and closing the drawer carefully.

"Come in," he shouted, and when the knob turned futilely, he got up and opened the locked door.

Kantner loomed in the doorway, his face seeming to flame.

"I waited until your TA left," Kantner said. "I've wanted to talk with you for a while. Is this an okay time?"

"Come in." Cole sat back down and motioned toward the other chair as he watched Kantner swing the door closed behind him. "What's up?"

Kantner looked at him in silence for a moment, the rainwater eyes depthless and intent. Finally he said, "I wanted to tell you how much your class means to me. You're not like the rest of these professors with their bullshit theory who just talk to hear themselves. You talk about true things."

Cole settled more deeply into his chair. In a student population of ten thousand, there were crazies, students like the white boy/girl at the fish pond or "I need" next door. A modernism class, with all the requisite talk of hanged gods and Christ and human responsibility, tended to fertilize their imaginations. It could be even worse in a Native American literature course, where they imagined themselves reincarnations of Crazy Horse and descendents of Indian princesses. Everyone had a Cherokee great-grandmother, never Paiute or Lummi. On weekends they found a feathered huckster to take their hundred bucks for a sweat ceremony or three hundred for a vision quest, and they returned hungry and dazed with an Indian name like Willow or Redbird. 21

Their lives seemed to open before them like terrifying chasms, and he had learned to just listen. There were white sweat lodges all over the county. Not only students but doctors and lawyers were out there beating on drums and muttering garbled Lakota prayers.

"Most of them talk and talk and don't say anything at all." Kantner's eyes were blue now and gleaming, as if wet with tears.

"I'm glad you like the course," Cole responded at last, thinking of the Jack Daniels and Tecate in the drawer.

"These students take drugs, you know, in the woods."

Cole nodded. He didn't know and preferred not to. Now he imagined all the be-ringed and tattooed students from his courses, the blue-haired girls and skinhead boys out in the woods, their eyes as big and depthless as Kantner's, easy prey for mountain lions. Probably the students were beyond sex by now, evolved into something else their baby-boom parents couldn't begin to fathom.

"They're so young, most of them. They need a teacher like you. But they're arrogant. I watch them when you lecture, and some of them aren't really listening. They pretend to. It makes me so fucking mad, sometimes."

"Did you have any questions about the readings?" Cole asked, longing for the Mexican beer.

"I like the Frost poem about the spider and moth."

"Yes, that's a powerful sonnet." Cole heard his own words as though on stage, the absurdity of them striking him with such force that he almost laughed. He imagined how his own father or Uncle Luther would hear such words. Someday, he knew, the university would find him out, would recognize him as an imposter and have him removed. The ones who really belonged there, by birthright and Yale, would know they'd been correct all along. Indians, even mixedbloods or especially mixedbloods, did not belong. Again he thought of Onatima, and a tremendous homesickness touched him.

"It's really all about communication, isn't it?" Kantner

went on. "I mean it's like that Eliot poem, what if nobody understands you? I do not think that they will sing to me, he says, and he's right. They never do. They never, ever do."

Cole watched Kantner with growing interest. The face up close looked older, and he realized that Paul Kantner was probably closer to his own age than to that of the other students.

"I was in the Army, Special Forces, but all we had was that joke called Nicaragua. At least you had Nam."

Cole shook his head. "My brother had Vietnam. I didn't. I was what you'd call a draft resister."

Kantner stared at him for a few seconds before saying, "I really just wanted to . . ."

The phone rang and Cole reached for it quickly.

"I'm so sorry to disturb you, Doctor McCurtain," a voice cooed, "but this is Vivian Sands calling on behalf of Vice Chancellor Spanner. We have a rather difficult situation at faculty housing, and we wonder if you might assist us."

He tried unsuccessfully to remember this woman or Spanner. "You must have me confused with somebody else," he said at last. "I don't have anything to do with faculty housing."

"It's a situation involving a Native American faculty member. And we thought perhaps you could help us." The woman's voice sounded delicate, and he had an image of an animal stepping through shards of glass.

"You must have me confused with an Indian," he said.

"Please, Doctor McCurtain," she continued. "This is very urgent."

Cole turned to Kantner, hearing relief in his own voice as he spoke. "I'm sorry, but there's some kind of Indian emergency. I have to go."

Four

When he parked his truck at the faculty complex, he saw a crowd gathered near one of the townhouse units. The vice chancellor, flanked by a campus cop, rushed toward Cole as soon as he stepped out of the pickup.

"He can't do this," Spanner said, his voice taut with desperation, and Cole noticed that the thin-shouldered vice chancellor was actually wringing his hands.

"It's a violation of state game laws as well as university regulations. I've told him this, but he won't stop. He just ignores me."

"I said we ought to just haul his ass in." As she spoke, the cop glared at Cole, her mouth a grim line, right hand on the butt of her pistol. Her buzzcut hair was so blond it seemed no color at all, and through the open leather jacket he could see that her breasts strained at the uniform shirt. At the same moment it occurred to him that the women of Santa Cruz were absolutely right. Here he was, in a critical situation, obsessed with the breasts of a campus cop. Even her anger had an erotic edge to it, and he wondered if it was just him, her, both of them, or the whole world. Or had he simply been alone too long?

"I thought you could talk to him," the vice chancellor added, the corners of his mouth twitching.

"Skin to Skin?" Cole turned from the cop to the administrator for a moment before he pushed his way through the two dozen gaping academics, spouses, and pale children.

The field-dressed carcass of a deer hung by its hind feet from an ornamental mulberry tree. A steaming pile of entrails lay on the manicured lawn beneath the two-point buck, and the smell of blood was warm and rich on the sea air. A dark, wiry young man with a long black ponytail, wearing only a black pleated skirt and running shoes with no socks, was skinning the animal, laying the hide off expertly with a large, curved knife.

Cole watched the man with the knife work, admiring the precise skill and trying to remember the last time he'd field dressed a buck. It had been twenty years, and it had been in the coast range to the south on a cold morning with his father.

He stepped close, watching the rapid movements of the knife and the sharp flexing of the skinner's hard muscles. "They seem to be upset," he said.

The young Indian looked up with a quick, gap-toothed grin, and the nearly black eyes, long face, and gaunt cheeks reminded Cole of a laughing predator, a fox or coyote or perhaps a scrawny prairie wolf. "Yes. I've gathered as much," the man said as he pulled the skin down over the deer's head like a sweat shirt and began to cut through the neck. Over his shoulder he said loudly, "One of these women came out screaming, 'He's killed his wife. He's killed his wife.'" Mimicking the words with a falsetto, he glanced up again and grinned the wide grin. "Too bad the liver and heart are on that grass. I wasn't thinking. I should have put a tarp or something down first. They use herbicides and pesticides on the lawn here, so now they're ruined. This place is poisoned."

"They say you can't hunt on campus," Cole explained.

"Oh, I know that." He made a final cut, and the head fell onto the entrails, the pale inside of the hide dropping to cover both. The audience gasped.

He smiled and looked at the carcass. "He's a good one. Probably a hundred and twenty dressed out like this. That wouldn't be much for a mule deer, but it's pretty big for one of these coastal bucks." Dropping the knife, he dipped his cupped hand into the chest cavity, and it came out filled with blood. With an index finger he drew two slashes of blood down each cheek and another across his forehead. Then he made full, bloody handprints on each breast. He looked directly at Cole, and one eye winked. He began to

25

do a shuffling dance around the headless carcass, singing a nasal *"hey-ah-nah, hey-ah-nah,"* over and over until he had completed seven rounds.

"Explain to him that it's against both state and university regulations," the vice chancellor said desperately at Cole's shoulder.

"You look Navajo," Cole said, turning away from Spanner. "Is that a skirt you're wearing?"

"Alex Yazzie. Salt Clan, Born-for-Water. Chinle." He extended a bloody hand and then looked down at the hand and took it back with a shrug. "It's an Evan Picone. You think it's too short, too daring?"

"Cole McCurtain. Choctaw-Cherokee-Irish-Cajun, Mississippi and Oklahoma by way of New Mexico and California. Looks the right length to me."

"They seem a bit nonplussed, don't they?" Alex Yazzie grinned. "This fine animal gave himself to me. I was driving up the hill over there, just going along you know like I always do, when he jumped in front of my truck. I didn't see him till it was too late. Luckily, I had pollen with me. You see, I need some sinew for a special project, and I figured I might as well also make some venison stew, maybe even turn out a little jerky in my townhouse and offer some to my colleagues." He glanced at the crowd and then looked down at the skirt. "Unfortunately, I stained my new skirt. As you can see, however, I had enough foresight to remove my blouse and jacket. Also my heels. You ever tried to field dress a buck in heels?"

Cole admired the dark muscle of the deer, noting the wide purple bruise on the front shoulder. "I doubt you'll be able to make venison stew. They seem pretty upset. It's against the law."

"Against the law is my middle name. Besides, whose law are we talking about? You're the new Indian they hired in literature, a poor mixedblood trapped between worlds and cultures if I can believe my eyes. I thought you'd never get here. Ever had green chile stew made with venison?"

"I should let them haul your ass off to jail," Cole replied. He turned to the campus cop, feeling the Tecate and Jack Daniels spinning in his head. "I guess you heard him explain that the deer committed suicide in front of his truck. He didn't want to waste the meat. We Indians are like that; it's a genetic thing like not stepping on twigs. Can't be helped. But what if we were to donate this carefully dressed venison to a homeless shelter?"

Before the woman could respond, Cole moved close to the vice chancellor and said in a near-whisper, "We have to be very, very careful. By the way he's painted himself, I can tell that this man is a Navajo *heyokah*, a sacred warrior-clown. They're notoriously volatile. You should also be aware that once a Navajo has completed his deer dance, he's bonded with the animal spirit. And Navajos are well-known in the Indian community for becoming insanely violent if separated from their meat once they've bonded. We could have a very politically incorrect situation here, not to mention a dangerous one. The political ramifications could be unpleasant at best for the university and everyone involved; after all, we're dealing with the cultural traditions of an indigenous person of color, a real Indian. However, as I said, there may be a way out. If the meat were given away—in the same spirit that the sacred animal gave itself to him—he *might* be appeased."

"I suppose we could give it to a homeless shelter," the cop said. "That might be okay."

The vice chancellor cleared his throat and spoke softly. "See what he says."

Cole stepped close to the deer, the smell of hide, entrails, and blood powerful and disturbing. He remembered suddenly, in bright detail, his father's face on that fall morning so many years before, and he felt the immensity of his isolation on this spear of land jutting into the sea. Behind the dressed buck, over the roofs of the lower townhouses, the water of the bay glistened, a line of white fog cutting across the far side. To the southeast, the Santa Lucia coast range stood in a black, uneven line.

27

"They say if you give it to a homeless shelter, they won't prosecute."

Yazzie patted a flank of the carcass, his bloody hand smacking loudly, and looked out over the water. "You can tell them the buck stops here." He kept his eyes focused eastward, across the bay, the knife half-raised in his right hand, offering the crowd the dramatic profile of a warrior.

"You'll be charged with a state fish and game violation," Cole said. "That's probably a large fine. And you might lose your job here. You have tenure yet?"

Yazzie sighed and looked around, lowering the knife to his side, his eyes catching Cole's for the first time. "I had a dream," he said. "I have to make seven arrows, and I have to have deer sinew to make them." He held up a bandaged thumb. "I've already cut the shit out of my hands chipping the points. And you're right, I don't have tenure."

Cole nodded. "You could get enough from the legs, couldn't you?"

Yazzie studied the deer for a moment. "It would be tight, but maybe I could. No venison stew, right?"

"Right."

"Okay."

Cole returned to Spanner and the cop, who stood crowding the vice chancellor's elbow. "He has to keep the legs," he said. "It's for ceremonial reasons only an Indian would understand. But he'll let us take the rest."

"Just a goddamned minute," the campus cop said, but the vice chancellor stepped in front of her and spoke to her quickly and quietly, glancing once at the skinning knife still in Yazzie's hand.

"All right. Tell him to take the legs and leave everything else just the way it is," the cop said. "My people will transport the corpse and clean this mess up."

As she spoke, Alex was already sawing at the legs, taking each off at the knee and laying them carefully on the grass. Behind him, Cole heard a woman murmur, "It's okay. He's an Indian."

Gathering the legs under his left arm, Alex stood with the knife in his right hand, staring at Cole. "Come to my house," he said. "We should talk."

Cole looked at the vice chancellor and shrugged before following the young man toward the closest townhouse. Inside, Alex Yazzie laid the deer legs on the kitchen counter and said, "Make yourself at home," before he disappeared up a flight of stairs.

Cole stood in the high-ceilinged living room and read the titles of Indian books in the built-in bookcase. On the walls were powwow posters and a large brownish gray Navajo rug. Next to the rug was a rack with three bows, two old-fashioned recurves and a compound that, with its intricate pulley system, looked like a science-fiction experiment. Also in the rack were a dozen razor-tipped hunting arrows.

"What kind of dance was that?" Cole asked as soon as Yazzie came back down the stairs. "And what was that *hey-ah-nah* stuff?"

Wearing a gold sweat shirt and sweat pants now, Yazzie laughed. "Pure improvisation. I thought I could get that deer dressed out and into my freezer before anyone noticed, but obviously I couldn't. Then when I saw all those people there thinking I was some kind of cross-dressing, primitive savage who couldn't control himself around fresh meat, I figured the best way to save my ass from that cop and still get to keep the buck was to make them think I was a real primitive, crazy Indian. What'd you tell the vice chancellor, anyway?"

"Nothing much. Just that you were a sacred clown who'd bonded with the deer in traditional Navajo fashion and might kill anyone who tried to take it. Why the skirt?"

Alex Yazzie had cocked his head and raised his eyebrows, and again Cole was reminded of a hungry coyote. "Sacred clown? Bonded with his meat?" He grinned widely. "That's very good. I'm jealous.

"You've really been hiding out, haven't you?" Yazzie went on. "Haven't seen you at a single meeting. How about a beer?"

"I don't go to meetings."

Yazzie pulled two Budweisers out of the refrigerator and returned to the table. Twisting the top off one, he handed it to Cole. When he had the second bottle opened, he raised it. "Real men don't drink micro-brewery bullshit. Here's to my new Indian colleague."

Cole raised his bottle, remembering again the morning of hunting twenty years before. He could still smell the wild oats at daybreak, see the oak shadows stepping out of the dark hillside. Hunched in his brother's fatigue jacket, he'd squatted in the tall grain and heard his father breathing. His brother had still been in Nam, and the world that had been all before them was closing in as the sun rose. He had felt it on the chilled air, in the wariness of his father's breath. Within a year he would walk the dry riverbed, seeking his brother's bones, and when the three-point buck drifted out of the tree shadows that morning he rose and sent a bullet through its heart.

"You want to know about the arrows I'm making?"

Cole shook his head.

"No? I guess you might really be an Indian. White people always want to know all the mystical secrets. All the Indian hocus-pocus."

"Excuse me for saying this, Alex, but you seem like a pretty strange mix."

"You mean because you just saw me wearing a skirt to dress out a deer?"

"That's a good point to begin with."

"You have to loosen up your imagination, Cole. Our ancestors used to wear breechcloths. If I did that now, I'd get arrested for indecent exposure. I'll bet some of your ancestors used to wear skirts and call them kilts. All you southeastern Indians are part Irish and Scotch, aren't you?"

"Right. You wouldn't get arrested in Santa Cruz. They'd just think you were a real Indian."

"Okay, not in Santa Cruz, but you know what I mean. We have to keep these white people thinking. Who says we have to wear pants to be men? You think I'm gay, right?"

"The thought crossed my mind."

"Let's just say that I like to keep all options open. Call me a creature of boundless interests." He grinned wolfishly once more.

Cole studied the empty bottle in his hand. "I'd better get back to my office," he said. "I have a couple of classes to teach."

Yazzie looked from his own nearly full bottle to Cole's. "Listen, the only two Indian faculty members on campus should get together. Elvin Bishop is playing at the Catalyst in town tonight. Why don't we go listen to Elvin and swap some stories?"

"The real Elvin Bishop?"

"Yeah."

"He's still alive?"

"Better than ever. And he's not just the king of blues any more; now he's the king of organic farming. Has a place in Lagunitas where he grows vegetables, thirty varieties of brassicas alone."

"Brassicas?"

"Brussels sprouts. Where do you live? I'll come by and pick you up about eight. We have to get there early to get good seats. Unless you'd just like to dance."

Cole considered the invitation. Even with the shower and change of clothes, the smell of blood lingered around Alex Yazzie so pungently that it seemed to come from within. But maybe if they stayed out late enough and got drunk enough, he wouldn't dream. "Who are you going to be?" he said.

Yazzie's mouth stretched in a toothy smile. "Just me."

Cole thought of Elvin Bishop, one of the great bluesmen of the sixties and seventies. "That was a long time ago," he said aloud, more to his beer than to Yazzie. Now the founders of the American Indian Movement were running sweat ceremonies for crystal gazers in Santa Cruz, playing Chingachgook in a Hollywood movie, and singing with an Indian rap group. Leonard Peltier was still in prison in a frame-up, and Elvin Bishop was growing thirty kinds of brussels sprouts. The anniversary of the Wounded Knee massacre had come and gone with the usual heartbreaking pictures of Bigfoot's band frozen in the snow and loaded onto wagons like driftwood. On television he'd watched as a group of Indians made the long Bigfoot Memorial Ride through a chill factor of forty below, glimpses of their stern faces through hats and scarves reminding him of eroded landscapes. On the faces he could see the runoff patterns of booze and drugs and hard lives, the contours of Indian country.

Now his ex-wife and his daughter were in a house in the mountains of New Mexico, at the tangled tail end of the Rockies, with snow piling up on the deck and a scrawny Appaloosa chewing on the corral. The seventies were a long way back. It was a very long road they'd all walked.

"Okay," he said.

"Great. Draw me a map to your place." Yazzie pushed a pen and paper toward him. "Sometime maybe I'll tell you about my dream."

Cole sketched a quick map and rose from the chair.

Yazzie turned the map to study it. "Pick you up at eight, and I won't be late."

"Thanks for the beer. Sometime maybe I'll tell you about my dream."

Outside the townhouse, Cole saw a crowd of children watching as two campus policemen put the deer carcass into the trunk of a patrol car. He looked quickly away. The legless, skinless, and headless deer had resembled a fetus through the clear plastic. Beneath the mulberry tree, grounds keepers had placed the head and other remains in garbage bags and were hosing down the bloody grass. As Cole watched, all signs of the deer vanished.

32

Five

A feather floated on the water. Coyote stood above the flood, on Pico Blanco, and sang his song. Eagle and Hummingbird answered, and together those three made the people. That was the sacred time. Then the ones with crosses came from the south, and the children began to die. Crouched at the window, Venancio heard the priest cry in his sleep and felt ghosts crowding the mission walls. The sun flamed across the sea, lighting the path westward to the Island of the Dead, but the dead were too many, so many that the earth shuddered with her burden. Venancio kept a secret name and learned power in the shadow of the fathers, hearing the bells and singing the bear into blood and bone.

Six

Late that afternoon Cole was in his kitchen, tying grizzly hackle on a number-sixteen Black River mosquito. His head ached, and he squinted through the drugstore glasses. To one side was a small plastic box with a dozen identical flies. It was a dark variation he'd invented for the Black, a beautiful stream that divided the White Mountain Apache and San Carlos Apache reservations in Arizona. Below the Blue River, the Black River flowed through the White Mountains, down toward the yellow sandstone of Cibecue and the Salt

33

River. Every year for ten years, until the last year, he'd sneaked onto the reservations with a couple of friends to fish. His Black River mosquito had big hackle wings, lots of glossy black body with no moose-mane striping, and dark hackle tail.

The whip finish kept slipping. The wings didn't divide right. His fingers and thumbs were too big and blunt and clumsy. A bead of head cement fell into his beer. He dropped a finished fly into his shot glass, where it did a persuasive imitation of a floating insect. "If the river was whiskey and I was a fish, I'd dive to the bottom and I'd eat that fly," he sang as he plucked it out. His hands shook from a solid workday of drinking, the still-vivid blood smell of the field-dressed deer, and the awful drive home.

It had begun as soon as he started the pickup and pulled out of the college parking lot. A grey squirrel had flung itself from a tree under the wheels of the truck. He saw the grey blur and felt the impact before he could react. When he got out, the squirrel was dead. He considered cutting the tail off for fly-tying material but instead laid the animal gently in the grass, running his finger over the soft head and back, and then drove on down the hill. He'd only gotten a few hundred yards when a dark-headed junco fluttered from the side of the road into the truck's grill. In the rearview mirror he saw the tiny fluff of gray and black bounce to the pavement and lie still, the feathers ruffling in the draft of the pickup. In more than twenty-five years of driving, he'd only run over one animal, a ground squirrel that had rushed to its death on the coast highway below Big Sur. Now, in less than two minutes he'd killed another squirrel and a bird.

He'd turned from the campus and started up Empire Grade when a barn owl inexplicably swooped from the canopy of trees over the road, flared its wings, and hit the windshield with a bone-crushing thud. For a moment he'd looked directly into the bird's eyes and he'd thought of the owl from the night before. When he pulled the truck to the side and walked back, the owl was a weightless pile of dead, disheveled feathers, its eyes open and fixed and blood seeping from its cracked beak. A half-mile further, he'd slammed the brakes as a doe and yearling fawn sprang from a poison-oak thicket directly into the path of the truck. The truck had slid on locked wheels, giving the yearling a glancing blow that sent it tumbling. Instantly the small deer was up and clearing the next fence into the trees.

He'd driven the rest of the way slowly, with both hands clenched on the wheel, watching as rabbits tried to dive beneath the truck's wheels, mourning doves tilted like ballerinas at the windshield, and songbirds erupted from thickets toward the grill. Once home, hands shaking, he'd poured a shot of Jack Daniels and opened a beer, deciding to tie flies because it was the only thing he could do almost without thinking.

The Black Elk lecture had been a failure. In trying to free Black Elk from the romantic visions of John Neihardt and the students, he'd confused everything. He could tell the students felt cheated, missing the truth of the beautiful, troubled old man, Nicholas Black Elk, the angry Catholic who had been born on the boundary of one world and survived far into another. He'd cut the class short with a promise to finish *Black Elk Speaks* next time.

The cheap glasses he used for fly tying slipped down the sweaty bridge of his nose, and he pushed them back up. His hand was shaking as he wrapped the shank of a new, barbless hook. "I ought to try a Humpy," he said aloud, "or an Adams Irresistible." He looked at the cover of the fly-tying manual he hadn't opened in months. Inside were photos and detailed instructions for such ephemeral beauties as Carmichael Indispensibles, Royal Wulffs, and Blue Duns. All the lovely whiffs of spun feather and fur so desired by trout.

He stood up, letting the bobbin dangle from the vise, and opened the refrigerator. The motion of the door sent grizzly neck hackle, blue dun, and green-black peacock herl floating across the table. He watched a downy film settle in the half-filled shot glass. At times, he felt that if he could tie a new pattern something substantial and significant would change in his life. Each time in the last months, he'd get out the blue dun, the lovely golden pheasant tippets, the deer and elk hair, moose mane, turkey quill, hare's mask, squirrel's tail, calf's hair, gold wire, and colorful dubbing, spreading it all out in a gossamer storm across the table. But he always ended up tying mosquitos. In his mind he could see them on the dark water of the Black, settling like a shadow on a rippling tail water, could feel the swirl of a rising rainbow or one of the big browns that lurked in the deep green water of weedy cutbanks. He knew them and he knew the river. He would enter the river when the sun rose and he would rise to consciousness again only when the air around him turned gray and it was time to find his way back to camp through the dark pines. At night he would lie in his sleeping bag and feel the current pushing against his legs, see with his eyes closed the curve and sweep of the water into shadowed corners, and hear in his sleep the spurling stream and quiet slap of the riffles.

Taking the beer with him, popping the top as he walked, he left the kitchen and went to the living-room window, stepping through the empty frame to the outside.

The clouds had dispersed and the winter sun lay passed out on the shabby tops of pines and oaks along the western ridge. Red and misshapen, it dripped in slow delirium tremens down the other side to darkness. He squinted at the oddly blurred mass, and after a moment of straining remembered the glasses. When he took them off and slipped them into his pocket, the sun seemed to tighten and sharpen its purpose, slithering quickly out of sight.

He looked around in the half-dark, breathing deeply to take in the cutting scent of bay trees and composting winter grasses, then walked to the white oak at one end of the house and climbed onto a massive limb that dipped almost to the ground. The limb curved, swaybacked, to within six inches of the earth and then rose, forming a seat and backrest, and he folded his legs and leaned back. He bent his neck to look at a crazy pattern of two-by-six boards nailed between limbs fifteen feet above him. Black lines thrown against the lighter form of the tree at this time of evening, in daylight the boards were so weathered that the raised grain patterns stood out almost white. Only three of the little climbing boards that had led up to the tree house remained, rotten and hanging awkwardly from the main trunk. He heard the voices of children in the branches, and it made his heart ache. Where were they now, those brave kids? He felt tears start to form.

When he'd first returned to California the previous summer, he'd made a pilgrimage down the coast in his pickup, cutting over the Santa Lucia range at Nacimiento Summit. He'd parked for a few minutes beneath the big Monterey pines at the top, remembering his father walking into the shadows of the trees twenty years before to cut his hair, mourning Attis, his other son. He remembered the last time he and Attis had climbed down the steep trail below the summit to fish the headwaters of the San Antonio River, the summer before Attis went to Vietnam.

Then he'd started the pickup and driven down into the wild Jolon Valley and south on little back roads through country where they'd hunted deer and quail. The grass had been thick and brown beneath the trees of the foothills, alive with ground squirrels, and meadowlarks had lined the fence posts. Finally, he'd taken the one-lane gravel road that led to their first house in California.

It was still there, tucked far back up a narrow cleft in the coast range, a little white house with flaking paint and slanting foundation, with a bare dirt yard where a half-dozen brown-and-white chickens still scratched. In the hillside behind the house he could see a depression where, when he was seven and Attis nine, they had dug a cave, finding at the bottom two arrowheads of obsidian and flint and a little white stone doll. In thirty-five years, nothing about the house had changed. The canyon was as still as the inside of a kiva. Not even a bird made a sound or mark against the sky. In the big black oak at the edge of the yard, a few rotten boards still suggested the rectangle of the tree fort he'd built with Attis. The thick buckbrush and manzanita through which they'd squirmed with slingshots and beebee guns still rose on both sides of the canyon walls, and the wild oats were tall and golden between the thickets on the hillside.

A deep quiet lay about the house and over the canyon. Though the house was clearly lived in, there was no sign of life except the chickens. He looked at the door, with its familiar torn screen, and felt a mounting terror that he'd see himself or Attis come running out or that his mother, so young then but gone now for more than half his lifetime, would come around the corner with a basket of laundry for the clothesline.

He'd turned the truck around as quietly as he could and driven back on the gravel road. In retrospect, it seemed as though that visit had begun something, put some kind of plot in motion.

He had continued further south to visit his oldest friend, Mundo Morales, finding Mundo on the porch of his big new house outside of La Luz, bouncing a baby on his knee. "Us Moraleses don't waste time making more Moraleses," he'd said with a grin. "Call me grampa." Gloria had appeared from the house, rushing to hug him, as darkly beautiful at forty-four as she'd been at twenty-two. "Did Mundo tell you he's the county sheriff?" she said, and Mundo had passed off his compliments with a grin and a shrug. "Nobody else would take the job."

"That's not true. He won the election. You're staying here tonight, Cole. Don't even bother saying anything. We won't let you go." Gloria had picked up the baby and gone back into the house.

"Things change a little bit here and there," Mundo had said. He'd patted his noticeable belly. "But not too much. I still shoot hoops at noon with the guys at work. Gloria's on the board of supervisors for the North County now." He raised his eyebrows. "Makes all those big political decisions Dan Nemi used to make. She's an environmentalist."

Mundo had glanced around him at the new house, built so that an ancient white oak spread its branches over one side. "This was the Viejo's land, the last little bit of the old grant." In the morning they'd sat long at breakfast, remembering carefully, skirting the things that couldn't be talked about, and then he'd aimed the pickup north again up the Big Sur coastline.

"I'm drunk," Cole said to himself, wiping his mouth with the back of a hand. "And maudlin and tired." The oak he sat in was hundreds of years old. He tried to remember his second lecture of the day. He liked having the classes back to back, the two worlds so close together. He loved the painful sincerity of the modernists, how hard they had tried to find the questions and then answer them. Their poignant attempts to rediscover or replace God attracted him. Like some of the old men and women he'd met on reservations, they knew they had lost something precious and indispensable and they lived in a world bereft and haunted. But they believed that what they'd lost was still there, somewhere, if they could only understand the clues. The solution was just out of reach. His heart went out to them in spite of all their white, racist, empirical superiority.

More conscious than ever of Kantner bulking large in the front row, he had talked about Eliot, beginning as he always did with the obvious. Because it hurts to wake up. And then he'd gone off track and ended up ranting about television, golf, Lazarus unrisen, Christ uncrucified with rings in nose and nipples. The blood-dimmed tide, the ceremony of innocence.

Shortly into that second lecture of the day, watching the pale, credulous faces of his students, he'd realized he was drunk. At one o'clock in the afternoon it was a new personal record. *What are the roots that clutch?* he'd chanted, glancing out the window at a stand of second-growth red-woods. *What branches grow out of this stony rubbish? Death, says Wallace Stevens. Death, says Mister Eliot. Mister Bones, says the man dancing on the brink of the bridge. Red wheelbarrows, says Williams. Rain and white chickens. What does it mean to say God gave his only begotten son, that Christ died for your sins, that Abraham would cut the throat of his child, that Osiris was torn to pieces so that his dick would fertilize the Nile*—had he really said dick? He had, he remembered their nervous grins. *What is the agony in the garden, in stony places, but a promise we make to the god of life? Look, I offer that which is most valuable as proof of my commitment to you. I offer this tobacco, this red cloth, my daughter—Iphigenia—my son—Jesus—my precious lamb so that new life will spring forth. I offer myself, this pain. Pierced and hung from the sacred cross of the Sun Dance tree. These hundred pieces of my flesh. That my people may live. It is our violent and bloody and holy and wonderful insistence that death is not an end but a beginning, that we have a profound and infinite commitment to the continuum we inhabit, that, above all, we accept responsibility for our place on earth.* He'd been shouting. *But the question remains.* His voice fell. *How can we account for the inexorable fact of our death, the death of everything?*

Listen to the words of a Luiseño singer, he'd chanted at them softly, *a California Indian song countless generations old. At the time of death, when I found there was to be death, I was very much surprised. All was failing. My home, I was sad to leave it. I had been looking far, sending my spirit north, south, east, and west, trying to escape from death, but I could find nothing, no way of escape.*

He had been silent for a moment, feeling a growing dizziness. *No way of escape. All was failing. How do we live with that extraordinary fact? We make a song, a poem, a story that comprehends the death of our life and the everlasting life of our spirit. We look to our relations in the cosmos, our relations in the earth. We make a story about the stars. Like the Pueblo dead, we return as rain clouds, the feet of our dead infants dancing the rain to our fields. We dance the Ghost Dance. We know the lonely dead seek us, and we honor life. Ah love, let us be true to one another, we pray, and mother earth is our love.*

He flinched at the memory. There had been a tension in the class, a confused stillness he hadn't felt before. Of course it was the murder and the missing women. What a stupid day for a drunken lecture on death. "They can't fire me," he said aloud to the tree. "I am a full professor with tenure."

"Of course they can't."

He lost his perch, catching himself with his free hand and a foot on the earth. Robert Malin stood two yards away, his hands in the pockets of a blue parka.

"Jesus Christ. What are you doing here?"

Robert took a couple of steps forward. "I like to walk up this way sometimes. There's a trail. Would you like me to show you?"

Cole braced himself against the limb. "Not right now."

"I hope I'm not intruding." Robert's eyes were two circles of shadow, and his hair was pulled back so tightly it seemed to gleam.

Cole sat up, swinging both legs to the ground and balancing the beer on his knee. "I rented this place because I like privacy. But I'm glad to see you, Robert. I'd offer you a beer, but I'm afraid I have to leave in a few minutes. Somebody's coming to pick me up."

"That's all right, Professor. I don't drink. Alcohol interferes with dreams."

Cole looked at the half-empty can. "Something has to. Call me Cole, okay?"

Malin looked toward the forest. "Walking up here, I kept thinking about what they've done to this forest. Sometimes at night it seems like I can hear the earth crying. It must be the sound trees make when the wind bends them, but it seems to begin deep in the ground."

Malin's voice took on a lecturing quality. "Redwoods have a shallow, interlacing root system, you know. They hold each other up. It's like a forest is all really just one tree. **41**

When one is cut, they must all feel the pain. When I walk around in the forest and see all the stumps, it feels to me like these mountains are drenched in death. They built that campus right in the middle of all of it—right on an Ohlone burial site, I've heard. The earth below the campus is limestone, hollow with caves that go for miles and miles. The voices must echo down there."

He reached to break a twig from the tree and snapped it into small pieces. "I don't believe it, of course, but Edgar Cayce and Nostradamus both predicted the great cataclysm. Cayce said, 'When many of the isles of the sea and many of the lands have come under the subjugation of those who fear neither man nor the devil, then shall thy own land see the blood flow, as in those periods when brother fought against brother.' With everything that's happening, it's tempting to think we've arrived at that time, and now we have to act responsibly. We can't hide. Just like Black Elk could not hide from the Thunder Beings, and Jonah couldn't hide even in the belly of a whale. They both tried, remember, and they almost died. Maybe that last earthquake was just a warning."

He tossed the remainder of the twig on the ground and shook his head as though a mosquito were buzzing in his ear. "That sounds crazy, I know. I don't really believe it all, of course."

"Did you walk all the way up here to tell me this, Robert?"

"No. I just went for a walk and found myself here. What'd you think about class today?"

Cole shrugged.

"They felt like you cheated them. That you took away the Black Elk they believed in and gave back nothing in return."

"An Indian giver? Well, the truth isn't always fun," Cole replied, surprised by his own anger. "They like to think Nicholas Black Elk was a one-dimensional holy man, Neihardt's romantic, tragic creation. That's what the whole fucking world wants, isn't it Robert? To see Indians as noble and mystical and, most important of all, impotent and doomed?

42

Then the whites can put on beads and leather and feathers and shed a little tear and be Indians."

Robert nodded. "But these students need something, and their parents haven't given them anything at all. Neihardt's Black Elk lets them think that the world is holy, filled with dreams, not just an empty place we fill with things we possess. Through him the students can believe that the world is alive, not dead, that it speaks to us. They can believe in the voices."

"Next lecture I'll give them back their Black Elk, Robert, but first they have to feel the loss, the sense of betrayal, the realization that words can say what they don't mean and mean what they don't say, that to an Indian every sentence in English may be a broken treaty. First we rescue Nicholas Black Elk from ethnostalgia, Robert, then we try to find him in all those words. All those fucking words, Robert."

"Maybe you could do it the other way around."

Cole drained the last of the beer and crushed the aluminum can in his fist. "Pain first, pleasure second," he said. "You should have done the lecture yourself, Robert. I gave you the opportunity."

Before Robert could answer, they heard the car and turned toward the approaching headlights.

"I have to go," Cole said. "I have promises to keep, and miles to go before I sleep."

Robert turned and began walking toward the line of trees.

Cole watched Robert approach the wall of redwoods and vanish. Then he moved toward the headlights, glancing back over his shoulder at the spot where his teaching assistant had disappeared.

Seven

He stood in the trees, listening, the dark almost complete. I'm in the middle place, he thought. It's just shadows and I'm inside and no one knows.

He lay on his side, imagining the great abyss that ran south and north, saw himself hurtling downward, falling through the earth.

There was a motion in the dark. The figure moved oddly, clumsily, and he peered sideways at it, his temple pressed against the leaves, knowing order would come of it all.

Eight

Alex Yazzie tucked a bra strap back under the shoulder of his black knit dress and pointed a finger at Cole with the hand that held the bottle. On stage a local all-woman blues band played a feminist version of "Backdoor Man," warming up for Elvin Bishop. "I'm a backdoor ma'am," the lead vocalist shrilled.

Cole listened to Alex's softly precise voice blend with the singer's contralto and said, "I thought you Navajos didn't talk very much."

"We just don't talk to outsiders. But already I consider you family. I might adopt you into the tribe. We could have a ceremony for you, give you a real Indian name. Middle-Aged-Man-Afraid-of-His-Students."

Cole looked at a red ceiling light through his Dos Equis bottle. "I already have an Indian name." He thought of Uncle Luther, who had given him his name.

"What is it?" Alex shut one eye and watched him with his head cocked in the posture of a crow or magpie.

Cole looked at the dancers and then back at Alex. He shook his head.

Alex opened both eyes and grinned. "Just testing. Say, remember how great you feel when you come out of a sweat lodge?"

"No, I don't remember. How do you make tits like that?"

Alex looked down. "Nylons. I stuffed nylons in my bra. You like them?"

Cole peeled the label off the beer bottle. "They're perfect. A little uneven, lopsided maybe. Maybe you could use pencil erasers, too. Your dress is resplendent, by the way."

"This old thing?" Alex smiled and glanced back down at his chest. "I saw an ad for prosthetics. I think that's the answer." He looked up. "By the way, I've noticed that you favor blue work shirts and Levi's. I've watched you, you know. You always wear the same thing."

Cole looked down at his shirt. "These shirts used to cost ten bucks at Penney's and now they're thirty-five from L. L. Bean. They're fake work shirts."

"You really should open more than one button at the neck, California style." Alex took a drink and looked out over the dance floor below their balcony table. When he spoke again, his voice was softer, with a sense of distance. "If I don't get tenure, I think I'll move back home, help with the sheep, maybe work for the tribe in Window Rock. I miss the rimrock country, the tall rain. The slim boys in black hats and the girls in turquoise. The way thunderstorms come up in the summer and you can see the sacred mountains. I miss my family, my clan, my horse."

"Bullshit. It's fun to picture you out there with the sheep in your dress, but there's no way in hell you won't get tenure. You'll forget all about frybread and mutton stew.

45

How old are you, thirty? You'll be a famous academic in ten years, the first gay American Indian full professor at Harvard. You'll forget your roots and travel to Paris to lecture about Indians and buy fashionable dresses. You'll be displaced and deracinated, part of the new Native American Lost Generation, the academic Indian diaspora. You'll wear turquoise and silver and have expensive Navajo blankets on your walls. Chiles will give you indigestion."

Alex grinned. "I refuse to be deracinated. I will never stoop so low."

Cole watched a group of women in leather jackets, white tee shirts, and short, spiky hair walk by, sullen and dangerous-looking with their tatoos and rings. "There goes one of my colleagues," he said, nodding at the group. "The one in front. She stole the wife of our most distinguished professor and then dumped her for a male grad student."

Alex shook his head. "Why can't everyone be normal? Is that too much to ask? By the way, I told you I'm not gay, and don't call me bisexual, either. Definitions are a form of oppression, right, Mister Indian? I prefer infinitions to definitions."

Cole took another drink and swirled the remaining beer in the bottle. "Mister Mixedblood to you, and I apologize for deracinating you. What I really want is to just go fishing. Flyfishing on the Black River."

The singer wailed, "What the men don't know, the little girls understand," to hoots and cheers from the mostly female crowd. Cole peeled the label from the bottle and rolled it between thumb and forefinger. The women with short hair had begun dancing, moving awkwardly to the blues tune. One of the dancers began to float, to rise very slowly from the floor. He could see her partner struggling to keep her from floating away, tugging at the elbows of her jacket. The music had turned blue, giving the pale hair and faces a ghostly sheen, and a rivulet of golden liquid had begun to pour from a corner of the room, flooding the dance floor. The women shuffled through the flood, sending ripples toward the watching crowd. Luminescent waves lapped at ankles.

Cole said, "I used to pretend I might go back to live in Mississippi where my father and grandmother and great uncle are. I'd go around saying the names to myself. Yazoo, Bogue Chitto, Bogue Homa, Red Water, Standing Pine, Conehatta, Pearl River—all those wonderful names. But I was just a visitor down there."

Alex watched a tall, hollow-cheeked youth dancing alone beneath the bandstand, eyeing the lesbians with suspicion. "You poor, homeless halfbreed," he said to Cole. "The real lost generation, trapped between worlds. Living your liminal life. If you were a fullblood like me, you wouldn't have this identity crisis. You'd have a card from the BIA telling you exactly who you are, so that whenever a shadow of self-doubt fell over you, you could just pull out your card and be happy again. You said you had a daughter?"

Cole drained the bottle. "My daughter graduated from high school and is living with her mom. She wants to go to college here."

"Here at Santa Cruz? That's great. What's her name?"

"Her name is Abby. And it's not great. I haven't encouraged her."

"Why not? It might be good for both of you if she was here. You have a lean and lonely cast. You need relations. Living alone is unnatural."

"You live alone."

"But not spiritually alone."

Cole shook his head. "There's something wrong with this place. This murder, and those missing women. I've been having dreams."

"You want to tell me about the dreams?"

When Cole remained silent Alex said, "It sounds like you spend too much time alone. Maybe you drink too much."

"You ought to come fishing with me in Arizona, Alex. We could go over in July, after the spring runoff, sneak onto the reservation. You've never seen anything more beautiful." 47

"Why'd you and your wife split up? Women? Men?"

Cole studied the crowd for a moment. "I've tried to figure it out, but I guess I don't know why. It was like everything dried up. We stopped touching, even talking. I tried to blame it on her. We were married fifteen years, and then she went back to school and became a lawyer and everything seemed different. But when I really think about it, I know it started a long time before that. She said I was the one who changed, and maybe she was right. I don't know. There was a point when I just didn't feel anything, nothing at all."

Cole paused and looked for the waitress. "Mara used to always eat ice cream out of the carton, one spoonful after another. Never from a bowl, like that would mean she was committed to eating it or something. It drove me crazy. You know, we tried to get to Wounded Knee during the occupation. Tried to drive there in a sixty-two bug, her pregnant as hell and throwing up all the way. The car blew up in Holbrook, and we came back by Greyhound, Mara throwing up in paper bags all the way home."

"That's a genuine Native American experience, the kind that should bind people for life. Maybe you were jealous when she finished law school. When she had her own life. Do you miss her? Why'd you come out here?"

"They made me one of those offers I couldn't refuse. Every time I said no, they made it better. But that wasn't the real reason either." He spotted the waitress and tried unsuccessfully to get her attention. "I thought Indians didn't pry. Why don't you lecture in drag? You'd be the star of the campus. The University of California's only cross-dressing Navajo." He watched the waitress move between tables a few yards away. "I've been thinking about my older brother. It must be this place. We spent a lot of time together in the coast range south of here when we were growing up, hunting and fishing and backpacking in the coast range. Sometimes I have the feeling he's close, right out there in the trees waiting for me."

48   "Where is he?"

Cole hesitated. "He died in Vietnam," he said, the words awkward.

Alex looked at him curiously, as if he might ask another question. Finally, he said, "I'm sorry. Why'd you really come here, Cole?"

Cole spotted the waitress and signaled, pointing with both hands at the empty bottles. "You ought to see the big rainbows in the Black River. Like this." He held his hands up and a neon trout flopped between them. "You can back-pack in for a week and never even see a human footprint. There are elk all over the place, and bear, wild turkeys, eagles, mountain lions. It's paradise. And those Apaches are your cousins. Maybe we wouldn't have to hide. You could just show your enrollment card." He released the fish, letting it fall to the pool of dancers below, where it flashed a rainbow tail and was gone upstream.

"Or we could just buy a permit from the tribe. Do you think you could trust me out there for a week, Cole, just the two of us?"

"I'm bigger than you. I could kick your ass."

"One thing you could not do to my ass is kick it. Don't let the dress fool you. You're looking at a sixth degree black belt. Had to have something to do during those Harvard winters."

"Black garter belt, maybe." Cole scanned the dancers, recognizing one of his students in a group of four young women swaying arm in arm. The music played across the liquid floor in gold-blue waves, lapping at their thighs. One of them reached down to scoop up a handful and rub it over her hair, where it hung in fluorescent ribbons. A second quickly stripped off her clothes and began flailing in the liquid, her face and breasts luminous. "Christ, I'm drunk," he said. "God knows why I came here." He paused for a long moment. "I took a year's leave from the university there, so I can always go back, at least until the year's up. I guess I just had to get away for a while."

"You're an articulate drunk, Professor McCurtain. But you should talk to somebody about these dreams. One of

49

my uncles is what you might call a medicine man. You could talk to him."

"Why?"

"He knows about dreams."

"What makes you think a Navajo medicine man could help me, or that I even need help?"

"We all need help."

"Thanks, Alex, but all the help I need is a river, a fly rod, and rainbow trout. You ever backpack?"

"That's for white people. We have horses. I guess those Indians down in the South never had horses."

"Are you kidding? Choctaws invented horses—blooded racehorses, thoroughbreds, quarter horses, even Tennessee Walkers and Shetland ponies. It's a little-known fact. The Spanish caught the ones that escaped from us. At first they just ate them, but soon the primitive Spaniards were veritable centaurs in armor. Choctaws even invented those little bitty suckers that were running around during the Paleozoic period. Navajos invented camels."

"The Paleozoic?" Alex grinned, his teeth white and sharp looking, and Cole had a sudden feeling he might be bitten. "I can see little bitty Choctaws riding those little bitty horses. Navajos invented Choctaws."

Cole lifted the bottle. "How come crazy white men want to be Indians?"

Alex took a pull on the bottle and winked. "How come crazy Indians want to be white men? Or women? There's Elvin."

Elvin Bishop stood on the edge of the stage, his face as seamed as redwood bark and his eyes huge and luminous. He looked directly at Cole and grinned. In his overalls and flannel shirt, with his wild, wired hair and gleaming teeth, he looked like a diabolical farmer.

The dance floor was now dry, a desert of blowing sand where the bones of fish lay scattered. The dancers' faces were sunbaked and desolate, and they looked up at Elvin 50 with the expressions of supplicants. Cole noticed that more males had appeared in the Catalyst, a mix of shaved-head students from the campus and long-haired bikers from up the San Lorenzo Valley, cutaway leathers showing a jungle of tattoos. Women and bikers and biker chicks stood in distinct, tense clusters, holding long-necked Budweisers and watching the dance floor and stage.

"They're not going to give me tenure," Alex said. "They don't want an Indian in their department unless he's in a museum, like Ishi. It makes them uncomfortable to have a live Indian around when they want to go dig up Chumash bones."

"Christ, I'm drunk," Cole answered. "Stop whining, Alex, and just publish. That's all they give a shit about. Words in little journals. Of course they're racist, but publish enough and even racists have to give you tenure. Publish enough and you can have the chancellor's wife if you want her."

"You think I ought to publish?" Alex said.

Cole peeled more of the beer label off with his thumbnail and shook his head. "I don't; they do. Have you heard anything about a murder around here, about somebody being cut up?"

Elvin Bishop started yelling words about a beer-drinking woman, with a saxophone ripping behind the song. The dancers began struggling, tripping and falling on the rocky terrain. Alex looked away as though embarrassed. "You didn't read about it?"

When Cole shook his head, Yazzie said, "It was a student from the campus. They think she tried to hitchhike home a few days ago, and they've been finding parts of her body all over the place."

Cole cupped the beer in both hands and watched the dancers belay one another in dangerous pitches.

"You look like you don't feel too well," Alex added.

"There's something going on," Cole replied. "You're an anthropologist, right? And you know California history. You ever hear the phrase '*gente de razón*'?"

Alex studied him for a moment. "Spanish."

51

"I know it's Spanish."

Alex looked down and adjusted one of his breasts with his hand before he spoke. "I definitely need a better breast system. The Spanish who built the missions in California called themselves *gente de razón*. They called the Indians *'bestes.'* Beasts. Because they were pagan. And *neófitos*, children. The Spanish were people of reason, you see, grownups. They gave syphilis to the Indians."

Cole nodded. "And God. Syphilis and God. You ever hear of a Padre Quintana?"

Yazzie looked at him quizzically. "Padre Andrés Quintana? He's somewhat famous around here. He was one of the Franciscans at the old Santa Cruz Mission. In 1812 the Indians killed him when they couldn't take his cruelty anymore. According to the Ohlone people in the mission he was a cruel bastard; he used a whip with wire ends to shred their backs."

Alex grimaced and took a long drink, glancing at the solitary boy on the dance floor before he continued. "*Cuarta de hierro*, they called it, the whip of steel. Imagine that. One of the guys who helped kill him said they tricked the priest into coming to the mission orchard one night and strangled him, then they hung him there by what the Ohlone informant called his *'conycañones.'* I think that means his balls. Ed Castillo, a brilliant Luiseño friend of mine, found the interview and translated it. I'll make a copy for you."

Alex closed his eyes for an instant, and Cole said, "So he got his own medicine?"

There was a commotion, and they turned to see Elvin Bishop climbing off the stage with his guitar. He leaped up the stairs to the balcony where they sat and began to strut and dip between the tables, leaning over men and women alike to grin and shout his lyrics. When he reached their table, he stopped and lifted the guitar before bringing the neck down so that, with an explosive riff, it pointed at Cole's chest. Sweat ran down the singer's forehead and dripped from his chin, and his eyes were huge, swirling pools. In spite of himself Cole drew back. With a wink at Alex, Bishop spun and clambered to the other end of the balcony and down the steps into the wild crowd.

When they could hear again, Alex said, "The Ohlone tried to cover it up by carrying the priest to the mission and tucking him into bed. But he came back to life. In the interview the old guy said, 'So we had to kill him again.' I love that. 'So we had to kill him again.'"

Cole used the beer-soaked napkin under his bottle to wipe his forehead, feeling the electricity of Elvin Bishop's guitar like an arrow in his chest.

"What's gotten you so interested in local history?" Alex asked.

"I came across some references." Cole paused, waiting for his thoughts to clear. "Did you ever hear the name Venancio Asisara?"

"That's one I don't know. Who is he?"

"The name was in my head when I woke up this morning. In fact, it woke me up. I don't know why, but I think he's an Indian from around here, from the old days. You know how dreams are."

Alex watched him curiously. "I know how dreams are. You don't sound drunk."

Cole glanced from the struggling dancers to Alex. "I feel drunk. Lord knows I try."

"The Ohlone don't say the names of the dead, Cole."

"You mean he must have said his own name in my dream, because no one else would have."

"Maybe. Hey, Elvin likes you. I'm jealous again." Alex wagged a finger around his beer bottle. "To say their names can attract them. They're lonely. But I don't have to tell you that, do I?"

"No."

"The Ohlone took it further than any people I know of. They obliterated everything connected to the dead—house, weapons, clothes, even memory. Absolutely nothing was left. It was all too dangerous."

53

"That's not uncommon, except the memory part." Cole held the bottle against his temple.

"It meant there wasn't any history, Cole, no yesterday. There was only sacred time—the time of creation—and today, with nothing in between. And then the Spanish came and taught them history and death in a single moment. Just imagine it. All of their care and precaution meant nothing. In one generation it was over. After ten thousand years, one morning they woke up and the world was unrecognizable. They must have felt like they were the dead and the Spanish were the living."

"Maybe I said his name."

"You have to be careful. There's a reason you heard that name."

Cole put the bottle down and rubbed his temple, which had begun to throb. "Know anybody who fixes windows?"

"Windows?"

"I shot out my front window last night."

"You have some trouble out there?"

"Just an accident."

"I don't know anybody. Coyote come by with a bottle last night?"

Cole shook his head and closed his eyes.

"You're alone too much, Cole. Your daughter would be good company. By the way, I've been thinking about a sweat ceremony. A friend of mine in San Jose, Emil Redbull, said he'd come over to run it. Emil's a Lakota pipe carrier, and he'll do it right. We need a place to build the sweat lodge. How about your house?"

"I don't want Abby here. And no sweat ceremony. I'm just renting the place."

"It wouldn't be much of an intrusion, just some canvas thrown over a few sticks. You told me the guy who owns your house lives in Vermont. He wouldn't even know."

Cole sighed. "When?"

"Next weekend? Emil's coming over then. I told him your place was perfect."

"You can build it behind the house. Just don't drag me into it."

"A sweat would be good for you. You need it. You ever take part in a Native American Church ceremony?"

Nine

At one in the morning, the little house was almost lost in shadows. The living-room lamp he'd left on was the only light visible on the ridge, and the house seemed to clutch itself against the cold.

Cole sat for a moment in Alex's Volvo, dizzy with the long day's drinking, wondering if he'd left the gas heater on so the house would be at least a little warm with the missing window.

"You going to invite me in for a nightcap?"

Cole watched the house as he spoke. "I don't make a practice of inviting strange men in dresses in for nightcaps. It's not the warrior tradition."

When he opened the front door, he felt the sensuous warmth of the overheated house passing across the room like a stream toward the empty window frame. "I've got to get that window fixed," he said.

"It's environmentally unsound not to," Alex responded, "but I like the feeling of hot and cold."

Cole headed for the kitchen. "Beer?" he said over his shoulder.

"Beer for me," Alex answered from the other side of the living room, where he was kneeling to look through a box of tape casettes beside the stereo.

As Cole carried the beers back into the living room, he heard Hank Williams begin to moan about cheatin' hearts.

"Care to dance, Professor?"

Alex shuffled up and lifted one of the cans from Cole's hand, taking a long pull. "I love Hank Williams. Old Hank just breaks my womanly heart."

"I don't dance. I especially don't dance with men." Cole felt his head spin with the music.

"Everybody knows how to two-step." Alex set his beer on the coffee table and put his hand on Cole's shoulder, the other hand cupped around the can in Cole's hand.

"You can lead," Alex said, and they began to dance. Slowly, carefully, they moved about the room, Cole with his eyes closed, hearing Hank sing about tears like falling rain, about sleep that will not come the whole night through. Alex moved with him, light on his feet, quick and graceful, his thighs touching Cole's, his head gradually sinking to rest on Cole's shoulder. Beyond the music Cole imagined the night air stirring the tops of the redwoods, the wide, smooth bay cupped by the mountains, and the vast, open sea.

When the song ended, Cole stepped back. "It's time to go, Alex."

Alex looked at him. "I think I'm in love," he said.

Cole shook his head slowly. "I know. So am I. But she divorced me." He walked to the door and held it open. "Be careful, Alex. It's a dangerous road."

When he couldn't hear the car anymore, Cole went to the bathroom and washed his face with soap and hot water. Slowly and thoroughly, he brushed and flossed his teeth and then drank three glasses of water and swallowed three aspirins for the headache he knew would come like falling rain. In the mirror he looked transparent.

Ten

Padre Quintana! The old priest stops at the orchard's edge, confused by the flames until a club smashes him to the earth. Venancio Asisara, naked, painted, and wearing the hands of a great bear, stands over him. Behind him is Nasarío Galindo, the alcalde. As others run from the darkness to cover him with pain, he sees her, her young face broken in hatred. *Forgive me Father.* He thinks of the time with the girl, young breasts and thighs, the terror of youth on her breath, and the great seas he has crossed. There is a river and sunlight. Taken by force, she has plunged him back to that moment of decision a world of years before when it was she whom he cast off before he could even know. He is swept with wonder at the great depth of his hatred and hers. Like the very seas. *Bestes.* He curses them in broken whispers. *La muerta, para siempre.* They will be swept from the earth, their children damned. The bear rises over him, its poisoned claws distended and blocking the flame of the fire.

The painted gambler stood before the empty window, hands outstretched.

Eleven

At four A.M. the owl called him from the seventh dream. Two hours before daylight, he sat at the kitchen table, his head aching, the shotgun against his leg, and wrote a letter.

At noon, his daughter knocked on the door.

When he opened it, she threw herself at him, pushing him over backwards so that they both landed on the coffee table, which tipped and splashed stale beer on his back.

"Jesus, Dad. What a mess."

Abby gazed around the little living room, her nose wrinkling. He lay on his back looking at her.

"You're drunk."

He sat up, conscious of the fact that he was dressed in a white tee shirt and boxer shorts, that he hadn't shaved in three days, and that the room looked worse than he did.

"I'm not drunk," he said. "I'm soaked. You spilled beer on me. And I've had trouble sleeping. I think you woke me up."

"You think?"

"Well, I don't remember what I was doing before you knocked me down. Maybe I was drunk, but I'm not now."

"I don't care if you are drunk. It's wonderful to see you." She threw herself on him again, hugging his head to her breasts.

"It's wonderful to see you, too, and I'm not drunk."

She pulled back and smiled, her green eyes shining. She wore her brown hair in a thick braid over a blue tee shirt and halfway to the waistband of her jeans. Her face still held the New Mexico sun, with a sprinkling of freckles. When the smile vanished, her serious mouth was pursed at the corners, as if prepared to utter hard truth.

"You're drunk as a skunk," she said as she stood up.

"Watch those boots." He nodded toward her cowboy boots. "They're dangerous. Why didn't you tell me you were coming?"

She smiled again. "I wanted to surprise you. I made Mom swear she wouldn't tell you. Go take a shower, shave, and get dressed."

He climbed stiffly to his feet. "You're giving orders like your mom."

"Because I love you. Hurry up—I'm starved. I'll fix us lunch."

"Well, I don't know. I haven't . . ."

"Take a shower. You look bad and smell worse." She shoved him toward the back of the house and turned to the kitchen.

Halfway through the bedroom door, he called out, "I don't have a shower. Watch out for that fly-tying equipment. That's expensive stuff, and there are number twenty hooks in that mess. I don't want to eat one of those."

Twenty minutes later he was at the table, scrubbed, shaven, dressed in wool socks, jeans, and a brown flannel shirt. Hot coffee, poached eggs, and toast sat in front of him, and he looked in surprise at the careful arrangement of materials in the fly box, each hackle and hair laid in precise organization.

"You're only tying mosquitos? There must be twenty there." She slid two eggs onto a second plate and sat down. "That's the pattern we used on the Chama. It was the only one you brought, and it didn't work, remember? Why don't you tie something more exciting?"

"There was some kind of hatch that day, stone fly or some damned thing. That's why they wouldn't hit mosquitoes. Besides, this isn't a standard mosquito; it's a variant I invented. I didn't know I had eggs in the refrigerator." He thought of the first time he'd taken her backpacking. It had been in the Pecos Wilderness. Five years old, she'd huddled next to the fire lost in his huge parka and wool hat, flakes of snow settling on her bent shoulders. More than a dozen years later, it was still the finest, purest, most splendid moment of his life, an awakening to love so immense it was like drowning.

She dipped a piece of toast into her coffee. "God only knows how old those eggs are. I hope we don't die of salmonella. I went up to the San Juan by myself this fall. The fishing was incredible." She glanced at the plastic box of dark flies. "I bought a new nine-foot graphite rod and new line. They're great. It's a kind of lime-green floating line with a slick shooting finish. I got to be pretty good at tying number twenty midges. That's the only thing they would hit." She nodded toward the gun leaning against the wall by the refrigerator. "I had to move the shotgun. Have you started hunting?"

He watched her closely, wondering what the weirdly rushed speech was for. "I usually keep it in my closet. I was just cleaning it." He rose and took the gun into the bedroom. "Big ones?"

She was ready when he sat back down. "All twenty inches or better. I want to study environmental science, and UCSC is a great place for it." She rushed on, as if delivering prepared lines. "I came now so that I can establish residency. It was too late to apply for next fall, so I'll have a whole extra year before I start. I figure I can sit in on some classes in the meantime." She broke a piece from the toast and dipped it in the egg yolk.

He listened, his cup halfway to his mouth, until she was finished. "I wish you had asked me first. The University of California is falling apart. The budget's destroyed. Everybody's leaving."

"I know you didn't want me to go to school here. You made that pretty clear, Dad. But I'm old enough to decide for myself. " She looked down at her plate. "If you don't want me to live here, it's okay. I understand. I can get my own place." Her voice thinned toward tears, and he thought of his wife, his former wife. So many of their words had ended that way. In his daughter's face, he saw Mara's.

60

When she looked back up, her eyes were shining, and her mouth was set in a firm line. "But I am going to school here."

He set the cup down and reached for her hands, holding both in his own. "I do want you here. I've missed you more than I can say. It's just that I worry."

He felt the way he had felt looking up at the ruins of the tree house. Children's voices haunted the edges of his thoughts, filtered through reaches of time.

She squeezed his hands. "You've always worried too much. You're like Garp; you always imagine every terrible thing that could possibly happen. You see undertoads everywhere."

He half smiled. "I can't believe your mother let you go."

"As I said, I can make my own decisions now. Mom knows that. Besides, she's really busy."

He studied her face, wondering what it was she wasn't telling him. Finally he said, "There are two bedrooms, but only one bathroom. No shower, just an old clawfoot tub."

"I love tubs, especially clawfoot tubs."

The relief in her voice made him feel like crying in return. "We're in the seventh year of a drought," he said. "That means only two baths a week."

"I love droughts. What's a clawfoot tub?"

"It has feet like claws. What did your mother say?"

She released his hands and lifted the cup. "She's thinking of selling the house and moving to Albuquerque."

He frowned. The house on the east side of the Sandia Mountains had been their dream home. Large, with a whole wall of glass looking across at the crest, five acres with a horse barn and corral bordering a national forest. At night, and sometimes even in daylight, the coyotes would surround the house and sing, and he'd go out onto the deck and sing back, yodeling at the stars or snow or moon. He'd turned the tack room in the barn into his office and written three books while the snow piled up on the roof and the wood stove glowed. In the morning he lifted weights, and every afternoon he ran for miles on the soft trails that

61

flowed through the juniper and piñon pine. In the winter, the three of them had skied right off the deck and out into the fragrant hills.

He'd left for California just after Christmas, rising before daylight to walk the five acres a last time. Through the windows, he could see that new snow had fallen during the night and lay in a thin coating on the gray branches of the junipers and pines and outcroppings of red rock. When he'd opened the door, he'd found a jackrabbit laid across the mat. He'd knelt and touched the thick fur, and his heart was pierced. The rabbit was still warm, and in the new snow around it were coyote tracks. In the dead of winter in a land of rock, withered trees, and scarce game, the rabbit represented an enormous, inconceivable offering.

"I guess it makes sense."

He could see his daughter thinking, deciding what information to parcel out, and again he saw her mother. "She's probably moving in with somebody."

He felt his heart contract and stay locked, like a pulled hamstring.

"He's a lawyer. He moved to Albuquerque from New York right after you left."

He nodded again.

"She asked me to remind you that you get half the profit if she sells the house, and the real-estate agent thinks it'll be a lot. She thought you'd probably forget."

"Has she put it on the market yet?"

"She can't do it unless you agree." She gave him a significant look. "It's still half yours. If you didn't want her to sell it, she couldn't." She studied him for a moment. "She told me she misses you, but that both of you had changed too much." She toyed with her cup, swirling the creamy coffee, and then said, "Someone named Rita called several times. She wanted your phone number."

"What'd you tell her?"

She shrugged. "I didn't talk to her. She just left messages on the answering machine."

"Who's taking care of Sage?"

"I left her with Christie, the girl who used to feed her when we were gone. She loves horses."

"Where's your stuff?"

"I forgot! I had the cabdriver pile it outside." She stood up and went to the front door, and he followed.

Two large suitcases and an aluminum flyrod tube lay in the gravel in front of the steps.

"I didn't bring much. I shipped some books. Mom's shipping a little more and storing the rest for me. What happened to your window?"

He looked at the empty frame and a feeling of urgency touched him, as though something important were about to happen. "An accident," he said. "Somebody's coming to fix it tomorrow."

"I hope it doesn't rain."

"We need the rain."

He helped her carry the suitcases and pile them in the spare bedroom.

"I saw an envelope on the table addressed to Grampa, Uncle Luther, and Onatima," she said, the statement ending with a question.

"You remember Uncle Luther and Onatima very well?"

"Of course. I was fourteen when we went down there last time."

He sat beside her on the edge of the bed, his hands clasped between his knees. "I forgot. There's a little creek here a mile or so north along the ridge. They say it has native rainbows. We could try it."

She put her arm around his back and leaned against his shoulder. "That would be nice," she said. "It would be wonderful. I could show you how to tie midges."

"I know how to tie midges."

Twelve

At night he walks beyond the mission walls, and the earth pulls at him, drawing his seed. A place irredeemably strange, beyond touch. He kneels at the stream, bringing the sweet water to his lips. He goes down to the sea, thinking of the girl. Where the surf swells toward shore a wake appears, a fin hissing from dark to dark. He drops his robe and wades toward the monster, his cut flesh burning with salt and the surge of the sea at his scrotum. The waves throw him back, and he lies curled on the sand like a white blossom, the cold night closing upon thin bones. She is there now in his thoughts, and Venancio.

He is lost in this new world. Out of his ancient home and up from Mexico he had soared, his robe spread like wings to save their souls, and now lustful for their world. Calls them *neófitos*, children, innocents, and knows all the while that their self-knowledge lies beyond his touch, that they are corrupt beyond measure and reach. He is outraged, horrified by their concupiscence, and desires them with a pain that drives him into the sea. Desires everything in this new world, the earth itself.

Father Quintana watches from the window, across five feet of adobe. Wind from the bay brings salt to his blue-white eyes, and he thinks of the time in Barcelona with the gypsies. *Forgive me, Father, for I. . . .* Father, Venancio has slain one of the great bears and boasts of his feat to the other neophytes, showing the necklace of claws and clawing the air. Venancio has dreamed and possesses bear medicine now, Father, and he casts his eye upon one of the young ones who walks out to wash cloth. Venancio Asisara, who would hunt in the old way despite the law, who shouts each dawn to wake the sun, his brute voice ringing over the mission.

Chin resting on the heavy adobe, the old priest watches, the wine in his hand forgotten. They worship the sun and would copulate in the open air. The flame of excrescence flickers in their dark souls.

The girl has small breasts and narrow waist. See how her eyes shine when she comes from the dark *monjerio,* how she smiles at the sky? Where she kneels to scrape cloth on stone, her small buttocks are like a boy's, her hair hanging down beside her face. Animal, *bestia,* she is lustful and bare-legged in the sun and sweating and whispering to the other women. His sackcloth woven with bristles and broken wire purifies his spirit beneath his robe. He will bear the heavy cross through fourteen stations. He will flagellate himself. He will sear his flesh with the four-pronged candle. He will hear her confession in the private room.

Venancio at the stone wall.

Like a great bear he rises on two legs and lusts after the girl, would take her there while the priest watches. He is confirmed, yet Nasarío Galindo, the alcalde, whispers that Venancio has a secret name, that he has dreamed of Raven, that he goes into the mountains by night and puts on paint, that he eats the witch's weed, *toloache,* and places feathered sticks in the earth. He encourages the *cimmarones,* the wild ones who run away. He is sly and has power among the neophytes, who believe he brings the rain, the thunder, that he makes the earth quake and becomes the great bear of his dreams. That he cannot die.

Venancio paints himself and gambles with the neophytes who have nothing to gamble, crouching by night in the forest beyond the mission walls, moving the bones with songs they cannot fathom. Venancio becomes the bear. His great shadow rears over the valley, its darkness cast upon the waters of the bay.

And tied to the oak tree Venancio will not cry out under twenty lashes for his lust, nor twenty for his crimes, confes-

65

sing nothing, his skin curled like the bloody bark from the madrone under the wire whip. Venancio will murder the old priest, crush his testicles and make him weep, will tell the story to Lorenzo, his green-eyed son from Manuela not yet born but fated to be set free when the missions die. Venancio will never die, will wander between worlds, his hate too strong for death, the violence of his people's life taken by the invaders become a mark upon the very earth. Venancio will inhabit the earth.

The old priest bends with the curl and flash of the whip, scourging the bestial land while gulls wheel and shrill, and he sees the small breasts, the smooth brown flesh, the death that awaits them all. *Espíritu Santu*, he thinks, the Indian will not cry for his flesh. The *esquilas*, the joyous bells, sing the death of another infant across the courtyard, an angel in heaven, and the great black cat prowls beyond the window, its scream like that of a woman in distress. His brother comes to him with hands outstretched—a lightning-struck obsidian point in his palm. The waves rear back and hurl bodies from the sea—heads, hands, arms, and legs—and the painted gambler beckons from beyond the adobe wall, hands outstretched, a severed head in each palm.

The girl bends beneath him like a willow branch, supple with terror.

Bestes.

I am dreaming, he warns himself, about to speak his brother's name.

Thirteen

The tall old man stood at the edge of the woods. Weeds had grown up around the silver trailer and vines climbed the sides and across the top, encircling the vent pipes and television antenna and reaching down to pry between window screens and glass. Underneath, where the trailer sat on cement blocks, a small tree had started and grown parallel to the earth for several feet until it could bend with the curve of the aluminum sides and lift itself vertically toward the sunlight. Behind the trailer, the chicken house and run had begun to fall into the weeds, the wire bowing beneath a weight of luxuriant vegetation.

A black, wide-brimmed hat dropped a shadow over the old man's face, so that the bones of his cheeks and forehead and the wide nostrils and thin mouth were planes of darkness. When he stepped fully into the clearing, the afternoon light caught up the white of his long, straight hair and shone dully on the red mackinaw and pale blue overalls.

He followed a faint path through the weeds to the door of the trailer, where the vines had been cut away. Without hesitation, he opened the door and stepped through.

Inside, the little trailer was cool and dark, everything coated with a fine dust. Pale green tendrils curled delicately through invisible cracks around the windows, and spider webs laced the corners and spread across the books that lined shelves below one window.

The old man removed his hat and sat in one of two straight-backed chairs at the little kitchen table. A shiny black spider paused in its journey across the tabletop, and the old man used his hat brim to hurry the creature to the far side.

"Go on home," he said, adding, "It's me, old lady."

Onatima imagines the clouds. They are billowy, blue-white and hard-surfaced, tall, piled one on top of another, lovely. They pass slowly, with a depth found in dreams.

She has been thinking of Cole, and the dreams they have both dreamt. But the clouds have sent her thoughts back to another lifetime.

She had walked out the front door while her father slept and her mother read a bible in the next room. In the kitchen Nancy had clattered supper pots, and the new man from the stables had sung a fine, monotonous song as he puttered in the side yard. The sun lay close to the earth and lined every action in a hot light, and he was there beneath the pecan tree, the reins held easily and his white hat low over his eyes. She hadn't even hurried, walking carefully down the raked path through the shrill of cicadas to the gate and out, feeling the stableboy's eyes on her back, aiming the will of her life with certain clarity. When he stepped down to help her, she pushed his hand aside and rose freely to the seat, her eyes laughing at him. His face was dark, darker than her own, his slanting eyes black and his moustache fine and drooping at the corners of his mouth. From his Choctaw mother he had cheekbones and eyes like hers, from his unknown white father an abiding anger that sharpened his senses and caused him to move with speed and precision so that when her father walked into the room in New Orleans exactly one week later he already had his gun in his hand beneath the coverlet and still, after almost three quarters of a century, she nearly hated him for letting the old man take her back as though he'd known her father would follow them easily downriver to the hotel and walk through the door at that moment and there wasn't a thing he could do about it. Keeping the pistol hidden, watching the old Choctaw man's shotgun and watching as she dressed and went away, with an ironic smile that would stay with her after seven decades as the single moment of her youth.

That had been her love, the one thrust of her life that her fullblood father had simply stopped, and as they returned by boat and carriage she looked not at him or even the thick woods but at the wonder of her self in her lover's arms. She had marveled at what men thought to be her beauty, looking in the mirror and wondering what there was about a particular quality of face, or eyes, or hair that could be called beautiful. In the mirror she saw still a reflection of someone who could outrun and outclimb most of the boys and sit a horse better than most of the men, strong shoulders and long, serviceable legs. It was, she had decided then, only the reflection of themselves in a woman's eyes that men called beauty. And when he took her to the country church a week later, a woman ruined, and made her marry Old Man Blue Wood, she looked still at neither of them but at the coil of memory in which she and her lover, two halfbreed gamblers of different games, twined their dark bodies again and again. Her white mother's loud anger and struggle to save her from the father had meant nothing because that had already been discarded and she knew with certainty what lay ahead over all the years of her life.

When the old man took her to the cabin across the river and beat her because she had been a younger man's prize, she looked away toward the slow water. It was only when she knew she would not survive the bitter and frightened beatings of the old man that she acted. And after that she lived alone in the old man's cabin, knowing through dreams when her mother died and her father drank all his land and horses away to the whites. When the crowfooted lawyer came across in a rowboat she already knew of her father's death, and she signed the papers and each month afterwards withdrew a few dollars from the bank in Vicksburg. Each night she brushed the length of her uncut hair and remembered the halfbreed gambler, knowing without bitterness finally what her gambler had understood all along.

In the little cabin she had let the dreams come to her night after night and sometimes even in a humid noonday and studied their meanings. She sought out the old women who lived alone, picking the frightened flesh from others' dreams, 69 learning to follow trails no one saw and listening to voices no one heard. And when she could know dreams, she began going again to the library in Vicksburg with a tote sack for books. And one day bought an Airstream trailer ferried across the muddy river, had electric wires run for reading lamps and appliances, and waited for the knock of the old man, Luther Cole. After thirty years, Luther was her second lover, and now he sat before her at the little table in her trailer, shaking his head.

"It ain't going to be easy getting there," he said, his long, carefully parted white hair moving with each shake of the bony head. "And it ain't going to be easy to fix. This is the boy's story." He lifted the hat from the table and hung it on the post of the chair. Around him, the interior of the Airstream was heavy with time that seemed to circle in the still air.

She sat across from him, radiant in the dim light, her silver hair shining and her filmy brown eyes wrinkled with laughter.

"Cole McCurtain isn't a boy any longer, Luther. He's a man with a grown daughter, and he needs our help. I think both of us had better be there when the time comes."

"This thing is big, old lady. Cole's story is just a little bit of it. It's different this time. Like you just said, he's a grown man and he's got to work through the changes. Besides, he's already got some powerful help out there."

Onatima's smile changed to a glare, her mouth fixed tightly in her taut face. A thin, almost transluscent hand reached for the braid of silver hair that hung over her shoulder and toyed with the red yarn at the end. Fingering the braid, she said, "What about last winter? He would have hit that tree." She looked away, her eyes traveling over the details of the little room, as though memorizing her home. When she looked back, her expression was focused inwardly. "I dreamt of a painted man in a clearing between tall trees, his body half black and half white."

Luther nodded. "It's that bone game. He's come back to gamble for his world. It started with Cole and those painted ones last winter." He glanced around the old trailer. "Your home is getting unnaturally dusty, Miz Blue Wood. Maybe I ought to trim some of them vines back."

"I like my little place just as it is, Luther Cole. These woods have a right to me and this trailer both. But since you know everything, you'd better get out there to California. No one can do these things alone; everybody needs help."

"It's one thing to know the story and another one to change it, old lady."

"Nonsense. You've already changed it when you helped last winter. You have a responsibility. It's going to take a long time to get there in that old truck, so you and Hoey had better start tomorrow morning. I'll go on ahead of you."

He watched, saying nothing. After a moment she reached across and laid a hand on his, and he felt a chill move up his arm and was struck with a profound loneliness.

He lifted a handful of his long hair and held it toward her. "Look at this white hair. We've done growed old together, Miz Blue Wood. I can almost see plumb through you now."

She raised his hand to her cold lips and leveled a steady gaze at him through clouded eyes. "I always could see through you, Luther Cole. Now I'm going to meet this gambler, all right, but you're the one that's full alive, Luther. So you have to go."

He let out a long, slow breath. "Ain't neither one of us full dead yet, neither. Being halfway to a ghost sure ain't made you no less stubborn." His fingers followed the thin outline of her cheek. "I ought to just move in here. Hoey could stay in my house."

She shook her head. "I always lived my own life, Luther Cole, and I don't plan to stop now. Besides, that will come in God's own time."

"You know what's going to happen, Onatima, good as I do. It'll most all be done by the time we get there. That whole

71

other part of the story's going on, and me and Hoey'll be right in the middle of it. Witches is just lousy out there."

The thin old lady arched her eyebrows and pursed her lips. "Witches," she said. "Don't be absurd."

He leaned back in his chair and said, "What in the world are you up to, Onatima Blue Wood? What in tarnation?"

Fourteen

Cusp of evening, and the sun caught in a red web on the sea's horizon. A drunken Indian, the sun thinks about yesterday and sleep, no investment in tomorrow. Its track across the sea another trail of poison, *chook-fa-hithla bogue*, the dancing rabbit.

Granite gnaws his back. On one side the Pacific Ocean, on the other the great bowl of Monterey Bay where points of white dip and skate. First they sail the Atlantic with bloody teeth, he thinks, the deaths of ten million in their invader's imagination, and then they pile their loot on little boats and let the wind drive them in circles upon the bay.

Cole lifted the pint, holding it against the dying sun, admiring amber light before he drank. His rented house lay on a lap of the ridge a half mile below, run to ground by the forest on three sides. Below that the coastal spine fell quickly to the shelf of the town five miles further down where the bay made a nearly full circle of darkening beach. The lights of the town shown brightly, and on the water's edge was the electric red-yellow-white of the Santa Cruz Boardwalk, where human beings tumbled free on the Big Dipper and spun balanced in the night on a great wheel. They had built machines to trick body and mind toward the terror of not-being, while a hundred yards away great white sharks hunted in a few feet of water.

There had been days when they yelled and he fled into the juniper hills to shout inside his head. He knew they were raging against the fact that they had inexplicably moved through their lives to arrive at that moment and death was no more than half a lifetime away. And after months of shouting there were months of silence, when he made his bed in the tack room–office and they walked through their home like ghosts without word or touch. Until the day Mara announced she had rented an apartment in town. As though he were a dull student, she had patiently explained about the divorce, looking directly at him all the while.

Through the disintegration he became aware that Abby had begun to avoid the house, staying with friends, vanishing from her parents' lives. He tried to bring his daughter back, letting his work at the university go in order to take her backpacking and fishing, yearning to find in the perfect flow of a roll cast some kind of continuum. They fished the fall rivers together, always within sight, the swirl of her cast looping his heart again and again. And then on a morning when ice rimed stream bank and fly line and the air was so clear it seemed to break with each sound, he told her of the California job. She'd listened and then walked away in silence, upstream, to fish alone and out of sight. After that trip he lived within himself, vaguely aware of Abby's comings and goings, mourning the loss of his family and wondering how such things had come to pass.

After his wife moved out, there were other women. First the former wife of a colleague, smart, fox-eyed, and wild. He'd come home after hours in her bed, dazed and guilty from the richness of her words and heated flesh, to the cold silence of his house in the mountains. He'd build a fire in the expensive wood stove and stare through the glass at the flames, wondering where his wife and daughter might be and on what date he would cease to be a husband.

And then there had been Rita, a student just a few years older than Abby, tall, dark as the shadows of his dreams, beautiful beyond description, and married. Who came to his office to invite him to her bed, simply and clearly. "This is not about love," she had said. "Remember that." They had met in motel rooms. And he had not remembered, had fallen in such love as he could conceive of, feeling tragedy in every shudder when she lay over him, shrouding him in the curtain of her black hair and dark eyes. "Tell me about your dreams," she had said the first afternoon when they lay listening to a summer thunderstorm. When he'd told her of the one he had over and over, the one in which Attis reached out to him, she'd sat up, placing both hands on his shoulders so that her eyes looked directly down into his. "That's a dangerous dream. My Jicarilla grandmothers would say you need a medicine woman," she'd said, "not just a good fuck." Three months later, lying in the same bed, she had kissed his forehead and said, "I can't see you anymore. I love my husband. But you're in love with the past. You're fucking the past, Cole, not me." He watched her dress, neither of them speaking until, with one hand on the door, she said, "Those who are drowning don't mean to take others with them, but they do, don't they? They must hold to something."

He'd put a case of Tecate and a road map on the seat of the pickup and driven a hundred and fifty miles south and east, drinking steadily until he came to a vast mound of grey stones rising above the empty plains of eastern New Mexico. In the last light of the winter solstice, while a gaunt wind threw handfuls of snow across the stones, he climbed drunkenly over the deserted ruins, trying to recall what had brought him there. In the middle, where the tumbled walls of a Spanish church had exposed the ancient circle of a kiva, he read a large, badly weathered plaque. The town had been Cueloze to its inhabitants but Pueblo de los Jumanos to the

74

first Spanish—the pueblo of the striped ones—and then Gran Quivira, the illusory city of gold. The Jumanos had ambushed a small party of Spaniards nearby and the conquistadors had killed nine hundred Indians in return, enslaving four hundred more. They had built the huge church over the kiva, the sacred middle place, using the stones of the town, but now the church and the pueblo had together gone back to the earth, the stones lying mixed in lines of convergence that seemed to sweep from far out on the darkening plains to the still center.

He climbed down the six-foot walls into the circle of the kiva. Then he lay on his back at the center, the earth like ice beneath him, and studied the winter sky. Beyond the swirling snow, the stars were holes in the dark, not relations in the sky, and he felt the immensity of his solitude. Everything familar had gone, and he had lost the path. Los Jumanos had called him.

The cold struck to his center, and he climbed from the ruins into driven snow that spiraled out of the northwest. Around him the earth was black, and ice stung his face. He knew that the snow would soon be drifting deep across the Llano Estacado. Back in the pickup, he drove northwest two hours before sunrise, staring into the blank face of the storm and so drunk that he missed the tree and instead took out a hundred yards of barbed-wire fence.

That same week he'd dismantled the pickup in front of the house, bolting new after-market metal in place of smashed fenders and hood. And when it was painted, looking better than before, he said goodby to his daughter, called his wife to say she should return home, and departed for California.

The sun slips the spider's filaments and falls to the sea behind him, and carnival lights quicken at the boardwalk in front of him. The path through manzanita and poison oak lies below, a darker line laid across the brush, and he slips from the rock and begins his descent, thinking of his daughter. The path is slick with leaves and soft with winter, and he ponders the possibility of turning around and going down the other side where the sun has laid a blade of red across the sea's throat.

Fifteen

The Father ordered that a wooden doll be made, like a recently born child; he took the doll to the whipped woman and told her to take that doll for her infant, and to carry it in front of all the people for nine days. The Father made the husband of that woman wear cattle horns affixed with leather. In this way they brought him daily to mass from the jail. And the other Indians jeered at him and teased him.

Sixteen

When the beam of the flashlight reached the water, four bodies screamed into the fire chief's life forever. Light from the burning house tumbled across the surface of the back-yard pool where they floated, and the woman's long, dark hair spread wide in the reflected fire, touching the arm of one child. The body of the other boy spun slowly in the rippling flames alongside that of his father.

Seventeen

*H*e *went at night into the forest, touching the bark of redwoods and calling to owls with their own words. His cheek lay close to the streams, and he felt the decay that covered the earth. Curled in the knuckled hollows of roots, he heard the songs of the ancient forest. He felt the weight of his lives. Deer moved beside the stream, their eyes sharp and painful stars, their antlers racks of flame that burned into the sky. Death prowled the ridge, and winter kept no warmth. The ocean beat at the night from the west, violent against the land. The bay lay to the east and south, inconceivable wonders sounding in its depths. The vision came to him once more, the voices telling him of things he would do.*

He dreamt of the gambler, the priest, and the Indians, and he listened to the key turn in the lock.

Eighteen

Hoey was crouched beside the little cabin, his broad shoulders bent as he skinned a big catfish. Three feet away, a black-and-tan bitch and a redbone hound sat watching with intense interest. A finishing nail through the head kept the fish in place as Hoey pulled the blueish-brown skin back with pliers. When he threw the skin, the dogs leapt together, each catching the prize in midair. With a snarl, the bluetick let go and slashed at the other dog's shoulder. The

77

redbone yelped and danced to the side, watching the bitch drag the fish skin a few yards away. Observing her rival through slitted eyes, she lay down and began chewing the tough skin with loud smacks.

"It's okay, Bony," Hoey said to the half-grown loser. "I saved the best for you." With a hard, sawing motion, he severed the mudcat's head and then, prying it from the nail with the pliers, he scooped head and entrails toward the redbone. The dog pounced and let out a yelp. He backed off and then crept close to sniff and lick at the guts.

"You'll learn about those spines," Hoey said, standing up with the four pounds of fish in one hand.

"That's a hard way to learn, ain't it, Hoey?"

Luther stood by the cabin steps. His rubber boots, patched in a dozen places, were splotched with black mud to the ankles, and in his right hand he held a wrinkled and muddied envelope.

"It's how you taught me, if I remember correctly."

Against the background of the brown, slow-moving Yazoo River a hundred yards away, the old man looked impossibly thin and brittle. "We got a letter," he said. "Addressed to Onatima Blue Wood, Luther Cole, and Hoey McCurtain." He held it out as if reading the address.

"Addressed to all of us? Mind if I take a look at it?"

Hoey laid the fish on the top step and took the letter. "It's from Cole. Why didn't you say that?"

"You didn't ask who it was from."

"It's already been opened, so you must've read it."

"Well, my name's second there, Luther Cole, and you were off catching that little bitty fish, so naturally I read it. Then I looked for you."

"What's Cole say?"

"You better just read it."

Hoey pulled the letter out of the envelope and read it slowly. When he was finished, he looked at the cabin steps for a long time before he spoke. "You know, I've been thinking of visiting my son. This would be a good time."

Luther's eyes wrinkled. "I think we ain't got no choice. That old lady'll skin us alive if we don't. Jobe says he'll feed these hounds while we're gone. I think you better fry up that fish for the trip. It's a long way to California, ain't it?"

Hoey nodded absentmindedly and looked around the half-acre clearing. "Hell of a long way. I guess Jobe'll feed these chickens, too?" He glanced toward the weathered chicken coop twenty feet from the cabin.

"Jobe'll take care of the whole shebang. It'll do that old black man some good to row across the river a few times."

Hoey picked up the fish and pulled the leather thong to open the cabin door. Over his shoulder he said, "I've been feeling kind of edgy about Cole for a while."

As he sat on the top step and pulled the rubber boots off, Luther said over his shoulder, "This story's so big Cole only sees a little bit of it."

"But you see all of it?" Hoey laid the fish on a bare-wood table and poured water from a bucket into a basin. He put the fish in the basin and washed it methodically. "That stove still hot?"

Luther came in and pulled the door shut behind him. He held his hand close to a rectangular wood stove and then opened the front of the stove and grabbed a large piece of split oak from a box nearby. "Not hot enough to fry them mudcats," he said, as he shoved the wood in and closed the stove. "It ain't like it was that other time. This here's mostly out of my hands, Hoey. You notice Cole just asked for advice. He didn't ask nobody to help. I suspect he knows he's gonna have to do this one by himself."

"Do what?"

Luther went to a cedar chest, opened it, and began to rummage around. "Cut that fish up small and use plenty of cornmeal. It tastes better that way after a couple days. I'll get this fire up. We still got some of that buttermilk?" He closed the chest and came to the table, setting a small leather pouch in the middle of the oiled wood.

"Do what?" Hoey put a black skillet on the stove and paused to look at the pouch.

"Cole left this here. I figure we better take it to him."

"I doubt that Dodge'll make it." Hoey spooned a mound of lard from a bucket into the skillet. "That truck's half as old as you."

"Oh, me and that truck will make it, all right," Luther responded. "Be sure you fry that catfish all the way through. I wonder what that old lady has in mind."

Nineteen

Cole was sitting at the kitchen table drinking coffee when Alex's Volvo pulled up. By the time he stood looking out the front door, Alex had the back of the station wagon open and was dragging a bale of hay out onto the driveway, holding the baling wire with leather gloves.

Letting the bale drop to the gravel, Alex looked up with a wave. "*Yatahey*," he shouted. In boots, Levis, flannel shirt, and down vest, with his hair pulled back in a ponytail, he reminded Cole of one of the tall Navajo cowboys from the New Mexico State Fair. The kind that made the teenage girls giggle behind their cotton candy.

"It's seven-thirty in the morning, Alex. And I don't have any horses."

Alex lifted the hay bale by the wires and, supporting much of the weight on his legs, shuffled to the doorstep, dropping it with a heavy thud at their feet.

"Thought we should get an early start on the practice.

Where do you think would be best? Probably over there by that oak." He lifted the bale and shuffled to the wide, flat area north of the house, upending the bale and carefully shifting it until it stood firmly on end.

"I brought one of the recurves this morning," he added when he returned.

"We have time for one cup of coffee, but no more, before practice begins," Alex said. "We're going to bring back all those bow-and-arrow skills. Give that memory in the blood a wake-up call, so to speak."

"I just made coffee," Cole replied. "And I have no memory in the blood. Where's your dress?"

"Can't draw a bow as well in a dress, Cole. Think about it."

Twenty

The pickup gained speed down the long hill, the battered body rattling and canvas water bags bouncing and swaying from both side mirrors. Luther watched out the window as a town slid past on the right, the descending sun and tattered clouds etching the plastered adobe with a fine gold. At the highest point of the old village, an earth-colored church rose up to a small steeple, as though surrounded and held captive by the ancient city.

"I wonder what kind of Indians these is," Luther said without taking his eyes from the pueblo. "They got nice-looking houses."

"They're Pueblos, Uncle Luther," Hoey responded, glancing from the road to take in the town. "The sign said

81

Laguna Pueblo. They've been in the Southwest for thousands of years."

"That's what they call themselves?" Luther looked around at Hoey with a trace of a smile.

"It's a name the Spanish gave them."

"They had trouble with them Spanish just like us Choctaws, huh? How come you know so much, Nephew? They don't make those Desoto cars no more, do they?"

Hoey lifted a hand from the wheel and gestured. "No. I used to read a lot, remember?"

"When you was trying to figure out how to be Indian?"

The highway had run like a rabbit path across Oklahoma and the Texas Panhandle. They had tumbled down out of the Sandia Mountains into Albuquerque, watching gray webs of rain and snow far out over the west and wet flakes that moved in long, slow lines toward the windshield.

"Everybody's mad," Luther had said, watching the cars fighting on the short stretch of freeway.

"Nuts," Hoey answered as they left the city and began to cross the Rio Grande. "Everybody's nuts."

"A famous river ought to have more water. John Wayne made this river famous." Luther craned to look northward at the wide stream.

"It ain't the Yazoo, is it," Hoey answered.

Luther continued to peer through the window. "You could walk across that river, Hoey, and you ain't tall. You see that movie where John Wayne killed those Spanish men and said all this land belonged to him? It was called Rio Grande."

"You remember every damned thing you see on tv."

The old man stared out at the darkening trees along both sides of the shallow brown river. After a long silence he added, "It don't look like a fishing river. I'm trying to think of the fish in there, and I can't do it. What kind of fish would be in such a river, Hoey?"

Hoey shook his head. "Suckers."

Luther turned away from the river. "Suckers. Ain't it

funny how Columbus Bailey quit fishing? Started hearing the fish scream when he took 'em out of the water. Said a big channel cat roared like a bear and a perch cried like a scared baby." He turned to look at Hoey. "Col said it pretty near broke his heart. I'm a old man and I ain't never heard a fish scream. I guess he got that power from his grampa."

"Col Bailey said that?" Hoey kept his eyes on the shining road.

Luther nodded toward the windshield. "I got to thinking that maybe them fish been screaming like that all along and couldn't nobody hear 'em before. Like a good dog smells things can't no people smell at all. Tonight's the gambler's moon, Hoey. It's taking us a long time already. Too bad you forgot you didn't have no jack."

"Forgot nothing. Jobe must've borrowed it and never told me. That old man always was light fingered."

"Well, it's good of Jobe to let you park it in his barn. Good thing that fella stopped by with the jack."

Hoey thought about the long first night they'd spent beside the highway in east Texas, trying to flag down somebody with a jack. And then the two hours in the gas station waiting for the flat to be fixed.

"Funny thing about them Baileys," Luther went on. "That Columbus says him and his brothers used to dream the same dream every night. Says the whole house used to sometimes get into one dream, and it'd be so crowded with them six kids and the old folks that they'd get to fighting for elbow room in their sleep and everybody'd wake up mad."

"What's a gambler's moon?" Hoey listened to the tappets sing their distress. All the way from the toll bridge over the Mississippi River, he had filled the crankcase and radiator with prudent regularity, listening and worrying about the nineteen-fifty Dodge.

Periodically the old man would seem to wake from his highway trance to speak. "I sure do wish I could drive one of these machines so I could help out," he had said more

83

than once. And at regular intervals, often from under the brim of the black hat, he commented upon a coyote that drifted across the highway in the headlights, or a low-swooping nighthawk. In the early hours of the first morning, an eternity before sunrise, Hoey had already begun to feel as though he were dreaming the trip and that the old man was there on the other side of the pickup cab just to wake him when it was over.

"Gambler's moon? That's what we're fixing to find out." Luther sat up and pushed the hat square on his head, looking around at the darkening landscape. "We ought to come to that Indian man pretty soon."

"What Indian man? I thought you'd never been here before. I thought you'd never left Mississippi except to go to that school in Kansas."

"That's right," Luther said genially. "I sure do wish . . ."

"That you could drive. For the past three hours I've been tempted to give you the wheel and let you take a shot at it. I figured you couldn't do much worse than me."

"I'm pretty near blind, Nephew."

"Only when you want to be. Other times you could see fly shit on soda cracker a hundred yards away."

"Well, she's home now."

"Who's home now?"

"Cole's girl, Abby. And she's done seen the gambler."

"You want to tell me a little more about all of this, Uncle Luther? Since I'm driving you two thousand miles?"

To the northwest, a mountain loomed, purple and black with the coming evening, and Luther leaned forward to see better through the windshield. "That's a sacred mountain," he said. "Cole's got himself into something out here big as that mountain. People try to get away from the past, and that's when most of the trouble gets 'em. This story ain't directly part of that other one, but everything's connected, you know."

A small owl swooped across the lights, dodging with a sudden flutter back to the sky.

They were silent for a few minutes, and then Luther said, "That old lady is full of surprises. There ain't much can stand against that woman when she gets her back up. And she never was one to let things be." He rolled the window down and took a deep breath of the cold air. "That California is a lot of trouble, Hoey. How'd you ever live out there so long?"

Hoey rubbed the glass cover of the gas gauge and strained to look closely. "I'm glad I gave up trying to understand you about forty years ago." He concentrated on the road for several minutes and then added, "I don't know. After the army, when I met Ida, it seemed like we'd stay there a little while and then go home, but then the boys came and I got busy trying to make a living, and the next thing I knew she was gone. It wasn't until I was standing there at the grave that it hit me. It was like I looked away for a minute, and all of a sudden twenty-five years was gone."

"You're saying her name, now."

"That's right. I guess enough time makes everything safe. But I sure do miss her."

"Twenty-five years ain't very much. It's all one time, Hoey." In a softer tone, Luther added, "You got to be careful."

"You know, Uncle Luther, I just don't care about that kind of thing anymore. I just can't seem to worry about it. Saying her name makes her feel closer."

"That's how it happens. That's how they work, and they don't mean no harm in the world. It's just loneliness. But you should be careful, especially where we're going."

Hoey took a deep breath before he spoke. "California is pretty nice country. The hills are full of deer, and there are some mountains near the ocean that have bear and wild pigs and turkeys and even mountain lions. There are draws close to where we used to live that have the best quail hunting you ever saw. California used to be awful nice."

A sleek automobile swept up on them from behind and swerved past to disappear almost instantly. Hoey stared straight ahead, both hands on the wheel. Luther kept his eyes on the landscape, where nothing showed now but silhouettes of mesas and bony trees. In the dim light the horizon looked like weathered bone.

Hoey watched in the rearview mirror as a semi came roaring down the grade at them, its lights blazing.

"They got strong medicine, these Pueblos," Luther said. "You can feel it, can't you? Did you see that bird back there, the one that come to look at us?"

Hoey shook his head, and his shoulders hunched deeper over the steering wheel. "I thought you didn't know anything about them."

Luther pushed his black hat further back on his head and seemed to listen. "Stop," he said suddenly.

Hoey braked and shifted the fragile transmission down into second. Where there had been nothing, a figure suddenly stood beside the road, a hand held up as though in greeting. As he pulled onto the shoulder of the freeway and felt the blast of the semi going by, Hoey marveled at the thin-faced old man who, framed in profile by the yellow headlights, resembled Luther. The long, gray hair was pulled back and bunched in what looked like a cloth-wrapped ponytail beneath a high-crowned and wide-brimmed hat. A Levi jacket was buttoned up to the throat, and stiff-looking blue jeans hung straight on spindly legs.

"He wants a ride," Luther said.

"Where'd he come from?" Hoey looked at the setting behind the old man. There wasn't a bush or a rock big enough to hide a chicken, and yet the old man had seemed to just step out of that landscape.

Luther beckoned with one hand, and the old man walked up to the passenger's side. When Luther opened the door, the man took off his hat and grinned widely at them, his teeth gapped and yellow.

"*Ya'hey*," he said. "I guess we better take off these big hats."

"I guess we better," Luther answered, sliding over to make room as the man climbed into the pickup and setting his own hat on his knees. "Welcome."

86

"It's only a couple miles. What took you so long?" The old man gestured with his chin and lips toward the freeway ahead, and Hoey quickly took in the man's deeply seamed face and dark, shadowed eyes.

"It's only a couple miles," Luther repeated, looking at Hoey. "Just up ahead on the right. We had a flat and my nephew here don't have no jack."

The hitchhiker nodded thoughtfully. "It's important to have a jack. My brother always used to drive up on rocks and change 'em that way, though. I give him a jack and he traded it for whiskey. Then he'd get a flat and have to drive around on the rim, cutting that tire to pieces. He'd trade his spare, too. Then they took his car away, too. Then he died."

"We have a jack now, remember, Uncle Luther? I bought one? Pleased to meet you, Grandfather." Hoey nodded at the new passenger and then pulled the truck back onto the freeway.

"Our guest is going home," Luther said.

The old man pulled a red bandana out of his hip pocket and wiped his face, and Hoey saw a large turquoise ring on his hand.

"You sure took your time." The hitchhiker turned to look at Luther, smiling the ragged smile again. "You are an old one, Grandfather. I bet you're a hundred years old."

Luther nodded. "It's an old truck, too. Hoey takes good care of it, so he don't drive fast. How old are you, young fellow?"

"It's a good truck. You can feel it. Not like these four-wheel-drive things all the young men buy now. Four-doubleyou-dees they call 'em. Drive all over the reservation drinking beer and throwing the cans around, with that music turned up loud. Scares the sheep. They get drunk in those trucks in the winter and then they freeze to death, too. Take that turnoff up there." The old man gestured with his chin, and Hoey slowed down for an off ramp that led to a thin asphalt road running toward black canyon walls.

"Just drive north, Grandson. It ain't far. I'm about

seventy we think, because I was born right after they had that first big war. Not the one with the code talkers."

"They had Choctaw code talkers in that first war, but everybody already forgot. My cousin did that," Luther said. "Hoey was in that other big one they had. They got any new wars now?"

When Hoey looked over, the old man was watching him steadily, leaning forward to see past Luther. Seemingly satisfied, he leaned back again. "That's a good boy," he said to Luther, nodding toward Hoey. "They always got new ones somewheres. You're Choctaw, from way over there."

"I'm sixty-one years old," Hoey started to say, but he watched the road silently instead.

In silence they drove northward. Beside the road, narrow washes and brown-gold canyons streamed away into shadow, and the old truck began to labor as it climbed. The moon rose and hung damply against the horizon.

"You got a pretty country here," Luther said.

"Indian country," the old man replied. "Everwhere you look, Navajo and Pueblo and Hopi land. We got sacred peaks in ever direction, and stories to tell us where we are. You know, them stories that tell us how to live here. Sacred geography my granddaughter calls it. She been to that college over there." He made a backhanded gesture toward the night.

"But now the white people got their own maps and different stories. I been looking at one of those government maps and traveling around, and you can see it clear. They got that Los Alamos up there in the north where they took Cochiti Indian land to plan that A-bomb. They got that Sandia laboratory over in Albuquerque in the east where they make nucular bombs. They got White Sands in the south where they fire them bombs and nucular missiles off to see if they work." He looked at Luther and shook his head. "And they got that uranium mine at Laguna where they made the water poison; that's the west. So you see how they got something in each one of those four directions like us Indians, but it's all about killing. And they got their stories, too. I went to this musuem they got in Albuquerque all about nucular bombs. They got them bombs they dropped on Japan in there, with little cards that tell a story about each one, how many people they killed. Fat Man and Little Boy they call them the way we give names to dogs and horses. They got the plane that carried them bombs where you can go inside it and make up a story about it being you. They got missiles in all kinds of colors with cards that say what they would or could do. For the museum they got this old airplane hangar with the ceiling painted black and little lights like stars up there. It's like the gambler's house where he put those storm clouds in the story. They have made a story about death."

"Our own chief's been trying to get the Choctaws to let 'em put a poison dump on our land," Luther said.

"Toxic waste dump," Hoey added, watching the road carefully. "We voted it down for now."

"Lots of Indians doing that. Just like white people, they're gonna kill the land for a little bit of money. They got our old tribal chairman in jail. He was making a lot of money. Now they got that thing they call a hantavirus that's killing us. Navajo Flu they call it. They say it come from mice and squirrels, but us Navajos know it come from them laboratories they got up in Los Alamos. Something that got away from them."

"It's funny," Luther said. "That word *hanta*, that's a Choctaw word meaning white. You got a white virus killing you. It's funny how everything's connected like that."

"Always been." They drove in silence for a moment and then the old man said, "There."

Hoey saw it as the word was uttered. A coyote in the middle of the road, its head turned toward them and red eyes flaring.

He slammed the brake on, and the truck locked into a shrieking slide.

"Don't stop," the old man said.

89

Just as the truck would have struck it, the coyote disappeared.

Hoey looked from one side of the road to the other, attempting to see the leaping shadow of the animal.

"Just keep driving, Grandson," the old man said.

"It was an owl before," Luther said.

"My name's Robert Jim." The old man held a hand out toward Luther, who grasped it for an instant in his own. Robert Jim reached his hand toward Hoey, who had taken the truck back into second gear. Hoey reached across Luther and felt the faint touch of the old man's fingers, the surface as soft and slick as snakeskin. He shifted the whining transmission into third as they topped a rise.

"We're very pleased to meet you, Robert Jim," Luther said. "My name's Luther Cole, and this is my nephew, Hoey McCurtain."

"That one is almost always somewhere around here. They get things beside the road, I think. But they're everwhere now. You need to be able to recognize them. Our people been disappearing. There's always been some that went away and never come back, but it's more than that now. They go and drink and nobody sees them no more. I think it's all connected, what they're doing here on the reservation and over there where you're going. That's why you two come.

"You can let me out there, by that fence. I live up that road." He nodded toward a faint dirt track that ran off at a right angle through a barbed-wire fence toward a high, dark canyon.

Hoey stopped the truck and the old man opened the door and climbed down. Once on the ground, he straightened and took something from the front pocket of his jacket.

"I almost forgot," he said, reaching a hand toward Luther.

Luther held out his own hand, and the old man placed a translucent rock in the middle of his palm. Next to the quartz he set a soft leather bag no bigger than a silver dollar. "You put this with your medicine, Grandfather," he said.

He pointed at the little bag. "That's pollen. I been saving it for you. Now turn around and drive to Gallup tonight. You walk around there a little bit and you'll see what I mean."

Luther nodded. "We'll go to Gallup, younger brother." He placed the gifts in the pocket of his mackinaw and stretched his hand toward the old man. By the tip of the blade he held a large black-handled knife, which Robert Jim accepted with a broad smile.

"Watch out for that coyote back there," the old man said. "Don't let him trick you." He stepped to the side as Hoey turned the truck around on the deserted road.

When they were headed south toward the freeway, Hoey said, "What was all that?"

Luther lifted his hat and adjusted it squarely on his head. "That was Robert Jim," he said. "Watch out you don't run over no witches."

In the dark cab of the truck, Hoey felt that his uncle was laughing at him, but he couldn't see the old man's face. "You had that knife since I was a boy," he said.

"Used to be boundaries, Hoey. Us Choctaws used to worry about them Chickasaws that was our brothers once, but we didn't know about all this other stuff. Then those Spanish come and started killing us. Come out of nowhere and killed us and went away for two hundred years and then come back again. Since that time things've been getting bigger and bigger. You remember souleater?"

Hoey nodded.

"Souleater's everywhere. He's been let go."

Twenty-One

Cole had pulled the door shut behind him, locked the dead bolt, and turned toward the pickup before he saw it. At the end of the path from door to driveway, the stick stood almost vertical, projecting three feet above the earth. Hanging from it were bright red and blue scraps and other, brownish objects.

He looked around and then strode quickly to the stick. The colorful scraps were the feathers of Steller's jays and several brilliant red woodpecker scalps. In the spaces between the feathers were reddish-brown strips of flesh. He pulled the prayer stick from the ground and laid it on the passenger's-side floor of the pickup. As he walked around to the driver's side, something else caught his attention.

Pressed into the soft, damp earth near the front of the pickup was a bear track. He stared at the imprint for several moments. He'd seen plenty of bear tracks before, but this one was different. From side to side it looked to be at least twelve inches, and he estimated the length to be nine or ten. Only one kind of bear ever made such tracks in California.

He followed the tracks across the dirt and into the grass, where a swath led into the redwoods. Inside the trees, the tracks vanished.

When he arrived at his office he called Alex Yazzie's home and university numbers. Alex answered at the university.

"It's a prayer stick," he said as soon as Cole had described the object.

"I know it's a prayer stick, but I need to know what kind and why."

"I'll be right over." Alex's voice was sharp with interest.

"One other thing," Cole said. "Are there any bears left in these mountains?"

He could feel Alex thinking for a moment. "There aren't

supposed to be any bears in the Santa Cruz Mountains. Used to be a lot of them, but they were killed out years ago."

"Well, I found bear tracks around my house."

"I guess you'd know bear tracks?"

"Yeah."

"Well, there's a population down below Big Sur. It wouldn't be impossible for one to work his way up this far, maybe a yearling pushed out by the older males."

"Any chance of grizzlies in this area?" Cole asked, knowing the answer.

There was a longer silence before Alex said, "The last grizzly in this part of California was killed by a farmer in Bonny Doon eighty-five years ago. An old female that was eating his pig. No one's even seen a track since."

"Well, I would appreciate it if you could come over and take a look at this stick. By the way, Abby's here."

He hung up, feeling the weight of last night's dream and this new mystery. He'd been eighteen years old when the world had opened itself up to him. He had made a journey with his brother's bones, taking them home to Mississippi, and discovered the reality of Uncle Luther and Onatima, a Choctaw world that lived beside this one like Black Elk's shadows, the way his own Indian blood seemed to shadow the whiteness of his other self. Now it seemed like that shadow world was threatening to subsume the life he'd constructed out of books.

Feeling the fatigue of the dream-filled night, he scanned the desk top and picked up a manila envelope that had come in the morning's mail. Out of habit he opened it and started to toss the flier in his recycling box, but the first words caught his eye.

The Santa Cruz area is precariously located in one of the seven spots on this planet where the magnetic radiation belts dip through the atmosphere and sweep quietly across Mother Earth. Sentient creatures, i.e., humans, animals, and plants, are attracted to this area, just as iron is to lodestone. Individuals, in particular, sense more strongly this peculiarity and

93

strive to express themselves in many creative forms. Numerous folks have likewise started to express a feeling of great spiritual intensity—a desire for reunion with the Universal One. Although the forms of expression are many, the goal is most definitely identical in all aspects: All Hail the One Mind!

He leaned back in his chair, wondering how he'd got on the mailing list of something called the Stoneybrook Correspondence School. "All hail the one mind," he said aloud. "They've been trying to do that for five hundred years."

He glanced at the stick and thought of the bear track and the night's dream, remembering the lash on his back and the butt of the whip in his hand, the girl, the spilled wine and hot sun. *Padre Quintana. Venancio Asisara.*

Alex knocked twice and pushed the door open. He stepped in and closed the door behind him, scanning the office with a glance at Cole. In western boots, Levis, chambray shirt, and sheepskin vest, he looked big and imposing in the small office. Seeing the prayer stick, he bent and picked it up, dropping into the extra chair and holding the stick horizontally while turning it at arm's length.

"Definitely a prayer stick. A lot like what the Ohlone are said to have made." He looked for the first time at Cole. "Where'd you find it?"

"Next to my truck. Where's the dress?"

Alex smiled. "What dress?"

"What do you make of that thing?"

Alex brought it closer and examined the feathers and strips of meat. Holding it close to his nose, he drew a long, slow breath through his nostrils and then quickly shoved it back toward Cole, who let it drop to the floor. "It's not beef or venison."

"What?"

"Look closely. Even dried out that way, you can tell it's not deer meat. Doesn't look like beef or pork either, too light and long-muscled."

"Any idea what it is?"

"For one thing somebody's knocking off protected wood-peckers. And that looks like a California laurel branch, which is probably authentic. The Ohlone used bay for such things. Bay makes nice straight shafts."

Cole leaned the stick against the desk. "Maybe it was left by some *Iron John* wannabe out wandering in the woods. Robert Bly's set Indians back about a hundred years."

"This isn't just New Age bullshit, Cole." Alex looked around the office, scanning books and posters, his vision finally settling on a clear vase half filled with brown water and a bunch of dead, half-petalless daisies. "Maybe you can tell me about those dreams."

"Are you a medicine man now?"

Alex shrugged.

Cole studied Alex for a moment. In the jeans, boots, and blue work shirt, with his long hair pulled back in a tight chongo knot, he looked once again like a Navajo cowboy. "Why not?"

When Cole had finished recounting the dreams, Alex was silent for a long time before saying, "You know, I guess it's lucky that I have all these years of European education behind me. I suppose it's desensitized me in crucial ways."

"The strangest thing," Cole went on, "is that I'm both of them. It's as if I'm everything and everyone at the same time. I'm the priest whipping the Indian's back to a bloody pulp, and I feel every second of it. And love it. I want to kill them all and spread their guts out to dry, hate them because their souls are somewhere I can't reach, and all the time I'm using that whip I'm praying and thinking of the girl. I know how she smells and tastes, and I want her. And it's me tied to the tree and getting my back cut to shreds, feeling like somebody's raking the flesh off my bones with steel claws and hating the priest and everything around me. It's me they call out to the orchard, and it's me who does the call-ing. And it's me standing above it all, seeing it like some-body watching a goddamned movie. And all the time I get the feeling there's someone or something else watching, just out of the picture. I wake up shaking, sweating, and thinking I smell blood everywhere." He stopped, staring for a moment at the cluttered bulletin board over his desk. "I'm seeing things, hearing voices, shooting at hallucinations."

The phone in the next office rang, and they sat listening to it ring a dozen times in the empty room. Alex said, "Some people might say you have ghost sickness. Ghosts send dreams. They take animal shapes, too, like owls. Look at yourself. You're sick."

Cole brushed his hair back with both hands. "I don't feel too bad," he said, his voice betraying him. "And I know a little about ghost sickness. I read Silko and Hillerman. He is Navajo, isn't he?"

"This isn't a time to joke around, Cole. Somebody wants you to know these things, to feel them. Who knows why? But you need to do something about it. You look awful."

"You should be a counselor, Alex. It's uncanny how you can make a person feel better. You know, Choctaws believe in two kinds of what you'd call ghosts, an inside shadow and an outside shadow. They can be dangerous. But the living can send dreams, too."

"What are you going to do?"

"I don't know. I guess I'll call the cops, but you know what that'll get me. They're so used to wackos a stick like this will seem normal."

"Wackos are killing people around here."

"I guess I'll call the cops."

"You have any relatives who could help?"

Cole thought of Onatima and Luther, seeing the old couple in his mind with sudden clarity.

When Cole didn't reply, Alex said, "In the meantime you ought to get a guard dog."

"No."

"I mean it. You should get a dog, especially now that Abby's here. Let him roam around your place. A big, mean one. And remember, dogs don't like ghosts or witches. We keep them around our hogans at home just for that."

96

"Absolutely no dog. Let me buy you a cup of coffee."

As they both stood up, Alex added, "Oh, yeah. One more thing. One of my uncles is coming out here to do a Native American Church service. I was wondering if we might be able to have it at your place. My house is technically on university property, and they might get a little weird if they found out about the service. I don't have tenure, you know."

"Before or after the sweat?"

"Well, the sweat's this weekend, and Uncle Emmet probably won't be here for a while."

"Peyote's just as illegal at my house as yours, Alex."

"Technically, yes."

"Hell, why not? Just don't expect me to eat any cactus."

"That's great. Uncle Emmet might be here in a week or so."

"Indian time, right?"

"Yeah. Tomorrow, next month, next year."

As they passed the college fishpond, Alex pointed at a big spotted carp. "That guy wouldn't last long on a reservation."

"Don't expect me to eat peyote," Cole replied. "No drugs."

"Peyote's not a drug. It's good for you," Alex said, waving his hands for emphasis. "It's an excellent antibiotic and antiseptic, with proven inhibitory value against eighteen strains of penicillin-resistant Staphylococcus. It's totally nontoxic, and it's spiritually nourishing to say the least. It's been used in childbirth for hundreds of years in Mexico. How's that archery practice coming?"

"It's not. Where do you come up with these didactic minutiae, Alex?"

"You ought to practice. I read books. I've always been inquisitive about what I eat, especially in church."

They paused to watch a young man jog by. Wearing only a book pack and a deep tan, the long-haired boy radiated health as he flopped across the quad.

Alex looked at Cole with raised eyebrows. "By the way," he said, "you should have the cops check out that prayer stick. I think it's human flesh. I think you've got a wolf on your hands."

97

Twenty-Two

Beyond the circle of light the darkness was almost complete. A misting fog had climbed up from the town and made a halo around the single streetlamp at the campus bus stop. The two young women stood side by side with arms interlocked. The taller one leaned over and nuzzled the other behind the ear and they both pulled closer.

The car came down from the center of campus, the headlights winding slowly through the fog. When it stopped in the light, they could see the **A** parking sticker on the front bumper. One of the girls gave a short hop. "It's okay," she whispered. They tumbled together into the backseat.

Workmen found the headless bodies in the Santa Cruz mountains two weeks later. "I'll never forget it," one of the road workers told the television camera.

Twenty-Three

Abby descended the steep bank, plunging the heels of her hiking boots deep into the soft duff to keep from slipping and holding the fly rod out away from the branches. In the bottom of the small canyon the stream dipped and fell in dark pools, and from above she saw the shadowed eddies where the trout would be. Tired of waiting for her father, she had walked out that morning after he left for school, borrowing his fishing vest and picking out the few number twenty Adamses in his fly box to add to her own midges and duns. The trout in such a stream would be miniscule, seven and eight inchers at the most if they existed at all, but they would also be wild and muscular and difficult to trick. In the depths of the canyon, they would feed all day, but in such a little stream they would be cautious and quick.

She cut down and across, plotting her path to arrive just above a waterfall that spilled over a rock ledge into a black pool six feet across. The stream gave no sign of ever having been fished, and as she walked she let the short leader swing free and felt her muscles tense with anticipation.

Two yards above the pool she stopped, leaning into the side of the hill, and let the leader drop so that the tiny gray fly settled almost motionless on the water. The fly had begun to curve upon the edge of the falls when it disappeared with a faint ripple. The trout darted and trembled across the pool, and she descended to the stream's edge before lifting the seven-inch rainbow from the water so that it hung shivering on the almost invisible tippet. Wetting her hand, she held the beautiful fish in her palm and slipped the hook from its mouth. When she lowered it to the pool, the trout vanished in a twist of shadow.

She began to work her way down stream, crouching so that the leader swung before her over the water, catching and releasing trout from nearly every pool, each fish an unexpected explosion of life. After releasing the sixth, she laid the fly rod on the bank and settled back against the steep hillside with a hand behind her head, closing her eyes and listening to the stream. The air of the canyon was cool and still, without even a birdcall to break the silence.

She thought about her father. When her parents had argued, she would go out to the barn to stroke the Appaloosa's neck and listen to the crows gossip in the piñons. She walked higher into the Ortiz Mountains to watch the double sunsets, the first for their side of the mountains and then the next that lay over Albuquerque to the west of the Sandia Crest. When the summer monsoons came, she crouched under thick-branched junipers until the afternoon rains passed, feeling the thunder reverberate in her bones and desiring those wonderful candelabras of lighting that lit up the sky, trying to imagine other possibilities. Then he'd started drinking, staying away from home on extended fishing trips, backpacking into remote corners of the Southwest. Her mother had immersed herself in the new law degree, rising early and coming home late, as though racing against a deadline.

With a kind of pity, she remembered the little girl she had been just two years before. She had begun to run with the long-haired, wild crowd from the American Indian Institute, mixing alcohol and drugs and an adrenalin rush of Indianness. Without her parents even noticing, she had begun to powwow dance, content at first to do the modest, traditional women's dances. But what drew her was the frenzy of the male fancy dancers, with their whirling colors and scalp-dance ecstasy. At each powwow—in Albuquerque, Santa Fe, Taos, Gallup, Flagstaff, or Phoenix—she would stand at the edge watching and envying the fancy dancers, knowing that what they danced for with their pounding feet and madness was nothing less than the end and beginning of the world. It was as though the women, with their slow, measured steps and close-eyed precision, as they moved carefully and inexorably in their circles, bore the burden of a fragile world, while the men, once again, were allowed the wild freedom of storm and fire. She longed for that freedom, for a fancy dance or, better yet, a Ghost Dance, the necessary violence that would inflame the stars. And because she couldn't have it, she quit dancing, stopped seeing the boy from White Mountain or any of the Institute crowd, and did not answer the phone. She began to savor solitude, the sensuality of being untouched.

It was on a weekend trip to the Black River that her father had told her of the new job in California and asked her to go with him. She had just shaken her head and walked, furious, upriver to a spot where the water ran deep and green under a grassy cutbank. In the past she had tried not to catch the big browns that spawned there, but that day she had wanted them.

After he'd wrecked his truck and left, she'd waited for the spring runoff to drop and then she'd begun fly-fishing in earnest, tying the most intricate patterns she could find, each fly like a tiny fancy dancer, rising at three in the morning to drive to the northern New Mexico rivers he'd shown her, abandoning boys and sex in favor of silence and cunning. Breast deep in the slow waters of the San Juan, a twenty-inch rainbow on the end of her line, she had felt the ultimate embrace of the water, and it was like going home to a place she had never imagined. Roll-casting for a riffle on the Chama River, she knew she had escaped something deadly. She hiked and camped alone, and alone she fished the best waters, climbing down cliffs to wade the fast, brown Rio Grande of the Taos Box, where big trout lay in the slipstreams of boulders.

Watching the spires of redwoods rise against vague sky, she had begun to wonder whether to fish another quarter-mile of the little stream or go back to her father's house when she heard a shuffling in the damp leaves.

She sat up.

A dozen feet away, a dark silhouette stood against the gray of the undergrowth.

A familiar voice said, "Hello."

He walked closer. "I like to hike up this creek. It runs out near where I live."

"Robert?"

His face came into focus as he stood there with his hands in the pockets of a hooded sweat shirt, a half-smile directed toward her. "I'm sorry if I startled you," he said.

"I didn't expect anyone to be out here."

He pushed the hood back, so that it bunched at his neck. "Catch any fish?"

She nodded. "Little rainbows. Have you seen them? They're almost black."

101

He sat down on the hillside close to her, drawing his knees up and wrapping his arms around them. "I don't fish, but I've seen them lots of times from above. They're beautiful. They look like little black arrows. I always liked to think about how they lived way up here in this canyon in the dark and nobody even knew they were here, how they could spend their whole lives up here and no one would ever know."

"I guess I spoiled that, huh? Now at least two of us know, and now they know I know."

He picked up a twig and began poking it into the earth, as though considering her statement. Finally he said, "It's okay, because you and I are different from all the others. The fish don't mind."

She smiled. "They probably mind being caught. But I try not to hurt them."

He reached behind him to slip the holder off his ponytail and pull his long brown hair tighter before he replaced the elastic band. "Hurting isn't always bad," he said, shifting his eyes from the stream to her and back quickly. "Creation has always existed in a matrix of pain. When a mountain lion brings down a deer, the pain is so deep that it fills the whole forest. You can feel it, it hangs in the air for days afterwards. It's the most beautiful thing of all, and somewhere in the screaming pain that's like music the deer, too, has to understand. It's the most awful kind of love. Like the pain of birth. God couldn't have made it otherwise, could He? How could He bear to see these things happen every fraction of every second if it weren't part of the plan? He created the world in such a way that all of his creations must sacrifice themselves at every moment of every day. It's like the way your people, Native Americans, know that animals give themselves to the hunter."

"I didn't know you were such a Christian, Robert. You know, the Choctaw believe that the Creator made the world and then went back to other business."

He had turned so that he was watching her steadily now.

"I'm not a Christian. Maybe I should say the Great Spirit or Creator instead of God. But now you're talking about the oral tradition. The stories that tell the people who tell the stories who they are. Native Americans are correct. If we don't know the stories we don't know how to behave, do we? We make mistakes. And often we don't even know we've made the mistakes until it's too late and everything is screwed up. Sometimes it doesn't seem fair. How can we be held responsible for breaking the rules if they never tell us the rules in the first place? We go out into a strange world and we're struck by lightning. Then only the aid of holy persons can help us. Isn't that what the stories teach us? And it isn't only ourselves that we screw up; it's the whole world, because nothing exists separate from anything else."

He stopped and watched her, as though waiting for approval. When she said nothing, he went on. "That's what I've learned from Native Americans. Every minute element is interrelated inextricably with every other element, and if we screw up one tiny part we screw it all up. Then we have to restore the balance somehow, make offerings, and propitiate the only forces that can help us, the way Native Americans have always known we must. The spirits guide us."

She looked at his bunched form and then at the creek. "That sounds like Black Elk and the Old Testament stirred together, Robert."

He laughed. "I guess it does, doesn't it? Well, everyone has oral traditions."

She studied the stream for a moment, and then she said, "Alex is going to have a Native American Church service at our house. Maybe he would invite you if I asked. You might learn a great deal."

"I'd like that." He leaned further back into the hillside, the uneven light shadowing his face, and said softly, "You are remarkably beautiful, Abby. I mean not just on the outside, but all the way through. Your eyes seem to gaze out of great depth at great distance."

103

She looked at him in surprise. His eyes were hidden. "Thank you."

"Would you like to have dinner with me sometime? It would be nice to talk again. I haven't met anyone else at the university with whom I think I could talk—except your father, of course."

She stood up, brushing the spiky redwood fronds off her pants. "That would be very nice sometime. But I have to get back home right now. My father's waiting for me to get back. He'll come looking for me pretty soon."

He rose beside her. "I'll call you, then," he said.

"So you just have to follow the creek back home?"

He nodded.

She picked up the fly rod. "It was a nice coincidence, running into you."

He smiled. "Some people think that nothing is coincidence, that everything is part of a plan. Be careful going home. I admire a woman who can be in the woods alone like you, especially after everything that's been happening. Many women would be frightened."

"Many men would be frightened, too," she replied. "Have a nice walk home, Robert."

He watched as she climbed the steep slope of the drainage, little avalanches of leaves and sticks tumbling in her wake. When he could no longer trace her path, he turned and began to walk back down alongside the stream, his head bent thoughtfully.

Twenty-Four

They found the young couple in one mountain cabin, a mother and daughter in another. In the state park, a hundred yards below the Garden of Eden overlook, four teenage boys were spread awkwardly about their campsite, as though a hard wind had scattered them like seeds.

The moon rose full, whitening the meadow and small house. From the western ridge, the great shadow reared to full height, falling across a corner of the house and across the thick redwoods and down to the bay, blotting out the moonbright waves.

Twenty-Five

The gambler's there, crouched in the clearing. Onatima's eyes take in the deep forest, the unnaturally straight trunks of trees that seem stitched to the curtain of the night. She smells the pungent air and sees his face lighted as though by fire. She clutches the pouch around her neck and hears the river, just outside the silver trailer, as it slides away in the dark.

What do you want, old one? she asks, feeling lost in her own dream for the first time since girlhood. The air tastes bitter and bitterly cold. She feels her blood slowing.

His eyes are as black as the raven cape he wears, his

mouth set in a line. He holds his hands in front of him, showing the bones, one pale and one dark.

Your world is gone, old one, she says, her words even and heavy as stone. Your children have gone from you, Grandfather. You should be sleeping. And she feels his hate taut on the night air as he begins to sing, moving the hands, his eyes on her own.

No use, she says. No use, and the words are like a song. We cannot help you. You can't win that world back, Grandfather. She shakes her head at the wavering hands and will not gamble. Our worlds are gone, old one.

The night grows colder yet. She feels a weight of death upon the air and closes her eyes. There is a sudden rush, and she is walking now through dead grasses that curve to her knees in a tangled mat.

Overhead, a mourning dove calls repeatedly, and she hears a muffled eruption of pigeon wings. The deer path winds through brush and trees, across ground thick with fronds and damp leaves that cushion her steps. She is about to turn back when she hears a faint thread of sound, just ahead.

In a few minutes she is there. In the center of a level clearing scarcely larger than her trailer, a stump stands black and massive. Squatting at the base of the stump is the gambler.

The gambling song fills the clearing with a sound so thin and uncertain that it might be the wind high in the trees. But she feels the song all the way to her marrow, a vibration that enters her and from her the earth and returns once more from feeling to sound.

She approaches, touching with one hand the pouch that hangs on a leather thong between her breasts, and when she can reach out and stroke the knot of hair and run a hand down the painted wires of moustache and beard, and trace with one finger the line between black and white from knotted hair to flaccid penis, she sits upon the ground. Folding her legs beneath her, she places her clasped hands in her lap and keeps her eyes unblinking on the singer.

The head moves in time to the song, up and down, back and forth, the eyes looking through her, beyond the circle of trees, beyond the clenched fists that are birds in looping flight, salmon in streams that have not run in a hundred years, nightbirds.

From a shirt pocket she brings a scrap of red wool, three inches square, which she lays before the gambler. *Immisa,* she says. An offering. She points with her lips at his right hand. I have come a long way, Grandfather.

The hands stop, and the gambler's eyes sharpen into focus. He looks at her, and both hands open. The painted bone lies in the palm of the right hand, the white bone in the left.

She hears the cries and scurrying feet, sees the orchard stooped in darkness and death.

Santísima Trinidad. Dios, Jesu Cristo, Espíritu Santo. Los padres españoles eran muy crueles con los indios. A fire and dancing. Jesús la muerta, para siempre . . . eran muy crueles. And she saw the teeming beaches of great bears and shrilling birds, clouds of geese over the marshes, deerness spread upon the meadows, antelope people and leaping silver fish. And the old priest whipping with wires a consumation of desire and death. . . . Thrice called him, los neófitos. Padre Quintana. Moonwhite it rode far over the wide bay where great fish dove in inexplicable wonder, dark and curving on the sea. And hung him there. Eran muy crueles. Bled into the earth conjoined like spreading roots of the great trees. Brought his lips to the bleeding backs, his hands upon the body hard and indivisible.

The bone game.

And down the shadows she hears the streams dance and sing as they have not sung in three hundred years, the sweep of god. . . .

She weeps and dreams of the other gambler. Desire and death. The bone game. She is alone in the little trailer, the night crowding close. "He wants his world," she whispers.

Twenty-Six

They drove for an hour in silence, Hoey watching the moon rise behind damp-looking tatters of cloud and the old man leaning back with his hat pulled over his eyes.

They approached a truck stop with an enormous electric sign across which rolled lighted advertisements. Hoey pulled into the gas pumps and filled the truck with gas, water, and oil. Huge semis came huffing off the freeway with air brakes belching, and Luther sat through it all with his hat over his face.

When they were back on the highway and the lights of the truck stop had vanished, Luther said from behind the hat, "That town Robert Jim talked about is coming up. We got to go through there."

"The highway goes right by Gallup now, Uncle Luther."

Luther straightened and lifted the hat from his head. In the high beams of an eighteen-wheeler bearing down from behind, his hair shone brightly. "That's it," he said, pointing at a flood of lights in the distance. "We'll just drive through and take a look."

Hoey squinted away from the glare in the rearview mirror and sighed. "Maybe we ought to find a room and get a little sleep."

Luther turned to look fully at his nephew, and his face was without humor. He turned back and gestured at an off ramp. "That's a good idea. Better take that one," he said.

"I don't know who's crazier, you or that old man back there," Hoey said, as he braked and swung the pickup off the freeway and under an overpass.

The road curved around to parallel the freeway, and in two minutes they were in the town, passing quick-stop stores and gas stations and motor-court motels with blinking cactuses and feathered headdresses. Hoey felt his uncle become fully alert as the old highway took them into the heart of the town, where traffic grew suddenly thick and slow, cars and trucks moving as though in dreams. They began to pass pawnshops with iron-barred windows and pictures of Indians and Indian designs. Surrounding the pawnshops, bars lined the road on both sides, each one with an electric sign and a dark doorway recessed from the street. Figures tilted in and out of the doorways, and others stumbled in the slits of alleys between buildings.

"Park over there, Hoey," Luther said, pointing toward a bare curb in the center of a block. "We'll walk around a little bit, like Robert Jim suggested."

"Are you crazy, Uncle?" Hoey pulled the Dodge to the curb and turned to face his uncle. "There's people out there'd cut our throats just for that hat you're wearing."

Luther lifted the hat from his lap and set it carefully on his head. "These Indians got better hats than this one. I guess you could stay in the truck for a while. Maybe guard it from Indians." He opened the door and swung his legs delicately toward the sidewalk.

"Lock the door," Hoey said. "Never mind, it won't lock."

When they were both on the sidewalk, Luther turned in a slow circle, looking carefully in all directions. "The Teepee Room," he said, reading a sign on the opposite side of the street. "That must be an Indian place."

"I think they're all Indian places. You're going to get us killed." Hoey began to walk beside the old man. "This town got rich killing Indians."

"This is a rich town?" Luther looked at a black-haired young man who lay on his side against a wall, a paper bag clutched in one hand and a clot of vomit covering a sleeve.

"These pawnshops," Hoey explained. "Rich white men live up in the hills and run these shops down here. They own the bars, too. That way they get everything."

Two men in cowboy hats bent over a woman whose black hair hung to her waist, the three of them awkward against the corner of a building. A streetlamp threw their silhouettes across the wall.

"Listen." Luther had stopped, his face lifted and his eyes closed. In the distance Hoey could make out a faint sound of drumming and singing.

Luther began walking, his head held up as though following a trail of sound.

Hoey walked quickly to keep up with the long-legged old man, and the drumming and singing grew louder. Finally Luther stopped in the mouth of an alley, and they both looked into the darkness of the space between two-story buildings.

Halfway down the alley a man beat the top of an oil drum with both fists. Flames leaped from a second barrel close by, reddening the drummer's bare chest and sweating face and touching the ends of his long hair with light. The drumming bounced off the close walls, and the man sang a high, nasal refrain, a few sounds woven together over and over. The man's face burned, as though the flesh itself had caught up and held the fire. And then he began to dance, turning from the fire and lifting his bare feet, his arms spread at the elbows, forearms and fists pointed in and downward, back curved and head bent toward the earth. With each foot lifted high and then dropped silently, the man began to move in a circle, head bobbing close to the earth, elbows out and fists clenched.

"He's hunting now," Luther said. And he turned and began to walk back toward the pickup.

For a long moment Hoey watched the dancing shadow and the fire. At the other end of the alley a second-floor window was suddenly illuminated and then plunged into darkness again. Below the window, thrown into relief for an instant, was what looked like a man with the head of a coyote. With a sense of something like terror, Hoey stared hard at the darkness where the figure had been. A hand gripped his bicep.

110   "We can't help that one," Luther said.

Hoey turned away and followed his uncle back in the direction of the truck. In his mind, the figure at the far end of the alley slowly resolved into the face and bare chest of a man with a coyote skin draped over forehead and shoulders. He felt a deep chill at his back, and he hurried to match strides with Luther.

"The Teepee Room," Luther said. "Let's go in there. I think we need a beer."

"You don't drink," Hoey said.

Luther looked at him with narrowed eyes. "You do."

The padded vinyl door of the Teepee Room swung outward, and two young men staggered out with their arms around each other's shoulders. Both wore black, high-crowned hats with a hawk feather in each band, and both were smiling broadly and chuckling.

Hoey stepped to the side to let the men stumble past, but upon seeing Luther the two stopped and swung about to face the old man.

"Hey, Grandfather," the long-haired one said. "You got the wrong hat." He turned to his friend. "He's got the wrong hat."

"Wrong hat?" the other repeated dully, his smile thinning out to a perplexed frown. Hoey noted that this one's hair was cut close and high, so that his ears stuck out comically from under the hat.

"Must be Ute," the drunker of the two muttered. "Ute hat."

"We are Chahta," Luther said, staring at both. "And we are your elders."

"Not my elders, old man," the long-hair began, but the other pulled his arm from his friend's shoulders and grabbed him hard by the elbow. "Shut up, Raymond," he said harshly. He nodded to Luther. "I'm sorry, Grandfather. My brother's drunk."

Luther nodded back, and Hoey said, "Then you better take your brother home."

Both young men turned toward Hoey as if seeing him for

111

the first time. For a moment they stared, and then they remembered their manners and looked away. At once the short-haired one began to urge his brother up the sidewalk in a stumbling retreat. Hoey heard one whisper, "Are you crazy, man? Didn't you fucking see it?"

Luther watched the two for a moment and then pulled the padded door open. Inside, the bar was crowded with Indians, tall and short ones, ones with long braids and loose black hair, ones with greased-back pompadours, and ones with crew cuts. Country-western music twanged, and through the blue air men and women smoked and lifted long-necked bottles and shouted at one another. At a pool table, a big man with braids and a sleeveless black tee shirt was bent over to line up a shot. A young man with an enormous belly and several chins stood to one side, holding a cue stick in his right hand and scratching beneath his flannel shirt with the left. His close-shaved head turned very slowly to take in the two men who had entered, and then the head turned back to the pool table.

Luther studied the scene, his eyes resting for an instant on a group of four young women piled together giggling and smoking in a narrow booth. The girls looked at him out of the corners of their heavily made-up eyes and then huddled with squeals of laughter.

"Would you like to sit down, Grandfather?"

A short, heavyset man in a black leather jacket, white tee shirt, and long, loose hair stood in front of them, his smile a stunning white in his dark face.

"Yes, Grandson." Luther nodded, and behind his uncle Hoey scanned the room for an empty table, finding none. He noticed the bartender watching them. A tall man with pale skin and short-cut, sparse hair, the bartender wore small, dark sunglasses that lay over his eyes like coins. His large lips seemed to have a bluish tinge, and he ran his tongue across them as he watched.

"Excuse me." The broad-shouldered Indian turned away and walked to a nearby table where three men and a young woman sat nursing beers and being careful not to look at Luther and Hoey. While Luther studied the room, Hoey saw the group at the table rise and, taking their bottles with them, drift toward the back of the bar, the woman watching Luther out of the corner of her vision.

"Some of my friends were just leaving," the man said, gesturing toward the table. "Welcome to Gallup, my grand-fathers. You have a long journey." He smiled and turned away, and as he did so, Hoey felt himself shiver.

They sat at the round table, and at once a plump barmaid set two bottles in front of them. When Hoey reached into his pocket, the woman shook her head and gestured toward the back of the bar. "He already paid," she said with a quick half-smile, before gathering two empty bottles and return-ing to the bar.

Hoey took a long pull on the beer and watched his uncle looking around him. "What's going on here, Uncle Luther?"

Luther focused on the bottle in front of him, turning it with a thumb and forefinger. "We better go, Hoey," he said. "We got to get up real early."

Hoey set the beer down and rubbed a hand across his forehead. "I'm not in the mood for beer, anyway," he said.

Luther stood up, heading for the door with such a weak, shambling stride that Hoey reached for the old man's elbow.

Saying nothing, Luther pushed at the vinyl door, but the door refused to budge until Hoey shoved with one hand.

Once outside, Luther turned in a half-circle to look up and down the street, saying in a voice deep with wonder, "I didn't know, Hoey. I never knew. This is where it begins."

"What begins?"

"We'll drive in your truck to find a place to sleep," Luther said, moving carefully in the direction of the Dodge. "There must be a Indian hotel in a town like this."

They got into the pickup and drove further down the main street, and when they stopped at a light, Luther raised a hand and pointed through the windshield.

"Look. It's like your boy's name. Coal Avenue."

113

Hoey followed the direction of the bony finger. "It's spelled different, though."

"It's a sign, Hoey."

"It's a street sign."

"What about one of those?" Luther asked, waving his hand toward a scattering of dimly lighted motel signs that punctuated the row of bars and pawn shops.

Hoey shook his head again. "Those kind rent rooms by the hour."

"Maybe that's good, Hoey. It's late and we got to get going pretty early, so maybe we could rent one for three or four hours."

"I think there were some better ones back on the east end of town."

Twenty-Seven

They left the motel room half an hour before sunrise and climbed back into the pickup.

"I need coffee," Hoey said as the pickup choked to life.

Luther finished running a comb through his hair and then reached with both arms to tie the hair in a ponytail. "We'll get some pretty soon."

"There was a truck stop coming into town. They're probably open." Hoey backed the pickup around and drove out onto the deserted street in the direction of the freeway. Sulphurous orange streetlights cast shadows from the dead facades of bars and motels.

"That was a Indian hotel," Luther said. "That manager last night said he was Indian."

"He told you he was from India, Uncle Luther. He was an Indian from India."

"He looked like that oldest Pike boy over to Satartia. The Pikes is Chickasaw and Cajun mixed. Feels good to be driving east this time of day, don't it?"

"Night," Hoey said. "There's that truck stop. It's open."

When Hoey had gone into the cafe and come out with paper cups of coffee, they continued driving east toward the freeway, coming quickly to the edge of town, where buildings gave way to tall weeds and ragged bushes lining both sides of the road. On the north side, a wide, crumbling arroyo cut deeply away toward distant train tracks. A quarter mile on the other side of the arroyo, beyond the tracks, sparse traffic on the interstate highway moved in the mixed light.

Hoey drove slowly, studying the growing light of daybreak ahead and smelling the sweet, cool air even through the closed windows. A mist rose from the weeds and lay alongside the straight, empty road. Hoey felt the old man grow tense, and when he took his eyes from the road to look at his uncle, Luther sat rigid, as though he were listening, the coffee held halfway to his mouth.

"You better pull in over there," Luther said quietly, gesturing with his coffee toward a turnout beside the road. "Something is going to happen."

Hoey swung the pickup off the road and into the turnout.

"Park it longways of the road, so we can watch," Luther said.

Hoey swung the truck slowly around so that it paralleled the road and turned off the engine. The truck shuddered and fell silent. "Watch what?"

Luther tasted the coffee and drew his mouth quickly away, keeping his eyes focused on the scene outside. "I don't know, nephew. Be careful. This coffee is real hot." He held the cup close to his mouth and blew before speaking. "Jobe pours his coffee in a saucer so it cools, then he drinks it from that saucer."

115

"If you don't explain what we're doing, old man, I'm going to start this truck and head for California right now."

Luther peered through the windshield. "We ain't actually going to California right now, Hoey," he said. "Look."

They watched as blue light moved slowly over the land from the east, layering red rock and stunted trees on the hillside south of the road and pouring like water into the ragged arroyo on the other side. Shadowy forms began to ascend like ghosts from the littered grass and shrubbery at the edge of the blacktop.

"I think Robert Jim wanted us to see this," Luther said quietly.

Fifty feet away, a man rose from the brush, his long, black hair slick with moisture, and even in the dim light they could see that his face was slack and empty as he looked about him, as though he were trying to remember something irretrievably beyond reach.

"Drunks," Hoey said. "This is as far as they get from the bars."

"Yes," Luther replied softly. "They think they're going home. Now watch."

A dark van was moving slowly along the road, close to the edge. A hundred yards away, a silhouette wavered upward from the grass, and Hoey saw the outlines of a woman. The side door of the van opened and two big men jumped out, seizing the insubstantial figure and dragging it to the vehicle. Throwing it inside, they leaped in, slamming the door closed. The van began to move away quickly, toward the interstate.

"Those are the witches," Luther said.

"They're kidnapping that woman." Hoey handed his cup to Luther and started the truck, spinning the tires as the Dodge hinged onto the road back toward the town. "We have to tell the police."

A cup in each hand, Luther turned to look over his shoulder at the several shadows still standing in the weeds, all gazing in the direction the van had taken. With the sweep of sun traveling from the east, he left the pickup and soared over yellow-brown earth and red rimrock toward the canyons, rising up to a blue-black mountain in the east and the four sacred peaks in the west. In the high desert, miles to the north, a round house squatted under a light blanket of snow, piñon and cedar smoke lacing the air. An old man and woman stood in front of the house, peering eastward, sniffing the gray dawn and listening. Two roan horses paced in a corral close to the house, snorting steam, and a black and white sheep dog prowled the corral fence. A mile beyond the small house, a pair of golden eagles rode updrafts along canyon walls, studying the restive earth where coyote paused, tongue out, laughing. The air was sweet and fragrant with cedar and sage, and snow lined the red and yellow shelves of canyon walls.

"It won't do no good," Luther said. "To tell the police."

"What else can we do?"

"Go on."

"We can call from the truck stop," Hoey said as he turned into the cafe lot.

Luther shook his head. "Witches already took that woman. The police don't care about Indians. This town is full of drunk Indians. The police will look at you and see you're just a Indian, too. Mixedbloods and fullbloods is all the same."

Hoey looked at his uncle for a long minute. "We have to do something," he said at last.

"We're supposed to try to get to California," the old man explained patiently. "Onatima is there already."

"You're not making any sense." Hoey rubbed his free hand across his forehead. "I'm getting damned tired of not knowing what's going on."

"I don't know neither, Hoey. Coyote's out there laughing at us; I just seen him."

"Do they kill that woman?" Hoey asked hopelessly as he started the truck once again.

117

Luther sipped the coffee. "They done killed that woman about a million times."

"Does somebody stop those guys?"

"I think maybe we do."

Twenty-Eight

Alex braked sharply to avoid the silver BMW that shot in front of them from a side road. "*Chinga tu madre, pendejo*," he said in a low voice. Turning to Robert, he added, "Spanish is a good language for cursing. The trouble with the Navajo language is we don't have words like that. And such things sound too crude in English, don't you think? Check out the license plate."

Robert leaned forward and read the letters aloud, "U R O K 2 B U."

"But it's great to be me. That asshole almost killed us," Alex said, hunching his shoulders inside the sheepskin vest. "Check out the bumper sticker."

"Practice random acts of kindness," Robert read before the BMW disappeared around a sharp turn.

"There it is in a nutshell, Robert. Words have ceased to have meaning in the Western world. There is no responsibility."

The redwoods on both sides of Highway 9 leaned inward, enclosing the twisting, two-lane road. Every quarter mile, thin waterfalls fell from folds in the hillside above them and vanished into culverts under the pavement. Robert leaned toward the side window, trying to see the San Lorenzo River in the deep drainage below the road.

The Volvo jolted over railroad tracks, and Robert pointed toward a trail that climbed into the trees beside the tracks.

"You can take that trail to campus," he said. "It comes out on the northeast side."

Alex smiled approvingly. "You know the region of your existence well, don't you, Robert? I'll bet you know every trail in this little range."

"I think I do. There are miles and miles of trails, from campus all the way to Big Basin twenty miles north. Almost no one uses them."

"Where were you born, Robert?"

"Right here. I've lived all my life here. My parents were born here."

Alex nodded. "A person should know the landscape of his dreams, huh Robert?"

"Dreams?"

"Abby told you about the peyote ceremony."

Robert nodded. "She said you might let me join."

"Join? That's an interesting way of expressing it." Alex turned fully toward Robert for an instant, and his face was serious. "Abby thinks it might be good for you. Do you think so?"

Robert nodded. "Yes, I think so."

"It's a Native American Church service, Robert. Why would you want to participate in an Indian religious service?"

"I want to learn. Native Americans have a lot to teach all of us."

"Like what?"

"How to live in harmony with the world, the environment."

"You ever see a reservation, Robert? Go to a reservation sometime, and you'll see junked cars, arroyos full of wrecked refrigerators, broken bottles, cans—all the same squalor you'll see anywhere, maybe worse. Not very harmonious."

"You know that's different," Robert replied. "You're testing me. That's poverty, the same everywhere. I'm talking about world view. I mean, the Ohlone people lived around Monterey Bay for maybe ten thousand years without destroying their environment, but look at what we whites have done in just two hundred. That river down there was full of salmon and steelhead fifty years ago, but now it's dead. Native Americans know how to live in balance, how to accept responsibility for their world."

"American Indian teenagers have the highest suicide rate in the world, Robert, a hundred times higher than white teenagers."

"It's because they've lost the way," Robert said evenly. "They've lost the sacred teachings of the elders."

Alex sighed. They passed a big yellow sign with a black dot in the middle advertising the Mystery Spot, a place in Santa Cruz where the laws of nature were confused, where trees grew perpendicular to the mountainside and water ran uphill. "A peyote ceremony isn't recreational, Robert. You understand that?"

"Of course."

"You have to approach it with a good heart, and respect."

Robert nodded. "I understand."

"The Peyote Chief knows dreams and reality are one thing, Robert. It can be hard." Alex kept his eyes on the winding road.

"You can drop me in front of that driveway," Robert said, pointing at a mailbox in front of a big gate of black iron spikes.

Through the trees, Alex could see the faint outlines of a very large house, and as if in response, Robert said, "My cabin is behind the house, down on the creek."

As Robert opened the door and stepped out, Alex said, "You're welcome to take part, Robert. Abby can tell you when."

"I'd like that. And thank you for the ride home."

"My pleasure. And remember, Robert. You're okay to be you."

For a few seconds, Alex sat in the car, watching Robert slip through the gate and vanish down the paved driveway.

Twenty-Nine

By the time the sound of Alex's car had disappeared, Robert stood balanced on a hanging bridge. Of rough-cut redwood two-by-tens nailed vertically, the little house sat on a platform overhanging a redwood stump. A tin chimney tilted out of the shake roof, and small windows in each wall were black squares in the shade of the forest. A shallow stream split around the stump, and the rope-and-plank bridge crossed ten feet of air to the door.

He paused for a note tacked to the doorframe and shoved the note into his pocket. "Got to watch the quality folks' house," he said aloud to himself.

"Quality folks?"

He spun toward the voice. A dark-haired young woman emerged from behind a hedge, arms crossed over her tee shirt, her smile a challenge.

"Hi, Brett," he said. "Just a little joke, from *Huckleberry Finn*."

"I know. We read that last year."

He shifted, squaring his shoulders. The rich man's daughter, she had watched him build his little house the previous summer.

"Joan and Peter went skiing," she said, speaking of her parents as though they were neighbors.

"Where are the twins?"

"In the house. I'm baby-sitter for the weekend."

"All by yourself?"

With an expression of disgust, she said, "I'm sixteen years old, or haven't you noticed?"

He looked at the big gray house, with its wide, close-cut lawn and tennis court. They had let him run PVC pipe from a garden connection for water, and he had use of the bath-

121

room and shower near the tennis court. For electricity, he'd tapped into a junction box at the tennis court and run a line along the bottom of the bridge into the cabin. Except from the back of the house, the little cabin was completely hidden from the world.

"I've never been inside your house," Brett said, her eyes drifting toward the front door.

"What about Ashley and Sarah? Should you leave them?"

"They're watching Kermit."

He looked at the clear water, where red and brown rocks covered the stream bed like autumn leaves. Sometimes he spent whole afternoons watching the fingerling trout that hung motionless in the shadow of his home, and the water striders that made disjointed patterns across the surface. At night he lay awake imagining racoons stirring the water's edge for crayfish. All his life he had dreamed of such a home, an island surrounded by steady motion, a house suspended above the heart of the world, inviolable. In the dark, he had but to wade the shallow stream to find deer trails on the other side that wound up into the coastal mountains, trails that followed the little stream canyons up to the crest. Sometimes at night his heart swelled with such love that he felt it would burst.

"Come in," he said at last, watching the perfect harmony of her young face.

"This is really cool." She stood looking around in the half-light. "And you built it all yourself." She examined the shelf that held his two-burner Coleman stove, and then stepped close to the plank table where his computer and reading lamp sat. Running a hand across the computer keys, she moved to peer out the little four-paned window.

"It's just like Swiss Family Robinson."

She glanced at the shelves of books that lined one wall from floor to ceiling, and then her gaze drifted further.

"I wish I could live like you do." Her fingers trailed across the books with a rhythmic sound. "I hate my life."

122   "You have a wonderful life. Your parents love you." He

remembered how golden she looked in the summer, as though she had taken in and held the sun from countless hours beside the pool.

"My parents love their Mercedes. They love being Joan and Peter. Have you read all of these books?"

"More or less."

She smiled sadly. "I'll bet you write poetry."

He shook his head. "A little."

"I'll bet you lie in this neat bed at night and think poetry. Can I try your bed?" Her eyes caught his, and she sat on the edge of the redwood frame and then rolled onto the bunk, her arms beside her and legs spread on the down comforter. Her fragrance filled the tiny room.

"My mother thinks you're brilliant, because you pretend to like her poetry. She also thinks you're gay, and I think she's disappointed. She has the hots for you." She gave him a suggestive look. "We talk about you at dinner. My father says you're a harmless fruitcake, but I can tell he likes having you live here. Like he has his own vassal or something."

"I'm not gay."

"It's okay. One of my best friends is gay. Well, really bisexual, I guess, since I know for a fact that he likes girls, too." She smiled, and he saw that her teeth were perfect, the kind of teeth rich people would arrange in advance along with the right preschool before a baby was born. With both hands she spread her hair upon the pillow. "We're a very strange family. I'd say we're full of Freudian tensions, but Freud is really outdated, isn't he? Real eighties. Sometimes my own father gives me the creeps. Sometimes I hate my parents."

"Your parents love you very much, Brett. You have to understand that they have a lot of stress in their lives. Things like skiing or having an expensive car are ways to cope with the stress. Life can be very difficult."

"Crap. You don't have any of those things. Your car is a million years old, and you live like one of Snow White's dwarves on top of a stump. I keep expecting Dopey and

Grumpy and all the rest to appear." She pushed hair away from her face. "Just kidding. I love your house."

"The love between a parent and child is special."

She made a face. "Good grief, Robert. Do you ever listen to yourself? You don't have to do that phony crap for me." The expression became an abrupt smile. "You never have girls out here, do you? I've never seen any. That's why my mother thinks you're gay. She watches."

Her fingers traced the length of his forearm.

Cautiously, he touched her cheek with the back of his hand, and she turned her head to take the edge of his hand between her teeth.

Releasing the hand, she said, "You're sweet, not like those jerky high-school boys. I like you." She pulled him toward her, and he let himself descend to her until they were kissing, her lips darting upon his and then drawing him in. He felt her hips begin to move beneath his.

Abuptly he locked his arms and shoved himself away, almost leaping from the narrow bed.

"I'm sorry, but you'd better go." He opened the door and stood there, hearing the stream and looking out to where shadows had begun to descend from the tall trees. "You see, I'm . . . I'm involved with someone."

Thirty

They caught up with the van at a rest stop ten miles east of Holbrook. "That's it," Luther said. "I guess you better stop."

Hoey turned the pickup off the highway and pulled into the parking lot.

"There ain't nobody else here," Luther said. "That's good. You got your deer rifle?"

Hoey turned from studying the van to stare at the old man. "You know it's behind the seat."

"Okay. Them fellows are taking a real long piss right now. So all you got to do is take that Krag in there and shoot 'em."

"Shoot 'em? You mean just go in there and kill those guys?"

"Sure."

"I ain't going to just kill nobody."

"Why not?"

"You ever killed anybody, Uncle Luther?"

The old man rubbed his chin with the back of his right hand, seeming to reflect for a moment. "Well, I never shot nobody. But you was in that war."

"Never again, Uncle."

"It's the most practical thing to do, Hoey. You shoot those witches, and they ain't going to do this kind of stuff anymore. Others will, there's so many, but these particular ones won't."

"It's crazy. Murder's against the law."

Luther took his hat off and looked at it. "Well, we better do something before they get their pissing done. It's going to seem unnatural long to them pretty soon."

"You fixed it this way didn't you? You knew we would catch up with these guys here."

Luther reached for the door handle. "They probably drunk too much beer, so now they got to piss like a Chickasaw racehorse."

They opened the doors and stepped out at the same time. Hoey pushed the back of the truck seat forward and pulled out the big deer rifle.

"Hide that rifle beside you, case there's somebody looking at us from that van," Luther said. "Though I don't believe there is."

Hoey held the rifle straight up beside his body, and they walked stiff-legged toward the bathroom, Luther watching Hoey with amusement.

125

"I feel like I'm in a goddamned parade," Hoey said.

"You sure you don't want to just shoot these witches?" Luther replied.

They rounded the corner of the small rest-room complex, and Hoey lifted the .30–40 Krag, slipping the safety off and working the bolt. "You stay behind me," he whispered.

They stepped around the cinder-block wall that covered the entrance to the men's room, and Hoey stopped just outside the doorway. Inside, a voice was saying, "I've never pissed this long in my life, Emo. You ever piss this much?"

"Jesus Christ," another voice answered. "Just shut up."

"I don't see you finishing neither. I bet I pissed two gallons by now."

Hoey stepped through the doorway, leveling the rifle at the three men lined up at the urinal trough.

"Hey!" one of the men shouted, jumping back and arcing a spray across the leg of the man next to him.

Behind him, Hoey heard Luther chuckling. "My nephew here says he don't want to shoot you men," Luther said. "But I told him it's the most practical thing to do. You can all stop that pissing now if you want."

The three men looked incredulously from Luther to the rifle and then down at themselves. Abruptly, the liquid had stopped falling.

"Take off your clothes." Hoey gestured with the rifle for emphasis as he spoke.

Immediately all three began to fumble with buttons and zippers. In seconds they stood naked in the tiled bathroom.

"Uncle Luther, you hold this rifle on 'em. And don't shoot." He handed the rifle to the old man, who looked at him quizzically and then raised the gun and squinted down the long barrel at each of the three in turn.

"My nephew just don't want us to shoot you," Luther said, his mouth close to the stock of the rifle. "Even though I tell him it's the practical thing to do. He must've seen this take-off-your-clothes part on television."

126   "Who the hell are you?" one of the three said at last,

watching the rifle swing from one to the other. "If you're after money, you're going to be disappointed." The speaker was short and brown skinned, with close-cut black hair and black eyes. The men on either side of him were both much taller, with white skin, sagging bellies, and pale hair.

"That little one talking's a Indian," Luther said, as Hoey pulled belts out of the men's pants. "You notice his pecker's a lot bigger than them others'. I always heard black folks had bigger ones than whites, but I never heard it about us Indians. Did you ever hear that, Hoey?"

They all looked at the crotch of the one in the middle. He looked down at himself in surprise.

"Don't you wonder why white people never made up stories about us Indians having big peckers, Nephew? That's something to think about."

"Jesus Christ," Hoey said. He gestured toward the three with the hand holding the belts. "Lay down on your bellies and put your hands behind your backs."

"That tile's colder than shit," one of the white men wailed.

"Shut up," the little dark one said. "You rather be shot?"

When the three were lying on the floor, Hoey tied each one's hands together with the belts.

When all three were tied, he stood up and began to gather the clothes.

"Why'd you tie them like that, Hoey? They look like a bunch of shoats all tied up naked like that."

Hoey shrugged. "It seemed like we ought to do something to these bastards. You keep that gun on them for a second. If any of you fellows decide to stand up, this old man will sure as hell shoot you. He wants to."

As soon as Hoey was out of the room, Luther said, "I know what you are, and I know what you been doing. You was going to do something with that woman you took this morning, but you ain't going to do that kind of thing no more. There's others will, but not you."

"What kind of Indian are you, old man?" the dark one asked, bending his neck to look.

127

"Chahta," Luther said. "What people call Choctaw. You must be one of these Indians from around here. Why are you doing this to your own people?"

The little man growled, seeming about to spit when he said, "Drunks and drug addicts and fucking white men's whores. Don't call them things my people." He squirmed around to glare at Luther and began to draw his feet beneath him.

"Well you better just lay still, because this rifle don't never miss. It's kind of like those missiles they showed on television, the ones that just follow whatever they're aimed at. These bullets just keep after you till they get you. This rifle's got some of that *fappuli* magic. One time I seen Hoey point it at the empty sky, not even a cloud, and when he shot, a airplane came spinning down out of that sky. Crashed right into a church full of white people and bad Indians. Killed a hundred people."

"Cracker Indian bullshit," the dark one snorted. "Bunch of cousin fuckers down there where you come from."

Hoey reappeared holding short lengths of rope. "There ain't nobody out there but the girl," he said. "Come on, you three, back to your van."

"Naked?" one of the white men asked, turning his head to look up toward Hoey.

"I told him to just shoot you," Luther said.

The men scrambled to their feet and followed Hoey out the door, with Luther and the rifle behind.

Hoey slid the door of the van open. "You three get in there," he said, and the men climbed through the open door, balancing precariously with tied hands.

"Lay down." When the three were once again lying on their bellies, Hoey tied the rope around their feet, running a length of rope from the bound feet to the belts around their wrists so that hands and feet were joined.

"You ain't got that rope too tight?" Luther asked.

Hoey shook his head. "I didn't cut off their circulation."

128   "What you want to do with these witches?" Luther asked.

"We ain't witches," one of the men said, his voice muffled by the mattress.

Hoey looked at his uncle and shook his head. "Christ if I know."

"We could burn 'em." Luther cocked his head as he looked at the three. "Onatima said white people used to do that with witches."

"We're not witches, for chrisesake," the other white man said out of the side of his mouth.

"What were you planning to do with that Indian woman?" Hoey asked.

"Nothing," the tallest one replied. "There's people in California buy 'em."

"Shut the fuck up," the Indian hissed. "You stupid mother-fucker."

"Or we could stake 'em to one of those great big anthills they got around here," Luther went on. "I saw that in a movie. Indians out here is supposed to do that."

Hoey looked at the old man and shook his head.

"I bet those Navajos know how to fix witches," Luther said. "Where's the girl?"

"I put her in the truck," Hoey answered. "I guess we can't just turn these fellows over to the cops, can we?"

Luther shook his head. "The police would say it's just a drunk Indian woman and two crazy Mississippi Indians causing trouble."

"You'll let us go if you know what's fucking good for you," one of the white men said.

Hoey stepped out of the van and slid the door closed. "I wish you could drive this thing."

Luther handed the rifle to Hoey and looked through the van's window. "Why can't I drive it?"

"You don't know how to drive anything, that's why. And you said you're nearly blind." Hoey glanced between the bucket seats at the steering column, seeing the keys hanging from the ignition. "It's an automatic, so you wouldn't have to shift. All you got to do is steer. Think you could do that?"

"Hmph. You get in that Dodge and let me drive this one."

"Okay. We can try it. Just keep that lever by the D. If you have to go backwards, which you won't have to, shift it to R." He watched as the old man settled behind the steering wheel, the brittle fingers divided exactly over both sides of the wheel. "You have to go first, since you say you know where she lives. Lucky thing they just filled it with gas." Hoey paused at the window and looked toward the rest-stop bathrooms. "You ever seen anybody piss that long?"

"Never did. It was like somebody put a piss-hex on them fellows. It's most peculiar."

"Well, I'll follow you. I hope we won't have to go too far on this highway."

Hoey got into the Dodge and started the motor, watching the old man in the mirror. The woman sat propped unconscious against the passenger door, slumped far back into the corner. The dark skin was swollen and pulpy from alcohol. Her flannel shirt reeked of vomit, and the synthetic pants were torn and filthy. Her black hair was long and tangled. He shook his head and thought that they would have to buy some clothes for her before they took her home, and then he pulled to the edge of the highway and stopped.

The van lurched past with gravel flying from the tires, skidded in a quick half-circle and came to a rest sideways in the road a few feet in front of the pickup. In the big side mirror of the van, he saw Luther lift a palm in greeting.

When no vehicles were in sight in either direction, the van jumped a few feet onto the highway and stopped and then jolted into motion, the rear end fishtailing. Hoey waited until the van was a hundred yards away and then accelerated onto the highway after it, heading back in the direction from which they had come. Ahead of the pickup the van swerved wildly and a mouse sprinted to the edge of the road, tail held high.

Hoey increased the speed of the truck until he could shift into third, all the time watching the other vehicle. The van raced ahead and dropped back and then jerked forward again, the edge of the black hat bouncing in the side window.

"Those boys are having a rough ride," Hoey said to himself as he watched a huge livestock truck appear suddenly on the horizon behind the pickup. The van seemed to nearly stop, and as Hoey slammed on the brakes, the loaded semi swung out to pass with a blast of horn. Hoey let out a long breath and began to scan the high desert on both sides of the four-lane highway.

Thirty-One

"What kind of place is this?"

Cole balanced a glass of lemonade on the newspaper in his lap, sitting back in the deck chair and seeming to address the question to the newspaper.

"Dangerous."

Alex, wearing a light-blue, flower-print sundress and white aerobics shoes, his long hair in a bun, sat in an identical chair, holding an identical glass. The sun had burned off the fog and now hung distantly over the tops of the trees, sending a smell of warm vegetation across the deck.

Cole stared at the *Santa Cruz Sentinel* in his lap. A black mountain lion had been seen in the Santa Cruz Mountains. "There's no doubt in my mind," a local building inspector told the reporter. "It was a pure, black mountain lion." Wildlife experts dismissed the four separate sitings. "While they are known to exist in South America," the experts noted, "there has never been hard evidence of a black lion in North America." A wildlife biologist explained that "It could have been a large house cat."

Cole closed his eyes and remembered Mississippi. The experts never talked to Choctaws, who'd always known about the black cats. He opened his eyes and searched for the sun through the oak branches. The panther that had screamed outside Uncle Luther's cabin twenty years before and still prowled Cole's dreams was black. *Nalusachito,* the old man had called it, souleater. Despite the sun's growing warmth, he shivered.

"It's just a cat," Alex said.

Cole looked up from the paper.

"I saw you obsessing on that story," Alex continued. "It's just a mountain lion. Sometimes, maybe in twenty years, maybe a hundred, they can be born black. It happens. Those scientists think they've got the whole world charted and graphed. What they don't see, they deny, and most of the world is invisible to them. They don't have the slightest idea."

The television went on through the open window. "The butcher murders are unique," the reporter's knowing voice said. "The decapitation and dismemberment are done with the skill of what the police say borders on professional medical knowledge.

"The pattern of the butcher killer is starting to emerge. He appears to strike only after dark. He travels certain routes in Santa Cruz, favoring the roads rimming the Santa Cruz campus. He has a knowledge of anatomy that, the sheriff's officials say, is good enough to make him a pathologist. Whoever he is, he knows the major roads through the Santa Cruz mountains and knows them quite well. Police tend to feel that there is a sexual deviation behind the butchery. Both the police and the sheriff's men admit they're getting nowhere, and have no leads."

"Do you believe that crap?"

Cole turned toward Alex's question. "Which crap?"

"About professional medical knowledge."

"No." Cole shook his head. "It's just the usual sensationalism. She's ignoring the fact that at least half of the bodies weren't mutilated at all. A dozen people have just been shot and left where they fell."

"The cops really said those strips of flesh were her?" Alex set the glass on one of his breasts and watched a red-tailed hawk circle.

"That's what they said. One of the missing students."

Alex's head moved very slightly with the arc of the bird, his eyes fixed on the sky. "On a prayer stick? Jesus Christ." He looked at Cole. "What'd they say they were going to do?"

"Send a patrol car up the road now and then. They're afraid of scaring the shit out of everybody."

"The truth is they're afraid of losing their jobs. These cops couldn't find their rectums unless they were doughnut holes. Did you tell Abby about the prayer stick?"

When Cole shook his head, Alex said, "You should. She ought to know what's going on. You aren't protecting her by not telling her."

"You may be right. I'll tell her when I get home tonight."

"I think you should. You know what we'd call this back home?"

Cole tilted the glass until it was empty.

"Skinwalkers, though nobody would really use that word."

"And what would you do?"

"We'd get stronger medicine, have a ceremony, or more than one. Find out who's doing it."

"And then?"

"Well, you have to deal with such things. They don't just go away. You have to stop them."

They sat in silence for a moment and then Alex added, "This is very bad, Cole. The best-case scenario is that some psychopath has you in his sights."

"Or her sights." He glanced at Alex's sundress.

"Maybe we should both leave, Cole. I mean, you've got cannibal prayer sticks and bear tracks turning up in your yard. There's a psycho out there killing people. I could get you a position at Navajo Community College. Five classes of composition."

133

"Dismemberment is preferable. Besides, we could leave, but this thing would still be going on."

"You're right, but what about Abby? I think you were right about that too. She shouldn't be here." Alex stood up. "You ready to go? The meeting starts in half an hour. By the way, where is Abby?"

"Watching the news."

"That news? We should bring her with us."

"I tried to talk her into it, but she won't do it."

Alex looked toward the house. "Maybe I should try."

"Abby's tired and wants to rest," Cole said. "She'll be okay. She's used to staying alone in the mountains back home, and she knows how to use a shotgun. Abby's a better shot than I am."

"Well, you know your daughter best."

"Do you plan to change first?"

"Clothes?"

Thirty-Two

Abby watched her father's pickup disappear down the gravel driveway. When she could no longer hear the high-pitched motor, she stretched, rising on her toes and yawning. She flicked the tv off with the remote control and turned on the portable radio in the kitchen. Going into the bedroom, she sat on the bed, tugging her boots off and admiring the view through the large bedroom window. A grassy meadow flowed away from the deck into the wall of timber a hundred yards further away. Opening a drawer, she rummaged for clean Levis, underwear, and tee shirt, piling them on the bed. Then she undressed and walked to the bathroom.

The old-fashioned tub was deep and long, made for giants, and she imagined how wonderful it would feel to lie there with it filled to the brim with hot water. Instead, she ran eight inches of water and sat in the tub, sponging herself and reexamining her father in her mind. He looked terrible, skinny and pale, much worse than he had before he'd left New Mexico. He'd stopped running, and it was obvious that until she'd shown up he'd been drinking too much. It was like her father had given up. And he seemed so alone. There was no sign at all in the house that anyone even visited, no signs of women, none of the little luxuries guests require, not even letters left on counters or coffee table. It was as if, except for Alex Yazzie, her father had spoken to no one since he'd loaded the pickup and driven out of the Sandia Mountains of New Mexico.

She ran the cloth between her toes and along her legs, wondering what her father was up to. There was obviously something he hadn't told her. Something that worried him. She held the cloth over her shoulders and squeezed, enjoying the warmth of the water on her breasts and stomach. Lying flat, she spread her hair so that it floated in a fan behind her. The stubble under her arms pricked where she was letting the hair grow out, and she ran a hand along one leg, wondering if she should let that hair grow as well. She pictured the shotgun where she'd found it in the kitchen. Her father had taught her to shoot and take care of guns, and she knew he wouldn't clean a shotgun unless he'd used it.

For several minutes she lay there, thinking of Alex Yazzie and enjoying the silence and warmth. Alex was a puzzle. He felt more male than any man she had ever known, making her dizzy sometimes. Even his smell was male. And then he would show up at the house in a dress, his hair in a beaded clasp, with dangling earrings and eye shadow. "Alex is nuts," her father said when she questioned him. "God

135

knows what he's doing." "But he's your friend, and I like him," she'd replied. Her father had looked hard at her, saying, "My friend is a trickster, Abby. Don't ever forget that."

She sat up and lathered her hair with her father's cheap shampoo, holding her head under the high bath tap to rinse. Finally she rose and rubbed the towel quickly over her hair and body. Half-dry, the towel wrapped turbanlike around her hair, she walked shivering out of the bathroom and into her new bedroom, where the full-length mirror on the closet door showed the approach of a body that had, in the last year, grown more full and rounded, no longer a fancy dancer's hard figure.

At the edge of the forest, a form moved from the shadows and sat cross-legged on the ground. The right half of the folded body was painted a dull white, the left half black. The hair, pulled back and tied behind the head, was parted in the middle, half-white and half-black. With eyes fixed upon the house, the naked figure held both fists with stiff forearms and moved them back and forth in a weaving pattern, chanting softly. One hand opened. In the cupped palm lay a fragment of white, a minute thread of flesh still adhering to the bone. The figure rose to its feet. With smooth, certain strides, it walked toward the house.

Abby was bent over, toweling her hair, when she caught the movement out of the corner of her vision. She straightened and saw the naked, nightmare figure walking evenly toward the window, fifty feet away. Without hesitation, she dropped the towel and ran to her father's room, grabbing the shotgun from the closet. She pumped a shell into the chamber and went to the phone in the kitchen. After the call, she stood with her bare back against the refrigerator, the shotgun ready, her eyes on the empty window frame in the living room.

Thirty-Three

Onatima watched through the cab window as they climbed up the shoulder of the coastal ridge above Santa Cruz. These were the trees of her dream, black-green and straight, with drooping, scaly branches. The winter air was thick with moist decay, and as they passed the turnoff to the university she saw seven deer grazing in a field near a fence. Looking back through the rear window, she could see the shrouded bay and faint lines of mountains on the far side of the water.

"Hurry, please," she said. All the way from the airport in the crowded city thirty minutes to the east, she had felt a pulsing warning, a moment approaching with deadly speed.

"It's a tricky road." The driver divided his gaze between the winding road and the rearview mirror, where the old woman with long, silver hair, flowing red dress, and red turban seemed almost transparent. From beneath the wraps of his own white turban, he stared in fascination at the illusion that gave him a wavering image of sea and green, falling hills right through his passenger. When their eyes met, he jerked his away as if burned.

She felt the cab jolt into slightly greater speed. Two miles past the university, they turned onto a rutted side road that wound higher up the ridge until, rounding a clump of shiny, red-barked trees, they were at the house she recognized from her dreams.

She stepped out as the car stopped. Without a backward look, she hurried up the graveled walk and knocked four times before pushing the door open.

"Hello!" she called. "Are you all right, Abby?"

"Who is it?" Abby stepped around the bar from the kitchen, the shotgun cradled beneath her breasts.

"It's okay now." Onatima reached for the gun with one arm and placed the other arm around the girl's shoulders. "You're safe now."

The driver stuck his bearded face through the door. "You owe me . . ."

He froze, staring for an instant at the girl and the shotgun before he backed out the door.

They sat on the couch, the shotgun laid on the floor. A siren began to wail in the distance, coming closer and louder until it was just outside the house.

The driver stuck his head through the door, looking carefully at the floor. "The policemen are here. Is everything okay?"

Onatima waved him away. "Come, Granddaughter," she said, "let's get you dressed before those fool police get in."

While the two deputy sheriffs took notes and walked around the house and to the edge of the woods, Onatima paid the cabdriver, who held the money as if he hadn't noticed it and stared with very large brown eyes at the house.

"If there is anything I can do to help," he began, pronouncing each word precisely.

She placed a hand on his shoulder and shook her head. "You're a good man. But we're fine now."

When the driver and deputies were gone, Onatima picked up the shotgun and went into the kitchen. Abby sat at the small table, her arms folded across her chest.

"We'll just keep this handy," the old lady said.

"They thought I was on drugs," Abby replied.

"Medication? That's why they asked those stupid questions?"

"Hallucinogens. Acid or something. Do you think I dreamed it?"

Onatima looked at her curiously. "No. There are tracks outside the window. It wasn't a dream."

"What was it?"

"A man, judging by your description and the tracks I found."

"He must be insane."

Onatima's lips pursed and she looked hard at Abby. "Undoubtedly. You know, the last time I saw you, you were just a little girl. After you left, I visited you in dreams. Do you remember?"

Abby's eyes widened. "I remember dreaming about you."

"There were things I tried to tell you."

Abby concentrated. "I only remember your face in the dreams."

"It was too difficult." Onatima folded her bony hands on the table and looked down at the veined knuckles. "I'm so old now that five years are like five minutes. You visited me five minutes ago when you were a little girl, and now we're sitting here like this and you're a woman. What I wanted to teach you was about power. I wanted to save you the years it's taken me to learn some things. But of course that never works.

"When I was a little girl I wanted to be like my mother, who was French. I loved her so much. My father was an important man among the Choctaw. He had a big house and fields and horses and was richer than any of our neighbors, including the whites. I was proud of him, but when we were with white people I saw my father grow small. My mother would take me with her to Vicksburg, where nobody knew us, and we'd pretend that I was just like all the rich white kids there. My father never went with us to Vicksburg. My mother and I would stay in a big hotel, and we would speak to each other in French. Even when I was a very little girl, I knew what she was doing, and I think I must have wanted the same thing.

"And then one day when I was at home playing with my dolls, I looked in a mirror and saw nothing. It was many years before I could see myself again, and now, as you can see, I'm disappearing once more."

She lifted a hand, and light from the ceiling fixture shone through the flesh and brittle bones. "My father's parents died before I was born. My father's mother, my Indian

139

grandmother, used to visit me on warm nights when I could hear the cotton fields moving like water all around the house. She called me *chahta alla*, her Choctaw child. She was very old and heavy, and when she sat on the side of my bed it would sag nearly to the floor. She loved pecans and would sit there with a paper sack full, cracking them between the heels of her hands and dropping the shells on the floor so that later I'd have to sneak around and sweep them up so I wouldn't step on them barefooted. She would brush the hair from my face and tell me stories about the way it had been, but her words were like water we try to hold in our hands. Many years later I told Luther, and he said I'd learned too many stories in school and from books to learn properly from a ghost with a mouth full of nuts. Luther Cole never did have enough respect for either school or ghosts. Finally, when I began to change into a woman, my grandmother didn't come anymore.

"Perhaps the man who frightened you today wants to make you see yourself only through his eyes, so that you can only imagine yourself from outside the window looking in. That way, every time you look in a mirror you will see only what the man sees. You will always be outside yourself, and your own reflection will be a trap. When that happens we become like ghosts who can't see our own bodies. Then we have to make others see us so we can know we exist, or we have to use others' lives as our own. That's what they want. It's a matter of power. They would imprison us in their vision and their stories, and we can't let them do that. We have to have our own stories. That's what my grandmother was trying to tell me."

Onatima placed both hands on the girl's shoulders and looked directly into her eyes. "There's a great deal of pain in these mountains. I can feel it the way you feel a cold day inside a warm room. I can feel it rushing toward this house. Why did you come here?"

"I thought my father needed me."

Onatima sat back, folding her hands once again on the

table. "He does. He needs all of us. When he was a little boy, four or five years old, I'd see him and his brother playing by the river, looking so much alike you'd think they were twins. Cole used to watch every move your uncle made so he could imitate him. He loved his brother more than the whole world."

"He's never talked about him," Abby said. "All I know is that he died in Vietnam."

Onatima looked up quickly. "Is that what your father told you?"

"Didn't he?"

"In a manner of speaking."

She patted Abby's arm and shook her head. "Now just look at me. I'm preposterously ancient. My teeth are new, and my hair hasn't been black since before your father was born." She smiled, and Abby realized the teeth were indeed too even and too white. "It's a good thing I have my herbs. Do you do aerobics with television?"

Thirty-Four

Abby, wrapped in a bathrobe, and Onatima were sitting at the kitchen table, drinking tea.

"Grandmother!" Cole rushed to throw his arms around the old lady, and she stood stiffly to let him hug her. Then she pushed him away and looked at him for a long moment before turning to Abby. "Your father is almost as skinny as Luther."

"And you are younger than you were five years ago." He looked at Abby. "Onatima uses witchcraft."

"Hogwash. I'm a hundred years old," the old lady said, looking from Cole to Abby. "I taught your father to read, when he was a callow youth."

"Onatima taught me how to think," he added.

"Not every experiment is a success." She turned back to Cole. "Your daughter had a fright. That gambler came to her window."

His smile disappeared. "What gambler? Are you all right, Abby?"

"The one in the dream. We can talk about that later, but we're going to have to watch Abby more closely from now on."

"I'm not a child who needs babysitting." Abby's words came out halfheartedly.

"Are you okay?"

"I'm fine," Abby said. "I had the shotgun. And then Onatima came. And the police."

"The police?"

"I called 911."

"That's good." He sat down at the table. "Tell me what happened."

When she was finished, he looked at Onatima and she nodded imperceptibly.

"How did you get here so quickly, Grandmother?" he asked.

"I flew, of course." She paused. "Luther and Hoey are on their way in Hoey's old truck, but I'm afraid they've been sidetracked already. Luther Cole never could stick to one idea. Lord only knows if those two will ever get here now."

"Why didn't you call first so we could meet your plane?"

She looked at him steadily for a few seconds. "I thought things had gone far enough without me. I flew in a 747. They have telephones in the backs of the seats. You can call people while you're flying. I was tempted, but you have to have a credit card. Money is no longer sufficient. Still, I enjoyed imagining those words spread out like birds on the wind. Progress can be very picturesque. Where will I sleep?"

Cole looked around the kitchen, as if an extra bedroom might materialize. After a moment, he said, "You can sleep in my room. I'll sleep on the couch."

"That's generous of you, Grandson. Already I miss my Airstream." She looked skeptically from the little kitchen across the bar into the living room. "You have cable?"

He shook his head. "Satellite dish."

She nodded. "Luther likes to watch that program in which the hero leaps back and forth into different bodies." She glanced at Abby. "When he looks in mirrors, he sees the other person he's supposed to be, and he has to live out that other person's story in each episode. Luther says it's the only realistic show on television. That old man lacks the ability to suspend disbelief, I'm afraid."

Abby yawned. "I think I'll lie down," she said.

When she had gone to her room, Cole and Onatima remained at the table, neither looking at the other. Finally, Onatima said, "This is a dangerous situation, Grandson. I don't know why Luther let it go so long."

"What does Uncle Luther have to do with it?"

"Luther Cole has something to do with everything. You should know that by now. The one in your dream seems to have a great deal of power, and there's something about you that has attracted him. Some of us, you know, are more receptive than others to such things. That's just the way it is. And you know I'm not talking about metaphors or psychic projections here. Maybe this bone gambler doesn't want to be dead. There are different kinds of dead, you know. Some are just lonesome and want company. You know about those.

"Others cannot accept death; they're lost. You might say that kind just want to use your life for a little while. When that happens, you will know it because it's an exhilaration like nothing else you can ever experience. Imagine how it must feel to suddenly be alive again after wanting it for so long. You feel like you're incredibly strong, powerful, that you're made of light that soars into the stars."

143

"You've felt that?"

"Of course. That kind of thing happens with a spirit that can't find the path, one that's caught in between. But this dream-sender is different. There's something more going on here, something I don't quite understand. Sometimes it feels like hatred and sometimes love."

"You know about the murders?"

She cupped her chin between thumb and forefinger and studied him for a long time. "I'm very curious, but each person has to face his own ghosts. The murders are related, certainly, but one thing at a time."

She sipped the tea and made a wry face. "Luther says I talk too much. But you have a complex problem here, much more so than what happened the other time. What Abby saw today wasn't a dream and it wasn't a ghost. The tracks go to the woods. I didn't follow them, but even I could see that they're just a man's tracks."

"But Abby's description sounded like my dream."

She cupped the tea with both hands halfway to her mouth. "Others dream also," she said. "Perhaps there are more actors in your story than you suspect. I want to see you lecture."

"What?"

"I haven't been in a classroom in thirty years. I think I would enjoy hearing you lecture. Elders teach, and I want to see you function as an elder. I won't frighten your students, will I?" She smiled. "I telephoned your wife last week."

"My former wife. Why?"

"Mara's my friend, and women have to help each other when you men screw everything up. She sounded relatively happy. Life's just like that, Grandson, and the sooner you adjust the better. It's time you got some perspective on this midlife crisis and stopped feeling sorry for yourself. You're very fortunate. You have a wonderful daughter and a wonderful former wife who will remain your friend if you let her. You have an education. If I had a Ph.D., I'd be in Wash-

ington, D.C., giving everybody hell. Indian male meno-
pause is a terrible thing."

"And I have a ghost. You left that part out."

"We all have ghosts, Grandson."

She stood up, smoothing her dress with fragile hands.
"Isn't it wonderful that life is interesting? Incidentally, you'll
stop drinking alcohol, too. That's the worst Indian cliché of
all. It's time to quit feeling sorry for yourself and start thinking about this situation here. It's your story, after all, and
people are dying."

Thirty-Five

The girl bends beneath him like a willow branch, supple
with terror. The spilled wine seeps like blood along cracks
in the stone floor. A late rooster crows in the courtyard
beyond the barred window, the sound disappearing in the
long tolling of vespers. Despite a life given to strange lands,
despite the agonizing trail of crosses, despite all, one's soul
is lost so easily between the thighs of beasts. *Delivered unto a
violent land.* He speaks the words in his mind. Now there
will be no escape.

Thirty-Six

Cole was splitting firewood when he heard the car. By the time he had walked around to the front of the house, Alex was there with the rear of the Volvo open. He held a heavy rope attached to something inside the car and was leaning back on the heels of his boots. Two thick, tawny legs protruded from the car.

Alex waved with his free hand, glancing at Cole but keeping his eyes on the car. "Hey, Cole,"

Cole tried to peer into the Volvo. "Good afternoon, Alex. What is it?"

Abby stood on the path to the house, watching. Behind Abby, Onatima looked on with eyes squinted and arms crossed.

"Dog." Alex pulled on the rope, and an immense yellow-brown animal tumbled onto the gravel, snarling.

"Sit!" Alex yelled and jumped backwards at the same time.

The dog sat, its drooping black eyes fixed grimly on the hand at the end of the rope.

"Don't worry." Alex waved a hand at Cole. "He always sits when you tell him to. He likes to sit."

"What is he?" Cole asked.

"Bull mastiff. A beauty, huh? Hundred and forty pounds if he's an ounce."

A profound growl rumbled out of the mastiff's broad chest, and the head swung toward Cole.

"He's gorgeous," Abby said, moving up to stand beside her father. "Can I pet him?"

Alex shook his head. "I think maybe you'd better let him get used to his new home first. I think he's a little bit nervous."

"New home?" Cole said. "What do you mean, new home?"

"He's for you. I was thinking about the trouble Abby had the other day, and I decided you needed a guard dog, so I went to the pound. He's a housewarming present for you."

"I've lived in this house eight months, Alex. It's already warm."

"Well, I felt bad because I never held a giveaway for you, or a blessing ceremony or something. This will make up for it."

"You don't have to make up for it, Alex. I told you I don't want a dog."

"Indians and dogs go together, Cole. It's an ancient, honorable alliance. A good dog warms the lodge during those hard winters and warns when the stealthy enemy approaches. And Custer's a sweet dog; look at that face. He's just a little nervous right now. That's a bumpy road you have, and he probably misses his former home."

"Custer?" Cole and Abby spoke at the same time.

"You named him Custer?" Abby's voice rose to a higher pitch.

"Well, I didn't. The cop did."

"Cop?"

"The one who arrested his owner."

"Custer?" Cole looked at the dog's enormous head, with jaws big enough to snap a small oak, and the neck and chest that didn't seem distinguishable. "Why?"

"Well, I don't know, but the cop was a Lakota guy over in San Jose. A lot of Indian cops around, you know. Maybe it's his hair. It's golden, like General George Armstrong Custer's— you know, Yellowhair. The pound people said he didn't have a name before. His owner was a crack dealer who just called him Dog. He had a deprived upbringing—a dog with no name, guarding a crack house—and I figured I could kill two birds with one stone, so to speak, by getting him for you. He's a professional guard dog. They said it took five animal control people with nets to get him out of that house. The Lakota cop said they wanted to shoot him. He

147

must have really felt like Custer, seeing all those guys coming. But he needs a regular home environment like you have here. It'll straighten him out, like therapy. You can keep him in the house for a while, and once he's used to the place, you can let him patrol outside, and nobody will bother you. Custer will protect you from attack."

Custer swivelled his head to look at Cole, the growl rumbling in a deeper note.

"I appreciate your thoughtfulness, Alex, but we don't need a killer to protect us from killers."

Alex glanced up, seeing the old lady for the first time, and waved, saying, "Good morning, Grandmother."

Cole looked at Onatima and then back toward Custer. "Alex, this is my grandmother, Onatima Blue Wood." He turned toward the old lady. "Grandmother, this is one of my colleagues from the university. He's a crazy Navajo transvestite."

"Come on, Cole. That's no way to introduce me to such a distinguished person as your grandmother. Besides, look at my wardrobe." Alex smiled at Onatima. "I've told him transvestite is not the technically correct term. It is an honor to meet you. Cole's told me splendid things about you."

Onatima nodded, watching with obvious amusement.

Abby stepped closer. "Oh, Dad, can't we keep him? Look how he's sitting there. He's well behaved. And if Alex takes him back to the pound, they may put him to sleep."

"That's what they would do for sure. The gas chamber. Don't you hate those white-man euphemisms? It's hard to believe people wouldn't snap up a pet like this, but they said I was his last hope, his stay of execution. He's my gift to your family. I already paid the animal control people for him, for shots and license and that stuff, and I won't get my money back. He'll be a sweet dog once he gets used to you." He took a step toward the dog, holding a hand out and crooning, "Good boy, Custer."

The growl rose in intensity and the dog snarled, saliva flying. Alex jerked his hand back. "Why don't you take him into the house and start getting him used to his new home?"

He looked around at the clearing and the ridge to the west. "You know, this is the perfect place for a dog like Custer. A clean, wholesome environment, lots of room to stretch his legs. Reminds me of home."

"You have redwoods at Chinle?"

"Please, Dad? We could just try him for a while."

"Abby, that dog is antisocial, probably a social psychopath. Probably damaged by drugs."

The dog braced its front feet and sat back on its haunches.

"I'm very pleased to meet you," Onatima said, walking toward the car.

As she approached, Alex looked at the old lady with interest.

"Let me have the rope." Onatima held out her hand, and when he handed her the rope she held it loosely, stepping close to the dog. The growl turned into a snarl again.

"Stop that nonsense," she said, bending slightly to look the dog in the face. "A dog with a name like Custer can't afford to alienate anyone. You'd better stop. Now come with me."

Custer stood up, unfolding to amazing height on his long legs, and followed her into the house.

Inside, she led the dog to a braided rug in the center of the living room. "Sit," she said, and Custer sat.

"Where would you like him?" She smiled at Cole, and it was the same smile he'd first seen twenty years before in Luther's cabin when his brother's ghost had stepped from the corner. The joke was on him, and she was enjoying it.

"Right there, I guess. Maybe you could tell him to lie down on the rug."

Onatima unhooked the rope from the dog's collar. "Lie down," she said.

Custer looked at her and walked to the couch, climbing clumsily onto the cushions and stretching full length on his side. With his head horizontal on a cushion, the accordian lips folded and salivating, he glared at them for a moment and then his eyes fluttered and closed. He began to breathe in deep, painful gasps that fell quickly to a wheezy snoring.

"Can you make him get down?" Cole asked, "That's my bed, remember? He's already slimed it."

Onatima shook her head. "I don't think so. Custer is not a particularly bright dog, Grandson, and he is certainly not a happy one. We should probably let him rest for now."

"Looks like he's asleep," Alex said. "They told me they found him on the couch in the crack house. He's probably used to a couch." He smiled expansively at the dog. "Isn't he a magnificent animal? Look at those shoulders. Maybe you should feed him. That way he'll bond faster."

He stepped to the door. "I have to get back to a class. Enjoy Custer."

"Could I catch a ride down with you, Alex?" Abby asked. "I hate to leave Custer, but there's an evening class I've been auditing."

"You're leaving us with this dog?" Cole looked from the mastiff to his daughter.

"Give him some meat or frybread or something. He'll love you." Alex backed toward the door. "Oh, I almost forgot. You'll need these." He pulled a bottle out of his pocket. "Custer's thyroid pills."

"Thyroid pills?" Cole looked at the dog, whose massive side rose and fell with slow regularity.

"Mastiffs have this thing about their thyroids. You have to give him eight of these every day. The human dose is one, but that's a very big animal you have. He'll sleep a lot. Those thyroid pills really slow him down. But don't worry; he's a killer when he's awake."

He tossed the bottle to Cole and started out the door before pausing once more. "Come to think of it, you'd better not let him have any frybread. The pound folks told me that mastiffs need a very precise diet. Human food gives them diarrhea. Could be a real mess."

Cole watched Alex and Abby leave and then turned to Onatima. The old lady's thin lips were pressed tightly together, and her eyes glistened.

150   "You think this is funny?" Cole said.

She glanced at the dog and back to Cole, the corners of her mouth moving toward a smile. "It's good to see you have friends," she said at last.

When they were on the main road descending toward the campus, Abby said, "That was really thoughtful of you, to get a dog for us."

He grinned at her. "He'll be a fine dog, once he gets used to his new environment. Your grandmother is very impressive."

"She's not really my grandmother. We just call her Grandmother."

He nodded. "We do that too."

"She's like my father's great uncle's friend, but the two of them have always been like his grandparents. It's complicated."

"Everybody's related," Alex said. "Everything's complicated. Your grandmother is a medicine woman."

Abby shrugged. "My father called her *apoluma* once. I think that's something like a medicine person in Choctaw, but there are different kinds. She's the smartest human being I've ever known." She watched the roadside for a moment. "Custer's a little scary, but he's beautiful," she replied. "He's a wonderful birthday present for my dad."

"Birthday?"

"His birthday's next week. I'm going to bake a cake. Will you come?"

"Wouldn't miss it." He glanced over at her and then back at a dry creekbed choked with bare poison-oak branches beside the road. "He's very happy you're here. You've already made a big difference."

"You really like my dad, don't you?"

"Yes. I think he's been very lonely."

"What about you? Are you lonely?" She reached to touch his arm lightly.

When he turned to look at her, it was the first time she had seen his face without a trace of laughter. "I'm so lonesome I could cry," he said.

151

Thirty-Seven

He feels her move beneath him. Deep inside, she trembles and breaks, shivering to her skin with a temblor that shakes them in their sleep. When the motion has stopped, he rises and goes into the night, his bare feet cupping the earth, walking fast on the narrow trail, eyes searching, hearing the voice and quickening to a loping run on the mountainside. A stream tumbles beside the trail, and the stars trace cold lines between the tops of trees. The cold caresses his flesh and thrills in his blood. And when she moves again he is high up the ridge, alone in a space between tall trees, his arms out to brace the night as he listens to her cries. He feels the bear, and he crouches. When the dreams come he is lifted and whirled through the darkness, given over to the sweetness of it.

The earth shakes. Venancio sends dreams. The bear is waiting now.

Thirty-Eight

A few miles east of Gallup Luther left the freeway, ignoring the stop sign at the bottom of the exit ramp and skidding sideways as the van turned north through an underpass.

Behind the van, Hoey watched in horror as the van tilted, rocked on two wheels, and fell back to the road. When the vehicle was moving on four wheels once more, Hoey eased the pickup out from the stop sign and followed. Beside him the young woman still slept, her head resting on the jacket he had folded against the passenger door and her filthy clothes covered by the green army blanket.

On the other side of the underpass, a teenager emerged from a desolate-looking gas station to watch them go by, his long black hair held back by a rolled blue bandanna. Hunched into a down jacket, he raised a candy bar to his mouth and held it there as they passed.

For an hour, Hoey watched the van waver from one edge of the empty road to the other, the tires squirming in deep sand and broken sandstone at the asphalt's edge. Red and black mesas cast geometrical shadows against the horizon in all directions. A coyote sprang out of a shallow arroyo a hundred yards from the road and began to trot across the sparse landscape, a limp rabbit hanging from its jaws. Instantly, a raven appeared in the air above the coyote, dropping to the ground a few feet away. The raven began to jump up and down, flapping its wings and feinting with open beak toward the coyote. The coyote dropped the rabbit and lunged toward the bird but wheeled instantly back to the rabbit as a second raven emerged from nowhere to swoop down on the meal. A fraction of a second faster, the coyote snapped the rabbit up once more and stood with it drooping from his jaws, his lowered head facing the two ravens that now barred his path.

Hoey slowed the truck and watched as the coyote turned to one side and begin trotting doggedly toward the east, away from its previous direction. At once the two birds were in the air, following.

When Hoey turned back to the road, the van was disappearing over a rise a quarter mile ahead. He pressed the accelerator and felt the old pickup struggle.

When he had caught up again, Hoey swung out beside the van and pulled even. Luther looked over with a grin, and Hoey waved toward the side of the road and then sped up to pass.

153

Luther steered the van onto the shoulder of the road, and in the mirror Hoey saw the heavy vehicle slide on locked wheels, hitting loose scree and bouncing over the berm into a cluster of creosote bushes.

When Hoey walked back to the van, he carried the rifle in one hand. Luther stood looking at the wheels buried in sand. "I got to get me one of these for home," he said. "You gonna shoot these witches now?"

Hoey looked at the trough where the van had smashed through the road berm and shook his head. "I suppose you know what I'm going to do?" he said.

"Well, it ain't like I didn't raise you my own self," Luther said, fighting off a grin. "But maybe you better tell me."

"Remember what you always said about evil?" Hoey replied. "How you can't kill it, and it's the white man's way to try? That all we can do is be conscious of it?"

Luther looked out at the mesas, saying nothing.

"I figure they'll get this thing out of the sand and drive back to California, where they belong. The important thing is we know about them, and she knows about them. Pretty soon everybody will."

Luther smiled. "I'm thinking of a story about these three. They're gonna freeze their peckers off before they get this thing back on the road. Others know about them, too, and will visit them, and their evil will turn against itself. Now we can take the woman home. Cole's going out there now to see him, but he ain't ready."

Hoey sighed. "To see who? Who ain't ready?"

"To see the gambler. I got to think about the boy now. He can't do this part by hisself."

"We can be there in one day if we don't stop," Hoey said. "You knew I wouldn't shoot these three. And you wouldn't have done it neither. Hell, I won't even ask. You hold the rifle while I untie these assholes."

Thirty-Nine

"Imagine what it would have been like if our ancestors had had CNN." Alex sat on the end of the couch, Abby beside him. The unconscious form of Custer lay sprawled across the rest of the couch, and Abby leaned away from the dog's massive, damp jowls into Alex.

A tall lamp cast a pool of light around Onatima, who sat reading a paperback in the overstuffed chair. At Alex's words the old lady looked up, reaching to pull the wire-rimmed glasses down on her nose. Her hair hung in braids over each shoulder, the silver taking on a deeper sheen against the black wool shirt she wore buttoned to the neck. Wide red suspenders held up baggy black wool pants, and high rag-wool slippers covered her feet.

"What a horrifying thought," she said, looking at Alex sternly over the glasses.

"Think of it," Cole said across the bar between kitchen and living room. "They'd cover all the raids, successful vision quests, hunting and trading parties, tribal politics." He stood over the stove, stirring a big pot with a wooden spoon.

"Right." Alex flicked the remote control to a different news channel, where soldiers in blue helmets were running for cover while black tribal people waved rifles. He flicked it back to the earthquake coverage and held the remote control up to his mouth like a microphone. "This is Heavy Bear reporting from among the southern Pikuni, where the people are still reeling from a major Crow horse-taking raid. Latest figures put the Pikuni losses at twenty animals, including two prized buffalo runners. Informed sources indicate the raid may have been in reprisal for recent Pikuni ventures against their neighbors. Back to you, Pretty Weasel."

From the kitchen, Cole said, "Thanks, Heavy Bear, and we go now to our Chinle correspondent, Alex Yazzie."

A profound growl began to rumble through Custer's chest, and the dog's head rose from the couch. Abby pushed herself farther into the crack between Alex and the back of the couch as Custer's legs bent and, with surprising speed, he swung his head and shoulders off the couch.

As he sat with his forelegs on the floor and hindquarters folded on the couch, the growl grew in volume, and the golden hair of his shoulders stood up.

There were three quick knocks, and Custer sprang from the couch, hurling himself at the door with an explosion of rage.

"I'll get the rope," Cole shouted, and seconds later he had the heavy rope attached to the dog's collar and was pulling backwards. Feeling the pressure, Custer turned and snarled, and Cole backed up a step, saying, "Good boy, Custer."

"Let me take him." Onatima grasped the rope near the dog's collar and led him toward the bedroom. Custer looked back over his shoulder, continuing to threaten the presence beyond the door with a steady, unbroken growl.

"That dog still hates me," Cole said, as he watched the dog vanish into the bedroom. "Just a moment," he shouted at the door.

"It's nothing personal." Alex replied from the couch. "He just knows he's no match for Onatima. But didn't I tell you he was a great guard dog? Have you ever seen him like that?"

"Never. It must be the cops, given Custer's past." Cole reached to open the door.

Robert stood on the doorstep, his hands in the pockets of his parka and a sheepish smile on his face.

"I didn't mean to cause such a fuss," he said.

"Robert!" Cole replied. "Come on in."

"Good evening, Robert," Alex said, rising from the couch. "That was Cole's new guard dog. A truly terrifying animal. All bite and no bark."

Robert stood in the middle of the room. "He didn't seem to like me," he said.

"Custer even hates his own master," Alex replied. "What can you do?"

"Custer?"

Cole waved a hand toward the bedroom. "It's one of those long stories. Robert, I'd like you to meet my grandmother, Mrs. Onatima Blue Wood." He grasped Robert's elbow to turn him toward the old lady, who stood in front of the bedroom door, watching Robert intently.

"I'm very pleased to meet you," Robert said. As he looked at her, his face seemed to pale.

Onatima stepped forward and took Robert's hand softly in her own. For a moment she held his hand between thumb and forefingers, as though testing the temperature, and looked deeply into his eyes.

"Robert's a Ph.D. student at the university," Cole said, "and my teaching assistant."

"I'm quite pleased to meet you, too, Robert," Onatima said, retaining her grip on his hand. "You have a remarkable effect on animals."

As she released his hand, Robert's sheepish smile returned. He looked toward Cole. "I felt like taking a walk and thought I'd drop off the latest exam papers." From beneath his parka he produced a large manila envelope, extending it toward Cole.

"Hi, Robert." Abby smiled and then half turned to look over the back of the couch toward the bedroom, where Custer's growl kept a steady tempo through the closed door. When she turned back she said, "You mean you walked up here in the dark? Through the woods?"

"Good evening, Abby. I like hiking at night." He glanced toward the bedroom, where Custer seemed to be choking on his own rage. "It's peaceful."

"Jesus Christ, Robert, you just got these exams," Cole said, taking the envelope. "Don't you ever sleep? Sit down. How about some coffee, or we have tea?"

"Actually, I don't sleep very much. Tea would be nice, if you have any without caffeine." He sat on the couch, at the end opposite Abby, and looked up at Cole. "The students did a good job. They're obviously learning."

"You don't worry about walking around out there at night?" Abby asked.

"No." He took off his parka and laid it over the back of the couch.

"Do dreams trouble your sleep, Robert?" Onatima asked, as she walked back to the chair.

He shrugged again, looking at her and quickly away toward the kitchen. "It gets dark so early this time of year," he said.

Cole went back to his cooking, dropping the papers on the kitchen table. "We have Indian tea, UPS delivery from Alex's grandmother. And I'm making green chile stew in honor of Alex," he said across the bar between the rooms. "Why don't you stay for dinner, Robert? The tea will soothe your spirit, and this stew'll clean out your pipes. Green chile stew's the real reason those Southwest tribes survived. It culls the weaklings from the herd." In the bedroom, Custer's rage increased, the growl breaking into a coughing snarl.

"Thanks very much, but I should head home. Actually, I'd better start back now."

"What about your tea?" Cole said.

"Thanks, but I forgot that I have to meet someone."

Robert stood up and put on the parka, saying, "It was very nice to meet you, Mrs. Blue Wood."

"Stay for dinner, Robert. I can give you a ride home afterwards," Cole said. "Alex made frybread, and we've got boiled hominy. It's your chance to experience real, tribally enrolled, BIA recognized Indian food."

Robert smiled. "Thanks, but I like walking, and I need to get back. I just thought I'd drop off the exams."

Before anyone could speak he had slipped out, closing the door behind him. Alex went to the bedroom and opened the door, standing carefully to the side as Custer lunged snarling into the living room, where he stood, his head lifted and lips pulled back over his teeth, the snarl falling to a growl once more. After a while, he turned his head slowly in each direction, pausing to growl toward the kitchen and then lumbering slowly back to the couch.

Abby shrank all the way into the end of the couch as Custer pulled himself onto the cushions, his stubby tail toward her and his head on a pillow at the other end. He lifted the head once to look back over the length of his body and rumble lightly at Abby, and then the head sank to the pillow, the eyes closed, and he began to breathe deeply.

"Custer seems to have strong feelings for Robert," Alex said from where he stood between couch and bedroom. "But I guess it's hard to keep up that intensity for long once he's had his medication," he added, as the rumbling in Custer's chest turned into strangled snores.

"Do you know Robert well?" Onatima asked, watching Cole.

Forty

Cole stumbled from the couch, fearing another earthquake, and went to look out the living-room window. A red, three-quarter-ton pickup with a camper shell was parked in front of the house. A hawk feather dangled from the mirror in the empty cab of the truck. He made his way to the kitchen and started a pot of coffee. As he stood looking out the kitchen window, listening to the pleasant bubbling from the enamel pot, a tall, skinny Indian wearing a black fedora

159

and long braids came around to the front of the house. Moving with extraordinary care, the old man dragged a heavy-looking square of folded green canvas out of the back of the truck and vanished around the house with the load.

When the coffee was ready, Cole poured a cup and carried it to the back door. The first thing he saw was the sweat lodge, arched saplings forming a circle about eight feet in diameter and five feet high at the center. The old man with the fedora was spreading the green tarp over the frame. Behind the framework of poles, wearing a heavy sweater and blue jeans, Alex reached to pull the tarp all the way over. A large fire burned a dozen feet away, and Cole could see that the pit for the rocks had already been made in the center of the lodge.

He walked close and held the cup out. "Good morning," he said. "I thought you might like to have some coffee." Sprawled on his side near the fire, Custer opened his eyes to glance at Cole and emit a faint, halfhearted growl before appearing to go back to sleep.

With amazingly long arms, the old man pulled a heavy wrinkle out of the canvas. When the canvas was smooth he turned to the east, where the sun was full over the ridge, and smiled as if the sun had just invited him in for coffee.

"Don't mind if I do," he said, addressing the eastern ridge.

Cole turned the cup so the handle faced outward, the heat searing his fingertips, and the old man hooked his forefinger delicately into the handle and smiled broadly at him, pleasantly surprised to find Cole attached to the other side of the cup.

"Thank you, Grandson." He looked at Alex. "Is this the one?"

"Good morning, Cole. I hope we didn't wake you," Alex said quickly, coming around the lodge. "This is my friend, Emil Redbull. Emil, this is Doctor Cole McCurtain."

Emil Redbull grinned. "Alex thought you wouldn't never get up. He started that truck again real loud because you didn't wake up the first time. That's a mean dog you got there. He told me and Alex he was gonna eat us for breakfast, but then he sort of tuckered out. Custer's a good name for that dog. He likes to be warm, I guess."

Alex said, "We got here before sunrise. I thought you'd want to be involved. Did you feel that temblor last night? Emil thought it was a good sign."

Cole held his hand out. "Yes, I did. I'm honored to meet you, Mr. Redbull. Alex can tell you about the dog. You take your coffee black, right, Alex?"

"Sure, black's fine, but maybe just a teaspoon of sugar."

"It's a beautiful morning out here. You live in a pretty place," the old man said as Cole headed back to the house.

"And a little cream," Alex shouted.

When Cole returned with two cups, handing one to Alex, Emil Redbull stood in the same place, the coffee cup held to his lips, his serious eyes studying the redwood forest across the meadow.

"You live here very long?" the old man said, still looking at the trees.

"Eight months or so."

"You know those woods?"

Cole shrugged. "I've been too busy to walk around much."

"I see. You ain't been out there?" Emil Redbull set the empty cup on the ground a few feet away and went back to work stretching the canvas over the poles, overlapping the edges generously. "What kind of doctoring do you do?" he asked without looking up.

"Cole's a teacher, like me," Alex explained. "He's good with a bow, too."

Emil stopped and looked from one of them to the other. "You're a doctor, too?" he said finally, addressing Alex. "A medicine man?" The corners of his mouth struggled to suppress a grin.

By the time Cole and Alex had finished their coffee, Emil was shoveling dirt to seal the bottom edges of the canvas.

Setting their cups aside, they rose guiltily to help the old man, completing the job in a few minutes.

Emil looked around. "I guess you got to be fire chief, Alex." He turned to Cole. "This'll be good for you."

"This isn't for me. Didn't you tell him, Alex?"

"You got any deer antlers?" Emil said.

Cole nodded. "There's half a rack on the ground over by the shed."

"That's good. Alex can use that to bring the rocks in. When's breakfast? I could eat that mean dog you got."

The smell of bacon hit them when they opened the door. Abby sat at the table drinking coffee. When she saw them she stood up.

"Mr. Redbull, this is my daughter, Abby," Cole said. "Abby, this is Emil Redbull."

"Good morning, Granddaughter. You are as beautiful as the sunrise."

"I'm honored to meet you, Mr. Redbull," she said, smiling broadly.

The old man turned to look suspiciously at Cole. "That a traditional greeting for you Choctaw people?" he asked. "How many horses will you take for this beautiful daughter?"

At noon, while Cole sat in a chair on the deck reading student papers and the old man slept on the couch, Alex built up the fire to heat the rocks. An hour later, when the fire was a heaped mound of red coals, Emil Redbull came walking around the corner of the house, wearing a pair of red gym shorts and a blue tee shirt that said, "Don't Worry, Be Hopi." With his thin, birdlike legs, he stepped daintily on the gravel and broken sticks of the yard, lifting his bony feet high and setting them down carefully.

"I hope you got yourselves some big towels," he said. "You can tell the veterans 'cause they got them great big towels. In the old days, sweats was only for men, but today we have special ones for women, too. Everybody needs to purify themselves these days." He looked closely at Cole. "You better get ready."

Cole shook his head. "I'm going to pass."

Emil studied him for a moment with a puzzled look and then turned and went back inside the house. A few minutes later Abby and Onatima came out. Abby had a towel wrapped around her, the top of her bathing suit showing at the edge of the towel. The old lady was covered from neck to knees by a red beach towel, her hair in a single braid over one shoulder and her legs sticking out of the towel like dry twigs. She stopped close to Cole and touched his arm, saying quietly, "This is necessary, Grandson. It's part of the whole thing."

Twenty minutes later, they were all huddled inside the canvas lodge, listening to Emil Redbull pray in Lakota. He sprinkled water on the rocks, and the darkness filled with a pleasant steam. Cole smelled cedar and sweet grass. Emil sang and passed a pipe, saying softly to Abby at his left, "Now you pray."

Cole heard his daughter ask the Creator to help the women who were missing in Santa Cruz, to help all those whom evil sought. Abby's brief words hung in the air, and then the pipe was passed and Onatima uttered a prayer in Choctaw. Amidst the foreign phrases, Cole could make out two clearly: *ippok nakni*—grandson—and *nita*—bear. And as she finished, he heard the name of Luther Cole, his father's uncle. The lodge flap opened, and Alex handed in another glowing rock on the deer antlers. Three times Emil sang and poured water on the lava rocks, and each time the steam grew more intense until it burned into Cole's thoat and chest, searing his lungs. When his turn arrived, Cole opened his mouth and only silence was there. He tried to form the words of a prayer in his mind, but his thoughts remained shapeless, inarticulate. A knot had formed beneath his chest and seemed to be working its way upward into his throat. He closed his burning eyes and in the darkness he saw the painted man and then a rearing bear, and then bear and man

163

merged into a single, one-dimensional figure like a shadow puppet that seemed to be reaching toward him. He forced his eyes open, and instantly they were flooded with hot, stinging liquid. Again he tried to think words, and the pressure in his throat rose to his mouth and emerged without sound. Alex reached a seventh rock through the flap, and Cole steeled himself as Emil took the pipe from his hand and then raised the dipper a fourth time over the rocks.

When they were all outside again, Cole stood apart from the others. He shivered and held his towel tightly across his chest, staring at the scattered coals of the fire. His body felt empty, like a woven basket set out to dry. The others stood close, also clutching their towels. To one side, Onatima and Emil Redbull spoke very quietly to one another, and across the fire Abby and Alex leaned into each other, so that their shoulders touched. Custer sat on his haunches on the deck, a torn and empty tortilla-chip bag by his feet, drooling and watching the humans with hostility.

Cole went into the house and ran cold water in the bath-tub, filling it almost to the brim. He took off the gym shorts and stepped into the tub and sat down. The water knifed through his groin and clinched a fist around his heart, and he gasped for breath. When he could control his muscles once more, he lowered himself further until his head, too, was beneath the surface. The cavern of his body seemed to echo, and he felt a shadow fall across his closed eyes.

He raised his head from the water and looked into the face of Emil Redbull. The wiry old man stood with his arms folded across his chest, the fedora pushed back from his forehead and his eyes creased and serious looking. He took off the hat and ran a finger along the sweat-stained rim. "Words ain't always important," he said, looking at the wall over Cole's head. "We just got to empty ourself of the stuff that gets in the way, and sometimes we don't know it worked till a long time later."

He set the hat back on his head and squared it carefully, still gazing at the wall. "You got something important to do here. I don't know what it is, but anybody can feel it. Lucky thing you got help." With those words he turned and left the room, shutting the door soundlessly behind him.

When Cole was dressed, he went to the kitchen and put on a pot of coffee, turning from the stove to find Onatima sitting at the table. She wore a thick red robe, with her long hair combed straight and shining to spill over both sides of the chair.

He sat down, resting both forearms on the table with his hands folded. "It was the dream," he said. "It's all I could see."

"I know. Maybe it's time, Cole. Maybe you can't put this thing off any longer." She lifted a thick strand of her hair and began toying with it. "He still troubles you, doesn't he?"

"Who?"

"It's very hard, I know. I've done it, too. But you brought your brother home. His bones are where they are supposed to be."

He looked at his hands. "I don't know . . ."

She cut him off gently. "It's not wrong to survive. I see Indians all the time who are ashamed of surviving, and they don't even know it. We have survived a five-hundred-year war in which millions of us were starved to death, burned in our homes, shot and killed with disease and alcohol. It's a miracle any Indian is alive today. Why us, we wonder. We read their books and find out we're supposed to die. That's the story they've made up for us. Survivor's guilt is a terrible burden, and so we feel guilty if we have enough food, a good home, a man or woman who loves us. You only have to realize that what Luther told you many years ago is true. You carry your brother inside you; he never left you. He wants you to be happy."

When he didn't respond, she added, "Now it's time to deal with the other one."

He closed his eyes. "Pretty soon. There's a lot . . ."

"Don't worry about Abby," she said, her voice brightening. "She's a smart young woman. We women don't need a man's advice in matters of the heart."

"What makes you think . . ."

She cut him off again with a wave of her hand. "Nonsense. You were about to talk hog talk just like Luther Cole and your father and all the other men I've ever known, and I won't let you do it. You have more pressing matters to consider, and you'd better act soon."

"I trust my daughter completely," he said.

She snorted. "More hog talk. No man trusts his daughter."

Forty-One

A stinging wind lifts the sand and cuts the tops off the waves, and Venancio tastes the salt on his lips. He holds his naked child in his broad hands, watching as sunlight strikes across the newborn face. Here, on this remote shore, the power of the priests is distant. The baby stares westward, and the eyes are the color of the water. In the infant's eyes Venancio sees the end of a world, but he cannot cast his son into the sea.

Venancio feels the muscles of his painted chest and shoulders contract with power that flows from all around, and he breathes the bitter air deep into his lungs. He knows he has the strength of the mountains, of the irresistible sea, and yet he is defeated by the eyes of an infant.

One of the great bears had come to the village beyond the mission on the night of his son's birth, calling his relatives into the dark. The bear is in the child now, and the blood of the priest, too, will fail.

Forty-Two

In the early afternoon, they stopped at a trading post that balanced on the edge of a dry riverbed. Around the little adobe-walled store, the sage-strewn desert stretched in a blue plain in four directions. For the past hour the woman had been awake, sitting upright beside Luther, wrapped in the blanket and staring out the window. None of them had spoken.

Hoey got out first and went to the other side of the truck, opening the door carefully and catching the woman as she half-fell toward him. When she was standing on the earth, clutching the blanket around her shoulders and leaning against the pickup door, he took a step backward.

The desert air was sweet and cold, and a dusting of snow still lay against the shadowed north wall of the store and under bushes along the dry wash. On the ridge of the store's rusting tin roof, a pair of ruffled crows bent their heads to watch, and one of them cawed a loud greeting. Fat-bellied clouds hung low and gray over the landscape, and a breeze carried the scent of snow to come. Hoey shivered and drew the delicious smell into his lungs.

"I know this place," the woman said abruptly.

Hoey turned back to her.

"I live over there," she said almost inaudibly, indicating the north with her lips and lifted chin.

"You'll be home soon," Hoey replied.

When they went into the store, they saw Luther standing next to a short, plump man with a shining bald head. The way the old man's head was bent, Hoey could tell he was explaining something to the white man.

Hoey looked around at the amazing mix of groceries, guns, flashlights, saddles, kerosene stoves and cans of fuel, and a thousand other things a person might need or desire. The

167

walls were decorated with beautiful blankets, and a big glass case under the cash register held racks and bowls of turquoise-and-silver rings, necklaces, and bracelets. A long shelf of ominous-looking dolls stood along the wall behind the cash register, above a shelf of rifle and shotgun cartridges.

"Witches tried to steal this young woman, and now me and my nephew are taking her home," Luther was explaining to the store owner. "My nephew and me are Chahta. We've come a long way."

The man glanced toward a door at the rear of the store and looked back at Luther nervously.

"Don't worry, young man," Luther said. "We ain't on the warpath right now. We have to return the young woman to her home so we can get to California."

"You ain't Navajo," the storekeeper replied.

Before Luther could respond, the front door opened and a tall old man walked in. He wore a sheepskin coat buttoned to the throat and a wide black hat, his hands shoved deep in the pockets of the coat.

"This here's Katherine Begay," the old man said to the storekeeper as he walked toward them. "You know Katherine Begay, Elmira's little girl."

"Hells bells," the white man stepped forward and held out his hand, smiling for the first time. "Robert Jim. I ain't seen you in months." The two shook hands, then the storekeeper turned toward the woman, peering at her the way he might have examined a new trade blanket.

"I had to wait for my grandson to drive me way over here in that old truck of his," Robert Jim replied to the man's back. "He went to visit one of his sweethearts up the road, but he'll be back soon. My tailbone tells me we drove two hundred miles." He looked at Luther. "My grandson has too many sweethearts. He's going to wear out that truck."

"Kate?" the store owner bent his head toward her face. "Hell, I've known you since you was a baby, but I sure wouldn't've recognized you."

168   "It's me, Mr. Oakes," the woman said. She leaned against

the glass case, holding the blanket closed at her neck and bending slightly away from the man.

The man stared at her. "It's really you, ain't it?" To Luther he said, "I've known Kate since she was a baby. Her family lives a few miles north of here. But I wouldn't've recognized her in a hundred years. She's been gone a long time."

"I smell something good," Robert Jim said, pretending to sniff the air.

Oakes grinned. "Care for a cup of coffee, Robert?" He looked at Luther. "Excuse my manners. I ain't had time to ask you fellows. How about it?"

"You got Hills Brothers?" Robert asked.

"French Roast," Oakes replied with a wider grin.

"A cup of coffee would be very nice," Luther said. "I bet this young woman would like some hot coffee."

As the store owner filled cups from the big aluminum pot behind the register, Robert placed a hand on the woman's shoulder. "Your grandparents will be very happy." He smiled at Luther. "It's good to see you again, Uncle. We have spoken with the ones you left by the road, and they will not return." He lifted his hand from Kate Begay's shoulder and gestured with an open palm. "Granddaughter, do you know who saved you? Luther Cole is a famous medicine man, known all over the world, and this here's his nephew, Hoey, a great hunter. They are on a journey." He reached inside his coat and brought out a purse. Extracting two twenty-dollar bills, he laid them on the counter. "Mr. Oakes will let you take a bath and pick out a nice dress. When my nephew returns, we will take you home. Then you can tell your story, and remember that you must tell everything. The people have to know the whole story."

Luther held his hand out and Robert Jim took it. For a moment the two looked like mirrored reflections.

"The boy is doing pretty good out there in California," Robert Jim said. "The grandmother is helping. Used to be the people could look around them and see where everything began, but now it goes on and on way past the sacred 169 mountains. All directions." He lifted his hand from Luther's and made a circular motion with his palm. "My relatives go to New York and Los Angeles and bring strange things back. Some of the young ones went to those new wars they got. The singers are sure busy."

Luther nodded. "The way is clear now." He glanced at Hoey. "That old lady's gonna skin us alive."

Forty-Three

The asphalt trail left Porter College and climbed over a small rise through thick redwoods. Robert walked with his eyes down, listening to the faint calling of quail in the brush close by. In the early evening, when day classes were over and night classes hadn't begun, the campus seemed empty and silent except for the animals. The trail joined a hanging bridge above a ravine, and he stopped in the middle of the span to watch a pair of does browsing in the dry creekbed below. In the shadowy light of the ravine, the coats of the deer were a steel gray, the outlines indistinct. The beauty of the deer was so great that he felt as though he would cry. So much, he thought, depended upon two deer, grayed by evening light, beside a dry creekbed.

After a moment he turned and continued across, his eyes downcast once again. He was stepping off the far end of the bridge when a huge hand shot out from behind a redwood and grasped his arm.

"Good evening, Robert." Paul Kantner stepped onto the asphalt.

"Let go." Robert jerked his arm away and turned to face the much bigger man.

"Oh, I'm sorry." Kantner's face seemed to crack in an anguished smile. "I didn't mean to startle you. I just wanted to get your attention. I've wanted to talk to you for a while."

"What about?" Even in the dim light, Kantner's face seemed to burn with red heat.

"Well, you're the TA for Doctor McCurtain's Native American course."

Struggling to control his voice, Robert said, "You're not in that class."

"Well, no, but I'm curious. I thought we could talk."

"I have office hours."

"But I like more informal discussions. After all, this is Santa Cruz, where we pride ourselves on intimate relationships between students and teachers."

"I'm in a hurry right now." Robert looked past Kantner toward steps that led away from the ravine.

"That's not what it seemed like to me." Kantner waved a hand toward the bridge. "You appeared to be sauntering along like the absentminded professor. Maybe you just don't want to talk to me."

"I have to get home. What did you want to discuss?"

Kantner moved to block the bridge exit, and the painful smile reappeared like a gash in his face. "Anxious to go meet the professor's beautiful daughter? She is beautiful, isn't she? Especially here, the campus where parents send their homely children." The smile vanished, replaced by a reflective expression. "That's actually what I wanted to talk about. I'll admit I'm curious about McCurtain and his family."

"I don't know anything about them," Robert said. "It's none of my business or yours. Now I have to go."

Kantner held up a hand, palm outward. "I've watched you, Robert. It's almost perverse. I can't really tell who you've got the hots for, the professor or his daughter. Could that be how he pays you? You get to fuck his daughter?"

"You're sick and disgusting. Now get out of my way." Robert's hand went into the pocket of his parka, and imme-

171

diately Kantner grabbed the arm with one hand while the other hand grasped Robert's throat.

"What do you have in there, a knife—a gun perhaps?" Kantner squeezed and Robert began gasping. "That's cute. I was in Special Forces, Robert. They taught us about knives and guns." He leaned in and thrust his weight down so that Robert's knees buckled and he folded toward the ground. "Surprise is the key. You should remember that."

Kantner released both grips and stepped back, watching the kneeling Robert intently. "Keep your hand in your pocket. I don't want to see what's in there, because somebody will get hurt if I do. I hate violence. It's pointless. I mean, here we are at the University of California at Santa Cruz, where language is god, so wouldn't it be ridiculous if we substituted physical conflict for intellectual discussion?" The smile flashed across his face and disappeared. "I apologise for my crudeness; it's a kind of atavism, I guess. It's just that I'm sick of these professors playing their language games. We pay money to sit there and listen to a bunch of faggots tell us everything is just language. That's because they don't know a fucking thing about reality, do they? They've never been hungry or had to kill so they could stay alive. They go to some goddamned prep school and then Yale or Harvard, and then they come here to teach us how to live. What a joke. Sometimes I want to stick a knife in their guts and ask them what that signifies.

"But Doctor McCurtain's not like that, is he? You see why I wanted to know more?"

When Robert said nothing, Kantner grasped both arms and lifted him gently to his feet. Then he stepped back again.

"You have to leave her alone, Robert." He nodded in agreement with himself. "You should stay away from her, don't you think? It would be more professional that way."

Kantner stepped to the side and began to walk away, crossing the bridge in the direction from which Robert had come, reaching the far end without looking back. Robert remained standing, listening without looking back until the heavy footsteps were gone. Then he moved slowly in the direction he had been going, rubbing his throat with one hand, his eyes peering down through thin slits in the nearly full darkness. When a student on a mountain bike swept past out of the dark, Robert didn't seem to notice. He thought of the deer, of the way they seemed to distill the beauty of the world in a nearly formless shadow.

Forty-Four

Onatima wore a long-sleeved, very loose-fitting dress of red cotton, the ruffled hem of the wide skirt touching the floor and hiding her heavy boots. Bands of white appliqué cutout in varying patterns of diamonds, circles, and elongated rectangles decorated the bosom, back, cuffs, and both ruffles. Her hair was braided and coiled beneath the red turban, and to the two hawk's feathers she had added a third, the long flight feather of a great horned owl. Beneath several strands of beads, the bulge of the medicine pouch showed below the neckline of the fitted dress.

Abby sat on the edge of the bed, watching.

Onatima smiled. "Let me tell you about these patterns. Every Choctaw woman should know these." She gestured with a rising hand toward the appliqué work on the dress. "This diamond design is that of the rattlesnake, *tiak i^{n}sinti*, the diamondback."

Abby looked closely at the patterns, surprised by the unexpected nasal shift of the Choctaw words.

"The diamondback is very, very powerful, and tonight I

173

might need that power. These," Onatima gestured toward the elongated rectangles, "represent the road of life which we all travel. It is important to stay on the road. And these circles represent our people, our tribe, all of us together. This is where real power comes from, from all of us— fullbloods and mixedbloods, those who live together and those who live apart. Like me. I'm wearing this dress tonight to remember who I am, because it's easy to forget, and when we forget we expose ourselves to unnecessary dangers." She placed the fingers of one hand in the hollow of her cheek. "We must rely on what we have. This dress was made for me when I was your age by a woman who even then was older than I am now. It was for a special day. I feel young, like I have ten lifetimes yet to live, but I'm not young. I think my breasts ran away years ago with somebody younger. I can't seem to find them anymore." She looked down at her flat chest. "And I think I must have been taller then.

"When I was your age I had already buried a husband I did not want, and I had already lost a man I wanted very much. For many years after I buried that husband, I lived alone and I listened. Often at night I went into the woods and listened there, just sitting and hearing what the woods said, because it's important to know that, too. Sometimes coon hunters would find me out there with their head lamps, and they'd get scared to death. You should have seen those men. They were a contemptibly ignorant lot, most of those hunters, white men and Indians and black men alike. They'd run around with their fool dogs and those stinking carbide lamps and shoot those poor raccoons. I'd see the little creatures up in the trees with their paws over their eyes—they knew that's how the men saw them, so they covered their eyes. Sometimes there would be a mother and one or two little cubs sitting with their paws like that. It broke my heart, so I was satisfied when word got around that I was a witch. The men became too frightened to come into that part of the woods any longer. Men

174

are always frightened by a woman who doesn't act the way they think we're supposed to act. Especially if they know we're not afraid of them.

"Those men thought I was a witch, and that was just their ignorance. They thought I was dangerous, though, and that was true. All those years before Luther, I looked and listened and felt and smelled and tasted the world very, very carefully. I lay down on my belly and looked into the little holes and cracks of the earth, shoving my face down through the leaves so that I could hear what moved and smell the lives there. I looked beneath the surface of those bayou waters and saw the creatures that swim in the dark there and heard their songs and finally came up with things tangled and moving in my hair. I'd come back from a day and night covered with dirt and mud and leaves, and evidence of my studies would terrify any hunters I met. It sometimes took two days to comb my hair out again, but it was worth it.

"Because I had already given up everything else then, I found power. That was how I helped Luther in the matter of your uncle's bones."

"My uncle's bones?"

Onatima frowned. "Your uncle died because of that war, but he had already come back. Your father did an extraordinary thing then. He found his brother's bones and brought them home, all the way to Mississippi. It took everything Luther and I had to make that story come out right. But it's not my place to tell it."

Abby opened her mouth to speak, but the old woman held up a palm to silence her. "I'd like to know more about this place. Your father is going to have to confront this thing eventually, but he isn't ready yet. So I want to know more."

They sat together in silence for a moment "Since I've been here, Granddaughter, I've been feeling something unusual. Something like loneliness. A long time ago, you see, I was in love with a man. With all of my being. He was one of those river gamblers, one they called a halfbreed, like me. I thought I'd put that man away over all these years, but lately I've been dreaming about him, and it's like he's here, very close, as though I could find him if I just looked hard enough. I can almost feel him out there in those trees." She was silent for a moment. "I've never felt a place so troubled by the past. And that, of course, is the essence of our problem. We pretend that the past is over, that ten or thirty or two hundred years puts a distance between us and what we were. But we know in our hearts there is no such thing as the past. I have always seen him for the first time and the last time, and I have always been here telling you this, feeling this. Your father has always grieved for his brother and yet never lost him. To believe otherwise is to deceive ourselves and to never be whole."

When Onatima stopped speaking, Abby took the old woman's hands in both of her own and was astonished by their weightlessness. "I'm glad you're here," she said.

Onatima retrieved her hands and patted the girl's shoulder. "There is a moon tonight, and it will be clear. I saw the satellite weather map on television. Now you should lock the doors and wait for your father. Don't worry, I'll only be gone a little while." She rose and went out the front door.

After a moment, Abby turned off the living-room lamp and stood looking through the new glass of the big window, watching the moonlight silver the grasses between the house and the redwoods. She shivered and tried in vain to make out the image of the old woman crossing the meadow.

Forty-Five

Alex looked over the top of the book. "Listen. *The Indians of California may be compared to a species of monkey, for naught do they express interest, except in imitating the actions of others . . . but in so doing, they are careful to select vice, in preference to virtue. This is the result, undoubtedly, of their corrupt and natural disposition. The Indian never looks at anyone, while in conversation, but has a wandering and malicious gaze.*"

"*Los padres españoles eran muy crueles.*" Cole rolled the *r*'s carefully and thought of the old Franciscan whipping backs to blood. "I wonder how many of those bastards took Indian mistresses."

Alex shook his head, the long, beaded earrings swaying.

"Those old priests were hard as cement nails," Alex said. "Not too many of them had mistresses, I imagine, since the odds of syphilis were high. It was so bad the Mission Indians had a saying: To marry is to die. I think the priests just lusted after altar boys."

"That's what you prefer to think." Cole kept his eyes on Alex's face.

He held up a hand. "You misunderstand me, Cole. But there's better stuff here." He put the book down and picked up another. "This is a book on the missions published in the forties by a guy named Berger. Listen to this guy. *The indigenous people, moreover, were often unfriendly to the newcomers and uninviting to behold. Both women and men were ugly, short, lumpish, and ungainly, with portly abdomens on scrawny legs. Straight coarse black hair was matted over their low foreheads; beady dull eyes were as repelling as the flat noses on their wide and shapeless faces.*"

He lowered the book.

Cole shook his head. "Hang him by his *conycañones.*"

"Here's what he says on the first page. *The entire history of human affairs relates no adventure of greater ambition and deals with no task more utterly hopeless than the noble effort of the Franciscan padres of California to raise a pagan Indian race to the white man's standards of living.* Can you believe this shit? Published in the nineteen forties? Did you know that in 1855 the good citizens of Shasta were paying five bucks for each Indian head brought in—man, woman, or child—and at Honey Lake the same year an Indian scalp was worth a quarter?"

When Cole didn't respond, Alex added, "Did you know that until 1867 it was legal to keep Indian slaves in California?"

"You're preaching to the converted, Alex. You should write an article for the *San Francisco Chronicle*, but of course they wouldn't publish it. Californians don't like to hear about their sordid pasts. No one's supposed to even have a past in California. It's considered in poor taste." Cole swiveled to look more fully out the window. Abby was walking across the quad in front of the cafe, and the tall student, Kantner, walked beside her. He was talking down at her and gesturing emphatically with his huge hands.

Alex swung around, his gaze following Cole's. "Who's that with Abby?"

Cole stood up. "He's in one of my classes. An odd bird."

"A big goddamned bird. How well does she know him? How well do you know him?"

Cole looked down at his friend. "Abby can take care of herself."

Alex kept his eyes on the couple. "What's his name? Has she been seeing this guy?"

Cole watched his daughter's retreating back as she and Kantner turned out of the quad past the provost's office. "Abby's smart enough to decide who to talk to. Besides, it's the middle of the day in the middle of campus. His name's Paul Kantner." He settled back into the chair, still looking in the direction they had taken.

"In the old tribal days Abby would have already been married by now, you know," Alex said.

"In the old tribal days I'd be a doddering elder already sucking venison broth, and you'd be a sacred clown playing with your wooden dick. I find it odd, Alex, that a man in a dress has such keen interest in my daughter's social life."

Alex spread the fingers of both hands and examined the nails. "Abby's special. I need a manicure. By the way, has it occurred to you that there must be rumors flying about us? I mean when the only two Indian profs hang out together and one of them wears a dress? I may have to change my style to save your reputation as a flaming heterosexual, Doctor McCurtain."

Cole watched his friend closely. "Good idea. My reputation is all I have. Meanwhile, why don't we drive up to my house for a beer? I have to pick up Abby in an hour and a half, so I can give you a ride back down then."

They stood up. "We stopped drinking," Alex said. "Remember? We'll drive up and have a glass of lemonade. I have a couple of ideas I wanted to bounce off you. I've been thinking of a Hollywood research project. You know how everybody's beautiful down there? It occurred to me that L.A. is just one huge eugenics experiment. For almost a century now all the physically perfect specimens of white America have been going there to be in the movies, right? And naturally they've been breeding. They're spiritually void, so basically all they do down there is have sex. So by now we have several generations of genetic experimentation going on, as though the Great Spirit created Hollywood just to have an experimental breeding program for beautiful white people. And of course all the other values—the kinds of things necessary for survival in Siberia or Standing Rock—have become vestigial, because in Hollywood everyone's survival depends purely on physical appearance. During the same period, they've been attracting and breeding Italians who look like Indians, so there's a whole subpopulation of them to study, too. What do you think?"

179

"I think it's politically incorrect. You'd never get funding."

"I thought you'd say that. I didn't have much faith in the idea anyway. But my second idea is better. Tell me what you think about this one. They have the remains of twelve thousand Native people in the Hearst Museum at Berkeley, right? The bones of our relations. Well, I've written an NSF proposal for a team of Indian anthropologists to do a dig in the cemetery at the Old North Church in Boston. That's where they buried all those Puritans. The Winthrops are buried there. My basic argument is that it's imperative we Indians learn more about Puritan culture. Puritans had a significant impact on us."

Cole began to smile. "Harvard should have stuck with Oliver LaFarge types. They made a big mistake taking an actual Navajo. I tried to tell them."

"Seriously, what do you think?" Alex held both palms out. "In the proposal I said we would document everything from the health and disease patterns of colonial settlers to burial customs, diet, nutrition, and social status. We'll do cranial measurements to figure out how intelligent the Puritans were, compared to us, and test teeth and bone samples for dietary information. Puritans were a primitive but fascinating people."

"I thought Navajos were terrified of the dead," Cole replied. "That you didn't even want your relatives' remains repatriated."

Alex held up both palms. "That's true, but I'm different. I've been corrupted by empirical science, the inheritance of logical positivism. Some of those Boston people may be a little squeamish about us digging up their ancestors, and that's understandable, but, hey, it's science, Cole. We can't allow their primitive superstitions to stand in the way of science. And here's the best part. Those graves are probably full of artifacts, buttons from Puritan clothes, whalebone corsets, dildos, things we can sell to collectors. And skeletons, of course.

180   "We'll donate most of the bones to Indian communities.

A lot of tribal museums would like to have Puritan skeletons on display, for educational purposes. Want to join the project? Maybe hang out in Boston collecting oral tradition while we're there? I hear they give great oral tradition in Boston."

When Cole just shook his head, Alex put a hand on his shoulder. "Think about it, Cole. By the way, Uncle Emmet called from Barstow yesterday. He's on his way and wants to have the ceremony tomorrow night. I invited Robert."

Forty-Six

"I'm surprised you haven't heard of Elfland."

"Well, I haven't been here very long." After thirty minutes of conversation, Abby was still amazed by the softness of Paul Kantner's voice. He was huge, the biggest person she'd ever met, yet his voice was almost delicate. It was the first thing she'd noticed when he sat down next to her and began to talk. She'd seen him in the modernism class and had felt something like revulsion at his mere size. Now, the guilt from that first reaction kept her walking beside him. It's like he's controlling his voice with enormous willpower, she thought. She wondered what his real voice might sound like.

"Elfland has been here since the campus was built, more than twenty-five years. It's a very strange place."

They left Porter College and crossed the ravine. She felt odd to be walking with him, but at the same time it was good to listen to someone besides her own family or Alex. Robert Malin had tried to be friendly, but Robert frustrated

181

her, constantly making her feel as though he were talking in a code she couldn't crack. The students on campus, men and women alike, struck her as children frantic for attention.

"I go up there sometimes," Kantner continued. "I'm trying to figure these students out."

"What do you mean?" She watched a girl on a mountain bike flash by on the winding path. Half the girl's hair was shaved and the other half hung down in a purple sheet to her shoulder. The paved path swung to the right, toward another college, and Kantner continued straight, leaving the official path and climbing up what looked like a firebreak. At his side she felt small and quick, like one of the gray squirrels that were everywhere on campus. And young. Paul Kantner, she decided, must be thirty at least. She wondered what he had been doing before, and why he was working on a literature degree. He didn't fit. Among the young students with their shaved heads, pierced body parts, dredlocks, and expensive torn jeans, he looked like a disapproving custodian. In class he sat in stern silence, seeming to hang on every word her father uttered.

"It's right up here, not very far. I'm curious about their impulses. What has brought them up here for all these years, all the different ones year after year, to do this? What kinds of mothers they had. You'll see what I mean. In a way it's like something your father would lecture about. Like they're trying to reinvent God."

Maybe he's in school to study the students, she thought. Then why not psychology instead of literature?

They left the fire road and entered a thick stand of tall second-growth redwoods, following a well-worn trail. The trail began to branch off into smaller trails, and Kantner kept to the middle. As it narrowed, she slipped behind, looking around her at the clear, parklike slope beneath the trees. Under the canopy the daylight was dim and patchy.

"This is Elfland." Kantner had stopped and turned to face her, towering over her from his uphill position and gesturing with both hands spread wide.

182

She looked around more carefully. In the shadows, she could make out brush fences woven in circles between clusters of redwoods.

"Redwoods grow from root systems, and where one of the old trees has died and rotted, or been cut down, young trees tend to grow in a circle from the roots of that tree. It's like children holding hands around a dead and vanished mother, the perfect mother who gives them life and then goes away. Like God. They're left staring at the empty center."

She looked from the nearest brush circle to Kantner, feeling a shiver probing her tensed shoulders. "This is interesting," she said. "But I . . ."

"They call these circles fairy rings. The students really eat that kind of poetic nonsense up. I call it the Hobbit heritage, vestiges of the seventies. Come on, I'll show you what they do." He gripped her arm above the elbow and stepped toward one of the circles.

"Excuse me." Abby pulled her arm free, and he looked curiously at her before going on.

She followed him, fascinated in spite of herself, trying to see the enclosure more clearly. Further up the hill another couple climbed hand in hand, and from somewhere to her right she heard a low, comforting chant. She began to hurry to match Kantner's long stride, drawn to this thing. Underfoot, the redwood humus silenced their steps completely.

Kantner led the way to the nearest circle and bent nearly double to stoop through a low opening in the brush wall. Following him inside, she saw that someone had woven a thick barrier of dead branches to connect the circle of four redwoods, each tree more than a hundred feet high. In the middle of the twelve-foot circle was a pile of stones covered with melted candles and beads, feathers, sticks of burnt incense, and scraps of paper soiled and melted by rain. Here and there bits of paper were also wedged into the stringy bark of the trees, some of the paper new and some moldering into the wood.

"There are half a dozen of these," Kantner said. "These are their churches, their new places of worship." His voice had become less soft. "They come up here and take drugs and burn candles and perform little ceremonies they invent. I've watched them. They think they're worshiping trees, or nature, or something. The women especially come up here. They don't shave their legs or armpits, and they come up here together, without men, and take off their clothes. They have rituals they've made up that they perform here in the place of the dead mother."

He paused and looked at her as if gauging the depth of her understanding. When she didn't reply, he went on. "I think this campus is unique, that it's a kind of magnetic center that draws children whose parents have abandoned them. I don't mean like physically or literally, but mostly symbolically. The parents who don't take responsibility for the souls of their children, who buy them cars and give them the money for drugs without asking. Like it's a campus for Lost Boys—and Girls—and they're all waiting for Peter Pan to save them from the pirates. They come up here with their drugs looking for Tinkerbell because their mommies left them a long time ago. It's like what your father talks about with the modernists when they thought God had died, like that Matthew Arnold poem he likes to quote in class all the time." He loomed over her, his expression turned inward as though entranced.

Abby moved backwards toward the tunnel-like entrance. "This is fascinating, Paul. I'm glad you showed me, but I need to get back. I have to catch a ride home with my father."

"I can give you a ride." He swung his huge head around to stare at her.

"No, my dad's waiting for me."

"You see what they're doing, don't you? They've been sent to this university by their rich parents. They've been given everything. But spiritually they have nothing." His voice had softened again, and he seemed to be almost talking to himself. "I come here at night and hear them, and I always get a terrible feeling of sadness. They're lost. They need guidance. Their mothers talk at them, but mothers never listen to their children. The children come here to escape that talking, talking, talking without listening. But they're all wrong. They come here for sex, too."

As he spoke, he had moved slowly until he had edged between her and the opening. Now he looked directly at her. "Let me show you something before we go."

He plucked a folded paper from the bark of one of the trees. "Listen to this." He unfolded the paper and began to read, his voice delicate once more.

> Your beauty, briefly seen,
> Like the shadow of a wild thing
> Skirting the camp at sundown
> In the darkness of the trees.
> Desiring to approach,
> But afraid of the bright fire.

He looked at her expectantly. "It's a love poem."

She glanced toward the opening in the brush wall. "It's nice. Who do you think wrote it, a man or a woman?"

"I wrote it. Do you really like it?"

For a moment she was speechless. Finally she said, "You wrote it? It's lovely."

"Do you understand it? Desiring to approach, but afraid of the bright fire? The shadow of a wild thing circling the camp. Can't you see it? Not the thing itself, but the shadow, at sundown in the darkness of the trees. The speaker is inside, near the fire, the keeper of the fire, and that which circles is both desired and desiring. Anything could be out there. The moment of desire is the moment of danger. To move out of the darkness is to offer oneself to the possession defined by fire. That's the ultimate danger. The possession of otherness. And to call the shadow into one's circle is, simultaneously, to offer oneself to the infinite potential of the unknown. Desire and death are shadow and light, but which defines which?"

185

He stopped, as though waiting for an answer. When she didn't respond, he said. "It's a love poem I wrote for someone very special."

She took an involuntary half-step backwards. "Did she like the poem, the one you wrote it for?"

He looked more intently at her. "I hadn't shown it to her. You see, it's unrequited love. She's sensitive, not like those others. It might frighten her. If things aren't handled very, very carefully, I've found, they become frightened." He glanced away from her at the disheveled altar and seemed to absentmindedly pluck a second paper from the bark. "They should never be frightened. It's unnecessary and clumsy."

"My father's going to worry about me," she said, bending and backing past him through the entrance.

Outside, she straightened and looked down the trail they had walked. Instantly and soundlessly, he was close behind her.

"When you're alone out here, there are voices. You think they're from people like you, but when you go in search of them, crawling on your hands and knees on the soft ground so that you're as silent as the bottom of the ocean, you never find the source."

She began walking ahead of him down the trail, looking through the trees on both sides for signs of the couple she'd seen on the way in.

"Wait." He clasped her shoulder and stopped her.

"Don't do that!" She jerked free and glared up at him. "I don't like anyone grabbing me."

He looked panicked. "Oh. I'm really sorry. I forget sometimes how strong my hands are." He held another creased paper in front of her. "This is another paper I found in there. I was just reading it. Listen."

He bent closely to read in the partial light.

> One person consenting to be murdered protects the millions of other human beings living in the cataclysmic earthquake/ tidal area. For this reason, the designated hero-leader has the

responsibility of getting enough people to commit suicide and/or consent to being murdered every day. Let it be known, therefore, to the nations of the earth and to the people that inhabit it, that the agony in stony places has begun. Fear death by water. A fortnight dead. The tragedy that has befallen us ought not to have befallen us and we will give of the first fruits of the earth.

She turned and began walking more quickly, and as he followed he said, "You have to be careful, Abby. Those are the words of a madman—or woman."

Forty-Seven

"Play you can't get away."

Robert sat on the damp lawn beside the pool, and the four-year-olds charged from two directions, one hurling herself at his back while the other dodged in front of him. With his left hand he hooked the one in front, and with his right he reached up to cup the other and flip her gently over his shoulder.

Wrapping both arms around the giggling and squirming twins, he chanted, "I gotcha where I wantcha and I wantcha where I gotcha, and I gotcha gotcha gotcha gotcha gotcha gotcha gotcha." The girls shrieked and squirmed in their pink corduroy jumpers, their identical faces contorted with delight. "Oh, I wantcha where I gotcha and I gotcha where I wantcha," he chanted.

"No tickling," one of the girls yelled, and then she collapsed in helpless giggles.

"Oh, no. She got away," he shouted, and one of the girls bolted out of his relaxed arm. Lunging for her, he let the second leap free. Instantly the twins circled and swooped in on him, and he trapped them in his long arms.

"Don't you ever ever ever ever ever ever say that you'll ever ever ever ever try to get away," he chanted, making the girls squirm and giggle more violently.

"Don't they drive you nuts?" Brett asked from the lawn chair where she sat watching.

He loosened his hold and let the twins break free, pretending to lunge at their fleeing heels. "Oh, no," he shouted. "You distracted me and they got away."

"Isn't that grass getting your butt wet?"

He shrugged. "It's worth it."

"You really like kids, don't you?"

"They are the most precious thing in the universe," he replied. "Beyond value. I want to eat them up." He lunged and scooped up one of the girls. Seeing her sister writhing in his arms, the other twin hurled herself onto his neck from behind, and again he flipped her gently over his shoulder and held them both in his lap, tickling and chanting, "You can't get away, you can't get away, oh you can't get away today."

One of the girls stopped squirming and looked up at him. "No tickling," she said. "Do shadowcats."

Brett leaned forward expectantly.

"Yeah, do shadowcats," the other twin said as they both stopped squirming and settled back in his lap.

He lowered his head toward them and made a serious face. "Oh, when you go to bed at night and pull your curtains down, you may be certain shadowcats are creeping through the town." He showed his teeth, exaggerating the sibilants, "You'll never, ever see them in the shadows of the night, for they'll be slipping through the alleys always slightly out of sight. But perhaps you'll get to meet them, if it's your house that they pick in the hours of the morning when the mist is growing thick. They will slide in through a window, just some shadows in the air, and they'll come to where you're sleeping, to perform their service there.

Perchance you may awaken just before it is too late, and they'll smile and lick their whiskers, but they'll never hesitate."

The girls squirmed, and one reached to put her arms around his neck. "That's scary. What's hesitate?" she asked. "Do another cat poem."

"Brett can tell you," he replied. He stood up, lifting the girls as he did so and then bending to set them on their feet. "But I have to go to school now."

Brett rose from the chair. "It's lunchtime anyway." She gave him a half-smile. "They love you. Everybody in the family loves you, even if Dad does think you're a fruitcake and Mom is so disappointed to think you're gay."

He patted the girls' heads. "You have a rare and beautiful thing, Brett, a family. Something valued by the gods above all else." He walked toward his cabin, pausing at the bridge to look back for a moment.

Forty-Eight

They found Custer beneath the oak where he was chained.

"Poison." Cole pointed to the froth on the dog's muzzle.

"Jesus," Alex said. "Why would anybody do that?"

Cole squatted and patted the dog's side. "Who knows why people do such things? It wasn't because he barked. Nobody lives close enough to hear him."

"Maybe one of those times he was loose he killed some-body's cat or something."

Cole shrugged. "Custer could have eaten somebody's kid. I wouldn't put it past him."

"There aren't any footprints except ours." Alex was walking in slow half-circles, looking at the ground.

"They probably stood in the grass and threw a piece of meat to him. Nobody would be stupid enough to get close." Cole stood up and let out a long breath. "You know, I don't think he ever stopped hating me."

"Don't feel bad about that, Cole. Custer hated the whole world. Except Abby and Onatima. And he had reason to hate the world. He was created by people to be exactly what he was, bred to be dependent upon prescription drugs, trained to be a crack puppy. He was just a projection of the European psyche."

"And you brought him to my home?"

Alex squatted and patted the dog's side. "You know how Indians are. We'll adopt anything, even bad habits. But I guess Custer was incorrigible, just like his namesake."

"You may recall that you didn't exactly adopt him. And I don't know. He almost seemed to be softening. Sometimes I didn't think he really wanted to rip my throat out, but that was probably the medicine."

"Poor fellow. A dog this big would feed a whole bunch of Lakota."

"No time for jokes, Alex."

Alex got to his feet. "I know. I feel bad, too, but humor's what gets Indians through the tough times, Cole. You hear the one about the Lakota and Navajo families who exchanged sons for the summer? When the Navajo kid got home his family asked him how it was, and he said, 'Ruff.' When the Lakota boy got home and his family asked him, he said, 'Baaaad.'"

Cole grimaced. "I don't want Abby to see him. I guess we'd better bury him."

Alex placed a hand on Cole's shoulder. "You have to pick up Abby in an hour, right?"

When Cole nodded, Alex said, "Maybe you should call the cops and then go get Abby. I'll stay here and bury Custer. I feel kind of responsible."

"No point in calling the cops. They'll just take a few notes and say they can't do anything. And it wasn't your fault. If I'd let him stay in the house during the day instead of chaining him up . . ."

"It's not your fault either. Maybe Custer had it coming. Maybe he was fated to come to a bad end, being raised the way he was. Who knows? Why don't you go on down to the university? By the time you and Abby get back, Custer will have a nice grave."

When Cole was gone, Alex went to the shed behind the house and returned with leather gloves and a shovel. He started to dig beneath the oak, and at once returned to the shed for a pick and a heavy metal bar. He drove the pick into the ground for several minutes and then used the bar to pry large rocks out of the earth. When he had a pile of gray and brown rocks at his back, he struck a layer of hardpan and had to return to the pick. After a few minutes, he took off his shirt and used it to wipe his sweating face.

For twenty minutes he swung the pick and scraped the shards out of the hole with the shovel. The rock-hard earth gave way to a layer of sandy gravel, and he sighed with pleasure as he dug the damp gravel and tossed it aside with the shovel. After six inches, he struck a layer of rock and reverted to the pick and bar.

After forty minutes, he stepped back and examined the hole. He remembered his father burying one of their sheep dogs who'd been bitten by a snake. His father had folded the dog's legs beneath it so that it looked like it was sleeping. The sheep camp had been in a hard and rocky place also.

He went to where Custer lay. With difficulty, he got both arms around the dog's vast midsection and began backing toward the grave. Dropping the body at the edge of the hole, he squatted to fold the long legs, only to discover that the legs were as rigid and unyielding as steel. Rigor mortis had seized Custer.

"Goddamnit." He swore the oath softly and wiped his forehead.

191

Laboriously, he raised Custer to his feet, propping the dead animal against his thigh. Hooking his arms around the midsection once again, he lifted the dog and stood it in the hole. The grave came up to the dog's belly.

"That was your last stand, Custer," he muttered as he dragged the animal out of the hole and laid it on the exhumed gravel.

Twenty minutes later, with the pick ringing on granite, he levered Custer back into the hole. The head, shoulders, back, and tail stood clearly above the surface of the earth.

Dragging the body from the hole, he dropped it and picked up the heavy bar. The bar bounced off the granite slab in the bottom of the grave, and he dropped it and shoved his hands beneath his armpits, wincing with pain.

He stood back and looked at the hole. To widen it enough for a sideways Custer would take too long. Abby would be home in fifteen or twenty minutes. It was too late to try a new hole somewhere else.

He went to the shed and emerged with a chain saw.

When Cole and Abby came out the back door twenty minutes later, Abby already in tears, Alex was placing a large white stone at the head of the carefully mounded grave. He rose and put his arm around Abby's shoulders. "May he rest in peace," he said.

Forty-Nine

The day after Custer's burial Cole was walking slowly toward his truck, thinking about the dog. In the novel they'd discussed in class that morning, the Indian narrator had confessed to shooting a dog just because he was drunk and it was moving. Custer's death, however, seemed part of something much bigger, part of everything that had been happening. Dogs didn't like witches, or ghosts. But ghosts didn't poison dogs. Witches might poison dogs, but he had ghosts, not witches. Not ghosts, just a ghost. Not witches, but psychos.

He felt a presence beside him and looked up to see Paul Kantner smiling down at him.

"Good afternoon, Paul," he said, relieved to know that his office hours for the day were over and he was on his way home.

"Hello, Professor McCurtain." Kantner bent his head slightly as he spoke, as if Cole were diminutive instead of merely a head shorter. "I was wondering if I could talk to you."

In his mind, Cole replayed the almost comical formality of their exchange. Nearly smiling at his own stiffness, a mixedblood clown playing the role of college professor, he said, "Of course, Paul, but I'm afraid I have to get home right now." At once his mind raced for convenient emergencies, responsibilities that would demand his time. "I'm expecting a crucial phone call from my publisher in New York," he added, grimacing inwardly at the lie, the broom-stick-up-his-own-ass sound of it.

"It's nothing important," Kantner went on. "I was just wondering about your daughter, Abby."

Cole stopped and looked at the student.

193

"We had a very nice walk recently, and I've wanted to see her again. But when I call, she always has some kind of excuse for not seeing me. Or even talking on the phone."

Cole waited, noticing the way Kantner's pupils seemed to have widened as the afternoon light dimmed. When no other words followed the statement, Cole said, "What do you want?"

Kantner ran a hand across his red hair and looked away toward the buildings and then back. "Well, I thought you might speak to her. Maybe tell her I'm okay."

Cole took a deep breath of sea air carried to campus by the afternoon thermals. After a moment he said, "You have to understand, Paul, that Abby is an adult. She has her own life. I can't speak to her for you."

Kantner seemed to stiffen. "But you're her father. You're always talking about responsibility in your lectures, all that 'give, sympathize, control' stuff. If you told her I was okay, she'd . . ."

"You can't buy my daughter with twenty horses, Paul. If Abby doesn't want to see you, or even talk to you, she has her own reasons. I won't discuss it, with her or with you." He stopped and waited for Kantner to respond, but the student stood watching him in silence, the muscles of his jaws taut.

After several seconds, Cole turned and continued alone to the parking lot. When he started the pickup and drove onto the road away from the campus, he looked in the mirror and saw Paul Kantner in the same spot, still watching him.

"I have a church service to attend," he said aloud to the mirror.

He really did have to go home, and he wondered why he hadn't thought of the truth instead of a ridiculous story. In fact, it had been a couple of years at least since he'd waited for an editor's or publisher's call. Even his agent had given up. She hadn't called in several months and had probably decided to write him off as a profitable client. For the first time in ages, he considered the writing he hadn't done, surprised to realize that he hadn't even thought of writing since he'd moved, until that moment hadn't even felt guilty about not doing it.

Fifty

Uncle Emmet turned out to be Great Uncle Emmet, a tall, wiry old man with a hatchet nose, wide-brimmed black hat, and white hair folded in a short ponytail and wrapped in red cloth behind his head. He sat before a horned moon on the floor of the darkened living room. In the center of the sand moon was a small ribbed cactus bulb, deep green with a tuft in the center. In one hand the old man held a gourd rattle, and in the other a beautifully quilled and beaded fan of mottled brown feathers and a short staff with lightning symbols.

A small fire burned in Cole's hibachi, and the seven of them, including one of Uncle Emmet's Navajo relatives from San Jose, a rail-thin young man with drooping mustache, were gathered in a circle around the fire and peyote altar. Already, they had smoked and rubbed themselves with sage. Now the old man sprinkled cedar on the fire and fanned the smoke over them with the peyote fan.

"My nephew Michael here can tell you I been a roadman twenty-five years now," Emmet was saying. "And I don't know hardly nothing yet. But I don't have to know nothing 'cause this here peyote chief always shows us the way. Alls we got to do is help each other and love each other and Jesus. We got to stay on the peyote road and don't take no shortcuts. It's a hard road, and it can show us how little and weak we are, but we got to stick to it." He shook the rattle once and sang a long, melodious song in Navajo. As he sang, he laid the rattle down and passed a flannel bag to the nephew on his left. The nephew removed a button and handed the bag to Alex, who passed it to Abby. As the bag made its way around, they all began chewing immediately, watching the fire.

"On the peyote road we got to love everything," the old man said, "and we got to always think about everybody we love and pray for them. Bad thoughts or selfish thoughts don't belong here. Like Jesus, we got to forgive everybody. That's real important. Sometimes we got to forgive ourself, too, and that's hardest maybe. We ought to have a drum, but I forgot mine back home."

The bag reached Onatima, who sat next to Cole. Cole remembered reading that the hairy fibers in each button were what made people ill. When Onatima handed him the bag, he took one of the buttons and gave the bag to Robert, who sat to his left. As subtly as possible, Cole tried to feel for and pluck out the fibers, but when he realized everybody else, including Abby directly across the circle, was already swallowing their buttons, he gave up and popped his in his mouth, chewing and swallowing the bitter cactus quickly.

"On the peyote road a man and woman who's married has to be faithful to each other. We can't drink alcohol or take drugs. We got to think all the time about the children and elders, and we got to have steady jobs. We got to think hard about the right way to stay on the road. It don't matter what religion you got or what tribe. It's all the same whether you're Navajo or Lakota, Catholic or Jehovah's Witness. There are so many good things to say about peyote. Peyote shows us how the world really is. Peyote brings us the knowledge of God being with us, and we see everything is related then. If we're scared, peyote tells us everthing's okay."

196

He sang the song three times more in quick succession and passed the rattle to Alex, who sang in Navajo, each word pronounced so carefully that Cole felt he should be able to understand. The rattle passed to each of them in succession.

The cotton bag made its way around four times, and each time, as he listened to the others sing, Cole chewed and swallowed the foul-tasting button. Then Onatima was handing the rattle to him. He stared at the fire, his stomach leaping and flaring just like the bitter flames. He remembered the sweat ceremony and tried to fight back a sense of panic. Frantically he searched his mind for an appropriate prayer, but the only words that came were those of a Luiseño song. "I had been looking far," he whispered, so quietly that he was certain no one could hear, "sending my spirit north, south, east, and west, but I could find nothing, no way of escape."

He passed the rattle to Robert, who reached for it slowly, keeping his face toward the big living-room window. Robert's eyes were wide, the pupils flaring, and the expression on his face was a fusion of joy and terror. As he released the gourd, Cole wondered if the peyote had transformed his own face the same way, and he looked to see if Alex, too, had been changed by the peyote chief.

Robert shook the rattle softly and seemed to hum rhythmically for a moment, his eyes never leaving the window, and then, without looking, he handed the gourd to the old man at his left.

Emmet sprinkled more cedar upon the hibachi and sang a long, soothing song that seemed to go on and on as Cole smelled the sweet juniper and watched the fire growing bigger and brighter. And then, in the middle of a phrase, the old man paused with the rattle half-raised, his eyes lifted toward the door.

"Nítchi bee íiniziinii," he murmured, and he cocked his head as if to listen.

Alex and the Navajo nephew turned their heads very

197

slowly so that they, too, could see the door. Cole saw the nephew's face reflect a sudden and abject terror.

"Ghost," the old man said, looking around the circle.

Suddenly Cole was sick. Lurching to his feet, he raced for the door.

"Don't!" Robert shouted, but already Cole had thrown the door open and stumbled outside, running to be clear of the house.

At once he bent over and spilled what felt like his life onto the earth. When the heaving stopped, he felt a deep hole in his center, and a strange buoyancy, as though his feet made no impression upon the grass. He raised his eyes, and the sky was an arc of cold stars swooping down upon him with the clear sound of steel on steel, and he could hear waves crashing on the far side of the ridge, battering the ancient coast range, pulverizing stone and working to free deep roots. A wind he couldn't feel stirred the tops of the tallest redwoods, layering the air with the sound of wings. There was a commotion high up on the ridge, and he straightened to look. Against the big, full moon the shadow of a bear rose until it stood outlined in light. Behind the bear, an unknown pattern of stars wheeled madly across the sky. Cole turned, wanting desperately to be back in with the others. A buck thrust into the clearing, its antlers flaming. The deer vanished, and there was a crashing in the brush. He felt the pulse of death like the peyote drum all about him, and he began to run.

He heard the rush of branches, the impact on the soft earth, the harsh intake of breath. He ran and stumbled, his feet catching on exposed roots and downed limbs, forearms raised to fend off branches that lashed at his face. At once it seemed he had run for hours, in terror of the tumult at his back. The pursuer kept up the frantic pace, and Cole could feel desire in the headlong rush, but the distance between them remained the same. He slowed, his breaths ripped from the cold air, and he felt that which sought him tear through the night with wild, loping strides, but the distance never closed.

His heart tightened, and he tasted fear like blood with each breath. Beneath his feet, the earth began to tremble, a tremor growing in intensity as a wave of motion swept through the trees. The earth snapped and hurled him against a redwood trunk at least ten feet through.

When he had pulled himself upright once again, the earth no longer shook. Around him the trees were enormous, eight and ten feet across and soaring toward the night sky. He began walking, feeling the earth shiver once more and knowing with certainty that something was just ahead, beyond the next stand of trees, around the next clump of brush. The bear was pursuing him through time but not space. He became aware of everything in the moon-pale forest, each infinitesimal movement, each rustle of sound.

When the forest parted, he knew where he was and at once saw his error. A fire burned with a phosphorescent brilliance in the center of the clearing, and the horned peyote moon hung in the tops of trees just beyond. Around the fire were scattered half a dozen domed huts of woven reeds. A young woman, outlined in light, crouched at the fire, ladling something from a basket into a wooden bowl, an infant in its cradle lying beside her. Men and women, their half-naked bodies dark and glimmering, were fixed in various postures between the huts, their still faces toward him. Shadowy children wrestled motionless in the dust, and objects hung from drying racks at the edge of the village. He felt a yearning, a homesickness that bore him toward the young woman and fire.

The gambler sat cross-legged on the ground at the edge of the village. A cape of raven feathers covered his shoulders, and an abalone shell necklace hung upon his painted chest. He looked up at Cole's approach and smiled, holding out both hands with the palms open. In the right hand Cole saw the painted bone.

The flames of the fire began to lick at the night, and people slipped into motion, turning their faces toward him. 199

A baby began to cry in one of the huts, and the people moved to stand in a dark crowd behind the gambler, who shook his fists, placed his hands beneath a woven mat, and sang. When he pulled the hands from beneath the mat, he began again the weaving and chanting, the free flight of clenched fists that Cole recognized. The people watched, and Cole felt plunged into a despair deeper than he had ever known.

Hopelessly, he went to the gambler and sat upon the ground. The gambler looked directly into Cole's eyes, and Cole looked back into the brown eyes of Attis, his brother, half a lifetime before. Attis sang and shook his fists and wove patterns in the air, his head bobbing in time to the gambling song. Cole reached to touch the left hand.

Movement stopped. Attis opened both fists, palms upward, and smiled. The painted bone lay in the right hand.

Cole sensed motion all around, and he rose and turned to run. The night opened before him. The Yazoo River was a dark swath bathed in the stench of decay, and they stood, two mixedblood children, holding hands before the falling cabin where they had been born. The cabin looked abandoned, tilting crazily in the weeds, and Cole knew that somewhere inside would be their mother. The door opened, and Attis freed his hand to step forward. *No!* Cole shouted, as his brother went up the broken steps and through the door. His mouth worked to form his brother's name, knowing that if he could shout "Attis!" his brother would not leave him. But he could not force the sound from his dry throat. Behind him he heard the panting breath of pursuit, and he started toward the cabin door.

Then Cole was alone and running. Attis stood in a clearing bathed by the moon, his face hidden, pointed toward the bright earth. At his back once more Cole heard the broken branches and stumbling footfalls, breaths torn from the air. Attis looked up, and his face had become Uncle Luther's, shining with love, and then Cole saw himself alone where his brother had stood. He felt a change in proportion, in distance. The choking breaths and plunging steps grew louder, and he saw the gambler, running not after him at all but to one side and beyond. Half black and half silver-white, from parted hair to feet, naked the gambler ran toward something he seemed to see through the trees. Cole strained to see as well, but what he saw was the gun in the gambler's hand.

It's time, now. The figure of Uncle Luther stepped out of the shadowed forest, a small bag dangling from his outstretched hand.

Cole reached to take the pouch, but he found himself in the midst of a river, fog shrouding the water and birdcalls lying heavy on the still air. The water was thick and black, and he struggled even downriver, making no headway. His brother's bones lay shining and silver in the limbs of a tree that rose too high out of the river, and Cole could only watch hopelessly as he was whirled slowly past.

He found himself walking toward the darkened windows of his home. Something heavy lay against his chest, and he reached up to find the little medicine pouch hanging from his neck. To the west a great white circle of moon was slipping behind the crest of the ridge, and in the east a pale band of light had appeared. The air was heavy with moisture, and from the big oak behind the house the owl called.

Finding the front door locked, he went to the sliding glass doors in back, but they, too, were locked. He moved around the house, trying doors and windows, but there was no way in.

He was back in the forest, and the pounding steps and frantic breaths rushed at him. *This is death,* he thought, and he heard the words as if another had spoken them. When he turned to face it, he saw his brother once more, this time standing in the depths of the trees, beckoning, the drowned face framed by long cords of black hair. Again he tried to form the shape of his brother's name, to draw out from his belly the cry that would join them together, but his throat was dry and cracked, incapable of sound.

201

He moved in the direction of his brother, but a form came from the shadows between them. The pale bear shuffled out of the dark, lifting its heavy head. The bear reared on two legs and became a man, the outstretched arms ending in the massive paws of a bear.

Black hair hung straight past the broad face and fell over the shoulders and chest. Cole heard the painful breaths and saw the painted chest heave. The hands, with their great claws, reached to strike him to the earth, and he felt his body give way before the weight. He smelled the salt of his own blood as the man-bear reared over him, and he began to understand the perfect logic of his death, the absurdity of forestalling the event of it.

"It's okay now, Grandson." The voice was Uncle Luther's, but when he sought the old man's face in the dark, it was Attis who reached toward him where he lay. His brother's hand closed on his, and he felt himself pulled from the earth with a force beyond any he had ever known.

Fifty-One

He awakened to faces peering down at him.

"Daddy!"

Abby bent and kissed his forehead, and he breathed in the warm fragrance of her hair.

"What?" he asked.

"You done slept a whole day." Cole searched for the face behind the words. "Uncle Luther?" he said.

"Yes, Grandson. We thought maybe you was going to hibernate this winter."

"Dad?"

Hoey nodded. "Good to see you, boy."

"Grampa and Uncle Luther got here last night, or I guess I should say this morning," Abby said.

"What happened?" Cole asked. He reached a hand up to trace the line of a welt across his cheek. His fingers found another welt just below the first, and then he realized his whole face stung and his body ached.

"You went outside from the ceremony for a moment, and you never came back." Alex stood at the foot of the bed wearing a blue robe and dangling earrings. His eyes, heavily made up with blue shadow, seemed to float all alone between the sparkling earrings. "We went to look for you, but you were gone. Your father and grandfather got here about daylight, and your grandfather found you."

"What happened to me?" Cole's hand had strayed to his chest, where he found a series of wide bandages.

"You got scratched pretty good," Luther said. "Onatima put some special medicine on them scratches and wrapped you up."

"I washed you and put Neosporin on the cuts," the old lady added.

"How'd I get scratched?"

Luther bent a little over the bed, and his face looked like a frowning mask. "If I didn't know better, Grandson, I'd say you tangled with a bear."

"Where are the others?"

"Uncle Emmet and Michael had to go home," Alex replied. "Robert was the first one to run outside after you, and he never came back."

"Has anybody called his house?" Cole asked.

"Robert doesn't have a phone," Alex said. "But after we found you, Abby and I drove to his house. He was sleeping. We looked through the window."

Fifty-Two

That afternoon, Cole sat in a chair on the deck, a blanket tucked up to his chin, watching two squirrels chase one another through the playground of the big oak. One hand lay inside the blanket, touching the pouch around his neck, fingering through the leather the sharp edges of the two arrowheads and the round surface of the tiny stone doll. Throughout the morning he had tried unsuccessfully to piece together the vision, coming always to the pouch and the sensation of being lifted from the earth by his brother's hand. As one of the squirrels took off in a soaring, five-foot leap, he felt his heart jump with it, and then the screen door banged.

"I made some coffee," Abby said, setting a cup on the little table beside him. "How do the cuts feel?"

He reached the arm from under the blanket and lifted the coffee cup. "Thanks, this is nice." He took a sip and tried to find the squirrels again among the twisting oak branches. "I feel pretty good," he added, surprised at the truth of the statement. "Sort of like I tried to bathe a bobcat."

Abby touched his blanketed arm. "The scratches aren't deep. You must have run into a lot of blackberry vines." She paused and breathed deeply. "Have you thought of coming home, Dad?"

He spotted one of the squirrels near the top of the tree, hunched on a branch that looked too small for its weight. "Home?"

"Mom won't sell the house if you want to keep it. She couldn't, anyway."

"I thought you wanted to go to school here?"

"Not anymore. I want to go back."

He nodded, thinking again of the peyote vision. Where was home?

She looked around them, her gaze moving from Custer's grave past the big oak to the trees beyond the grassy field. "I'm frightened here."

He set the glass on the table and drew the blanket more tightly around him, the hand returning once more to the deerskin pouch. In the oak the squirrel appeared to be turning something over and over in its paws. "I took a leave of absence, so I could go back if I wanted to," he said. "But I'd have to tell them right away." Suddenly the idea of returning was exciting. "I'll have to finish out the academic year here."

"That would be so great," she placed her hand on his shoulder again.

"But you can't expect me and your mother . . ."

"I know," she cut in. "But I miss her. You'll have to buy her half of the house."

He raised his eyebrows. "Right. With what?"

"You can refinance. I checked it out already. There's enough equity."

When he turned to look at his daughter, she was beaming. "Okay," he said, surprised it was all so simple. "We'll go back in June. I'll tell the university today. Now tell me about Paul Kantner. Alex and I saw you two walking off together the other day."

"Alex and you?" She made a face. "Paul wanted to show me the place the students call Elfland. The whole thing is really strange, but fascinating. But Paul's too bizarre for words. I don't like him. He gives me the creeps. Did Alex say anything?"

"He didn't seem happy about it. Do you want me to have a talk with Paul Kantner?"

She rolled her eyes and grimaced. "Good God, no. Alex didn't seem happy about it?" The grimace became a smile. "Don't worry about Paul Kantner. I told him not to call me anymore, so he stopped. When we go back home, I'll show you how to tie midges and paradrakes. We can fish the Gila like you always said we would."

205

"Midges are the easiest flies in the world, Abby. I was tying midges when you were a baby. You'll have to go to the University of New Mexico, you know."

"My father lies. You were fishing with worms until you were thirty. It's a great university. I think Alex is very nice, and very handsome."

He sipped the coffee. "Don't get your hopes up. You may have noticed that Alex often wears dresses. What about Robert?"

She shook her head. "Alex just likes to shock people. Robert's nice, but he makes me nervous. I've never met anyone so intense. It's like he has an energy field around him. And half his mind is always somewhere else when he's talking to you."

Cole was silent for a moment before he said, "Robert's a funny mix. He's smart as hell, but he's a simple-minded romantic at the same time. He's one of those white people who suspect all the evil their ancestors have done to the earth and feel the need to atone somehow. What he really wants is to be a white Indian, the Natty Bumppo of Santa Cruz. I guess that would make me his Chingachgook and Alex his Uncas. Only thing missing is Magua." He raised his eyebrows. "And you must be Cora, the beautiful maiden with the cross in her blood."

"You're making my skin crawl, Dad. You read too much."

"It's my job. The students think Robert's the best thing they've ever seen, with that lean and hungry look of his. They're all nuts for him, probably the boys and girls both, but I don't think he even notices. But Robert has a good heart. Maybe, as you said, he just feels things too deeply. He's in love with mother earth."

"Is Robert coming tonight?"

"I invited him last week, so we'll see if he remembers. He's never had traditional Choctaw birthday cake. I told him to be here about eight, that that's when you and Alex would get here for the Choctaw chocolate hominy cake ceremony. I said we'd be in traditional costume."

"Have you rented a tuxedo?" She stood up. "Isn't it incredible to have your whole family here for your birthday?"

"Incredible," he replied, thinking that it was too incredible, in fact, to be believed. Something was going on. "Like witchcraft."

"You're finally an elder, Dad."

"I'm finally an idiot dad," he said, thinking of the bear. "A fool dad. I should have left this place months ago."

"Before I go down to campus, we could tie some flies. I'll get set up." She patted his arm and went into the house, and almost at once, as though changing shifts, Onatima and Luther appeared, pulling chairs close on either side of him.

"Abby's baking a cake," Luther said. "Chocolate." The old man wore khaki hiking shorts, a red-flowered Hawaiian shirt with a black down vest over it, and sandals with calf-high black socks. The shorts, several sizes too large, were bunched around the waist with a floppy braided belt, and the shirt-sleeves hung to his elbows. His bony arms and legs were brittle and fragile looking. "Hoey said you liked chocolate cake with chocolate frosting, but I think that's the kind Hoey likes."

"You're right. You look good in my clothes, Uncle Luther," Cole said. "I'd forgotten I owned those. But you should have something warmer on."

"The day is not cold, Grandson," Onatima said from the other side. When he turned toward her voice, he felt a surge of warmth.

"You brought the medicine pouch," Cole said.

Luther nodded. "I found it in that little locker you used when you was a boy. I thought you would need it."

Cole lifted the pouch off of his neck and held it in the palm of his hand, staring at it for a long time. His brother had made it for him before going to Vietnam. He probed through the thin leather with his fingers, seeing in his mind the two arrowheads, the black obsidian with the white lightning bolt through it and the other that looked like

207

brown flint. The two-inch doll was of white stone, its outlines worn smooth. All three had been dug from a single spot in the coastal mountains and had lain on Attis's shelf for several years. He hadn't thought of the little deerskin bag as medicine until Uncle Luther had called it that twenty years before. Until then he had thought it was just a bag his brother had made to hold Indian things.

"I thought I'd lost it," Cole said at last, deciding not to ask how it came to be around his neck.

"Nothing's lost, Grandson," Onatima replied, touching his shoulder.

Cole slipped the leather thong around his neck once more and opened the blanket to tuck the bag inside his shirt. "Thank you," he said.

"Robert Jim gave you some pollen, too." Luther brought the tiny leather bag from the pocket of the down vest and placed it in Cole's hand. "You best add that to your medicine there. This thing ain't finished, but we think you may be ready to meet that gambler."

"Who's Robert Jim? I guess you'll have to explain everything." Cole remembered the image of the painted man in his vision—what had the figure held, a gun? The picture seemed wrong, somehow distorted.

"You have prepared yourself well, Grandson. For many months now you have put away the appetites of men. You have fasted and gone into the sweat lodge, and you have prayed and been given a vision."

Cole shook his head. "I think we may be dealing with semantics here, Uncle Luther. The truth is that I haven't been with a woman for all these months not because I was being pure, but because I was afraid." He glanced at Onatima. "I've done what you call fasting only because until Abby came I was too sick to eat. Alex dragged me into the sweat lodge and into another ceremony in which I ate a hallucinogenic drug that nearly killed me. To call all of that purification is wish fulfillment, I'm afraid."

208   "What you call it don't matter. Onatima always says the

Good Lord works in mysterious ways." He winked at her, but her eyes were fastened on Cole.

Onatima spoke up abruptly, saying, "Luther's right, but there's still one crucial thing you have to understand, Grandson. No matter what else you do, you should know that you can't win over this dream. He's part of something too big. It's everywhere now. We all have to live with this thing."

"But it's not dreams that are killing people," Cole responded, listening to the chattering of one of the squirrels. "It's somebody who leaves footprints, maybe the same psychopath who terrified Abby."

"The gambler is part of this place now. He doesn't know anything else," Onatima said.

"You mean the dreams."

Luther nodded. "People got to live with what they made here, just like everywhere." He rose from the chair, unfolding slowly until he stood straight and tall against the sky. "The gambler wants power, Grandson. And he thinks you brung it to him. He thinks you are a warrior like him." He looked down at Cole with a rare, serious expression. "Only thing is, don't say his name no more. He wants you to say his name. Now we better get ready for your birthday party. Hoey walked up to look at the ocean. Soon as Hoey gets back, he's going to take me and this old lady into town."

Onatima patted Cole on the arm and then stood and followed the old man into the house.

Fifty-Three

Abby stood next to her father's chair, leaning over the vise and pointing with a needlelike bodkin. The warm smell of freshly baked cake filled the kitchen. "You have to get the tips of the calf tail exactly even, Dad. Now wrap both sides of the wing nice and tight so it divides well. That's crucial. Now do the crossing tie to separate the wings."

Cole stopped with the bobbin raised above the fly and looked at his daughter, his face deadpan.

She smiled back. "You're cute when you're exasperated. The Royal Humpy is the best dry fly in the West. It killed them on the Black River this fall."

"You went there by yourself? That's dangerous with all the rattlesnakes."

"You've done it lots of times. It was gorgeous. The water was perfect, and the elk were bugling everywhere. I saw that herd of bighorn sheep, too." She pointed at the fly. "Get a good wrap behind the wings. When are Grampa and Onatima and Uncle Luther coming back from town?"

He finished tying in the wing and added two brown hackles. "I don't know. They went to buy me a new Jeep for my birthday. You and Alex seem to have gotten close." He squinted as he began wrapping the tiny hackle feathers toward the eye of the hook, unable to get the old couple's words out of his mind. Venancio Asisara was out there. Venancio had stood outside his window. Had he said the gambler's name himself, in his dream? Had it been his own voice he heard in the dark hours of the morning?

"A toy Jeep maybe. I like Alex. Make sure you get an even amount of hackle on both sides of the wing, and watch the eye. You used to wrap the eye on your mosquitoes sometimes, and I couldn't get the leader through. Maybe you should get one of those little cones you put over the eye before you tie off."

He looked at her. "I was tying flies before you were a gleam in your mother's eye."

She smiled again. "That's not true. You're a novice, a recently reformed bait fisherman. And I like Alex very much."

He tied off with the whip finisher and applied a drop of head cement. "I like Alex, too," he said. "But he's a lot older than you, and his life is very complicated."

She unclamped the vise and lifted the fly between thumb and forefinger, holding it up to the light. "It's perfect. See, you can tie something besides mosquitoes. Alex is only thirty-two." She dropped the fly into the box. "Let's try an Adams Irresistible. Alex is picking me up pretty soon. I'll ride back up with him, too."

He sighed. "Enough fly tying. I think I'll take a walk."

Fifty-Four

Leaving Abby at the house, he walked through the grass, pausing at the edge of the forest to look around, wondering if that was where Uncle Luther had found him. He continued into the trees, thinking of Emil Redbull's question. It was true that he didn't know the woods around his home, that he hadn't ventured beyond the big oak that marked some kind of boundary for him. He'd never lived anywhere before where he didn't know the terrain of his existence. But he had avoided the forests of the Santa Cruz Mountains, 211 staying within the clearings where the sun and stars, even veiled in fog, were constant markers.

Within the trees, he began to follow a deer path that climbed a small rise, enjoying the quiet of his steps in the damp leaves. It might be the same path, he thought as he topped the knoll and started down into a canyon, that had brought Robert Malin to his house.

The trail cut steeply across the hillside, dropping him into the dim bottom of the canyon. Soon he could hear the sounds of a stream, and then he found himself at the edge of the water and realized it must be the stream he had recommended on hearsay to his daughter, the one where without him she had caught the little rainbows. The stream dropped sharply from pool to pool, the surface of each an impenetrable black broken only by the gray wrinkles of water striders, and he remained on the trail as it edged the water, following the canyon in its quick descent. At regular intervals, pigeons erupted invisibly from the tops of the redwoods, the sounds of their wings tolling like bells.

After forty-five minutes the canyon began to open and level off, and he heard the sound of an automobile. A few minutes later, he was at a juncture where the stream he had been following ran perpendicularly into another one. In the middle of the larger stream, a little house of unpainted redwood sat on top of a giant stump, and at once he knew it was the cabin Robert had told him about, the one Robert had built.

Beyond the cabin he could make out the back and roof of a very large house, with a column of smoke coming out of a chimney. But the cabin was dark and uninhabited looking, the windows gray squares.

He started wading across the stream, jerking awake when the cold water flooded into his running shoes but continuing until he reached the other bank. He scrambled up the bank and onto the hanging bridge, with a glance toward the big house before crossing.

At the door he knocked and waited. When there was no

response, he leaned to look through the window beside the door. His heart froze. Three bodies lay tangled together on the floor of the cabin, a girl and two tiny children, their clothes soaked in blood and a pool of blood spreading around them. He held to the wooden door handle for a moment and then pushed at it. When the door swung open, he breathed deeply and stepped inside.

There were no bodies. Where the children had been, the floor was clean and bare. Everything about the room was orderly, the books shelved in precise lines, computer paper stacked neatly, even the little bunk made up without a wrinkle. It was the cell of a scholarly monk.

He sat on the sideboard of the bed and leaned his head into his cupped hands. The bodies had been as real as anything in his world, the faces fixed in expressions of terror, the blood liquid and shining. Two toddlers and a young woman, tumbled atop one another as though hastily discarded.

When the dizziness had eased he left the cabin and crossed the stream, following the thread of trail back up the canyon. Late afternoon had begun to solidify in the narrowing vee of the stream, and the sound of moving water was louder and more distinct than before. The image of the children stayed before him in horrifying, heartbreaking clarity as he bent into the climb.

He felt something wet on his face and reached a hand toward it. More drops struck his forearm and the back of his hand. He looked up from the trail to see lines of rain all around, sweeping down the canyon in strangely dark and heavy-looking curves. On the backs of his hands the rain was thick, and when he reached to wipe it from his face his fingers came away covered with a viscous liquid. Then he smelled it and raised his arms to cover his face.

He crouched on the trail, his face hidden, and heard the blood-rain sweep down the canyon in sodden waves that beat rhythmically in time with his own pulse. The liquid was hot, weighting his shoulders and back, covering him

213

with the odor that had come from Alex's deer—the fragrance of new death.

He cowered, the picture of the children never leaving him, until he could feel, smell, and hear nothing. Then into the emptiness came the sound of a stringed instrument, just touched and offered to the wind. The beautiful, pulsing note approached through the trees, growing stronger until it was inside his head, and when he pressed his hands against his own lips he knew that what he heard was himself.

He raised his head from his hands and saw air turning toward the dusk of evening, trees that were straight and curved lines of gray and black, earth hidden beneath a spongy layer of leaves, branches, and small plants. The little canyon smelled of damp and decay, with the fine, humid aroma of layer upon layer of death. Except for the cuffs of his pants, his clothes were dry, and there was no sign anywhere of the terrifying rain.

He rose stiffly, balancing with great effort, and began to move up the slope. The short afternoon had become evening, the light in the treetops deepening to near-black around his feet. He began to quicken his steps until he rounded the top of the small ridge in a shambling run. At the edge of the trees he stopped and looked at his own house. A coil of smoke rose from the chimney into the gray sky, and a warm light shone through the glass doors in back. He went to the drooping limb of the big oak and leaned into its solid curve, resting his arms and head against it. "I've lost my mind," he said aloud.

Fifty-Five

Alex Yazzie stood naked before the full-length mirror, turned so that the light made shadowy signs along his brown rib cage and across his groin. He bent and pulled the black bikini panties up, tucking himself inside them. Then he picked up a black garter belt from the bed and held it in his hand, studying it.

"Abby, could you give me some advice?" he said loudly.

Abby came into the room, stopping abruptly, her eyes fastening on the black panties.

"It's this garter belt. I've never used one before."

She remained where she was for a moment longer and then walked to him, keeping her eyes on his face. "You want me to show you?"

"Please." He held the belt out and she took it.

"I've never used one either, but I've seen girls at school with them. It goes like this." She held it in front of his waist. "This part goes in front."

As she fastened the belt, her fingers brushed across his thigh, and they both tensed. She kept her eyes focused on the belt.

"The stockings fasten here." She pointed.

"Um. Do you think you could show me how that works?"

He rolled the stockings slowly up each leg, and as she gathered the silk into the garter-belt clamps her fingers traced patterns on his skin. When she was finished, she let her hand travel up his leg to the flatness of his groin and belly, keeping her eyes averted.

He reached down to grasp her wrist and lift the hand, until her face rose and they looked at each other. He bent toward her for an instant, and then he stepped back.

She looked away. "I'm sorry."

215

He cupped her hand in both of his. "I am not to be trusted, Abby. You are beautiful and desirable and wonderful."

"I feel like an idiot," she said.

"No. You are very, very special. But you understand, don't you?" He looked down to where the evidence of his desire was obvious and raised his eyebrows. "I'm weak in all ways."

He bent to kiss her, and she pressed herself to him. When he pulled away, he studied her for a long moment and watched as she began to undress. When she was naked, she knelt to unfasten the garter belt and then slid his stockings and panties to the floor. He took both of her hands and lifted her, turning in the process so that together they fell back upon the bed. He began to kiss her body, his lips moving from her hair and face down over her breasts and belly and thighs until he kissed the soles of her feet and began to move upward again, his tongue tracing the length of her calf and thigh and belly. His lips touched her eyes, his tongue marking the hollows of her cheeks and descending again to her breasts, and then she began kissing him, touching every part of his body.

"A woman's body is a beautiful creation," he said. "The most beautiful in the world."

When they lay side by side on the bed, Alex raised up on one elbow and looked down at her. He traced the contours of her lips with his finger. "This is most strange."

She turned into his shoulder, and her hand reached toward his face and then settled onto his thigh.

"We fall in love with the wrong people, don't we, Abby?"

She touched the angle of his cheek. "I don't think so."

When they were both dressed, Alex spun on one toe and placed both hands flat over his belly, admiring the black wool skirt and red blouse he wore. While Abby sat on the edge of the bed watching, he moved closer to the mirror and scrutinized his face. Finally, he pulled on a short wool jacket, picked up a red-wrapped package from the bed, and placed his hand on her shoulder.

"Let's go to your father's birthday party."

When he turned the key in the ignition, the Volvo remained silent. He jiggled the key and sighed.

"You left the lights on." She pointed at the knob.

"Its dead as a doornail."

"Maybe one of your neighbors has jumper cables."

He shook his head. "Maybe, but I'm not really dressed for that kind of neighborly exchange. And none of my neighbors is very fond of me since the deer incident. Word got out somehow that I was a sacred warrior clown and potentially dangerous."

"There's a bus stop across the road, isn't there?"

"That's right. Let's go before we miss the last one."

As they walked toward the road, Alex said, "The only other time I left my headlights on I was way the hell and gone out in the middle of nowhere, miles outside of Kayenta on the res, where we'd gone for a naming ceremony. My younger brother, Tony, and I were the last guests to leave, and then we couldn't leave because our battery was dead. The guy whose house we were at couldn't jump us because his truck battery was also dead." He reached for her hand and held it as they walked. "So we stayed two extra days, lying in the shade and listening to stories and eating frybread and mutton stew until a relative came by to give us a jump start. I had a good time teasing Tony and the fourteen-year-old daughter of the family. They kept disappearing behind a mesa and coming back with sand on their clothes. That was the last summer I spent at home. Now I can't even imagine a time when two lost days could mean nothing, when I hadn't looked at a calendar for weeks at a time. It was really beautiful out there."

They crossed the road to stand outside the bus shelter. In the apartment nearest the road, a curtain parted for a moment and he saw a silhouette in the lighted window, and then the curtain closed again. Waiting in the cold, he remembered the way his brother held his hand up to hide his broken teeth when he laughed, the sounds of his mother shuffling around in the hogan before daylight, and the smell of juniper smoke and coffee on summer mornings outside. For the first time in years, he remembered the sound of a flock of milling sheep, and the smell of sheep mingled with dust and sage, and a sharp pang of homesickness pierced him. "I think I'll go home this summer," he said aloud. "I'll spend the whole summer there, up at the sheep camp with Tony. I miss being Navajo."

They heard a car coming down the hill from the campus, and he stepped onto the road and stuck out his thumb.

Fifty-Six

The driver had the gun pointed at Alex before either of them was aware of his movement. "If you both do what I want, I won't hurt you," he said.

From the backseat, Abby recognized the voice. The bulky head and shoulders had looked vaguely familiar from behind, but the voice made it certain. "You're Paul Kantner," she exclaimed.

Keeping the gun leveled at Alex in the front seat, Kantner half-turned toward her. "I didn't realize it was you until you got in. What a fortunate coincidence. There you were, desiring to approach but afraid of the bright fire. Remember? But now you've stepped into the circle."

He turned the car away from town, on the crest road. Behind them another car turned out of the campus and followed.

"You both smell like sex. Did you know that? We'll just drive around a little, I think." He looked in the rearview mirror. "Like the shadow of a wild thing. I've watched you, you know, since you showed up in class. Your father understands so much. He knows about the way women talk, talk, talk without saying anything at all. Cunts. I do not think that they will sing to me. I've learned so much in his class."

He swerved the car suddenly onto a dirt road and the car behind continued up the grade. A hundred yards into the forest, the road ended against a bulldozed mound of earth, and he stopped and let the motor idle. For a moment he sat aiming the gun at Alex, saying nothing. The smooth branches of big madrones snaked overhead, forming a canopy, and the tall, straight trunks of redwoods, mixed with the madrones and oaks, formed a close wall on three sides.

Kantner spoke to Abby in the mirror. "I tried to talk with you in Elfland. I took you there so I could read my poem to you. I knew you'd never find it, otherwise. I mean what were the chances of you going up there and just happening to pick up that piece of paper? That's crazy. So I had to show you. But I saw right away that I made you uneasy. All you wanted to do was get away from me. Do you realize how hard it was for me to read that poem to you? How much courage it took?"

"If you let us go now," Abby said, "we'll walk back to the road and say nothing about this."

Kantner jerked his eyes back to Abby. "I hate to see you stoop to a lie like that. We both know you would feel morally constrained to tell the authorities. I'm too dangerous to just let go. Now both of you get out on this side."

He shut off the motor, leaving the headlights on so that they pointed into the deeper forest, forming a half-circle of light around the front of the car. Then he opened the door and backed out, the gun pointed at Alex. "If you try to run, I'll kill her," he said to Abby. "And I would just find you, anyway. Some of the others tried to run, and I found them easily. They ran and tripped and became hysterical in these thick woods, and that made it much harder on them. You see it in the movies, how people run and look back and trip, and you think that's just Hollywood, nobody would really do that. But that's what happens. It's almost comical."

They got out of the car at the same time, and Kantner made a circular motion with the gun. "You turn around, Miss McCurtain. She's going to tie your hands behind you." He pulled several pieces of heavy cord from his jacket pocket with his left hand and pushed them toward Alex. "Make sure you don't hurt her," he said. "I'll tell you what no one else knows. I buried their heads in my backyard, facing my bedroom. Every night I talk to them. I say affectionate things, like you would say to a girlfriend or even a wife. Death never entered into it, you have to understand; death's a transition I didn't pay any attention to. I was trying to establish a relationship, that's all. Just a relationship. Is that so fucking much to ask?"

He jerked the barrel of the pistol toward Alex. "What are you doing?"

Alex had slipped his shoes off and stood in stocking feet, and he was slowly pulling the minidress higher, so that the hem now reached just below his crotch.

"Do you think that's what I want? You think you're going to offer your cunt and that will be all?"

Alex looked at Abby.

"You won't hurt me, will you?" Abby said. "I wasn't trying to get away from you at Elfland. It's just that my father was waiting. I loved your poem. In fact," she spread her hands, palms outward, and looked down, "I was really hoping you would write more poetry for me."

Kantner turned his attention fully upon her, the gun shifting so that it aimed haphazardly toward her abdomen. "God, that's pathetic. You really think I'm a moron, don't you? You're doing what they all did when it was too late. A lousy job of acting. Now you'll talk to me, but it's just lying bullshit to try to save your life. Even my mother tried that crap, but it was too late for her, too. They'll find her in the bathtub, most of her anyway." He grinned, his mouth enormous and dark, as Alex very slowly shifted his stance.

Kantner swung the gun back toward Alex at the same time that Alex pivoted, catching the gun hand with the side of his foot so that the pistol flew to the ground behind Abby.

Kantner was staring in the direction the gun had gone when Alex's foot came forward a second time, striking the big man's knee. Kantner screamed and crumbled, scrambling backwards in the same motion.

Suddenly Abby was between them, pointing the pistol at Kantner. "Be still," she shouted. "Don't fucking move."

Kantner seemed to relax all at once. He sat back on the ground, his arms lying helplessly in his lap, and stared up at her. "It's finally over," he said, his voice filled with wonder.

"Tie him up, Alex," she said. "If he moves at all, I'll shoot him."

"Alex? Doctor Yazzie?" Kantner was looking at both of them in confusion when his body abruptly stiffened and lurched sideways, the arms flailing for an instant before he collapsed. The quiet *pok* of a pistol seemed unrelated to the spectacle of the huge body becoming disjointed.

A voice from the dark said, "He was going to kill you."

Robert Malin appeared beside Alex, looking down at Kantner's body, where a small black spot showed in one temple. A line of blood ran from the hole down across Kantner's jaw and neck, disappearing into the collar of his flannel shirt. Robert held a small pistol pointed toward the ground.

Abby knelt beside Kantner. "He's dead," she said. "Why did you . . ."

"He was going to kill you," Robert repeated, looking at Abby. "Like he killed the others. I heard what he told you."

"No. He wasn't going to kill us," Alex said. "Didn't you see that Abby had the gun?"

Robert looked from one of them to the other. "I saw him

221

pick you up. I followed, and when he turned off I knew what he was doing. So I parked out of sight and cut through the woods." He looked at Alex with a strange expression. "I had to. I knew what he was going to do."

Fifty-Seven

"Thank heaven it's over." The vice chancellor spoke directly into the camera, his face pallid and insecure.

Gathered around the television, the whole family watched as the camera shifted to focus on a young Asian American reporter. "Was Paul Kantner the serial killer of Santa Cruz, the butcher murderer?" she asked, her voice deep with portent. "Is Santa Cruz's reign of terror over, thanks to the courage of two Native Americans and the alert response of a student?"

The screen showed a picture of Alex, tall and imposing in his boots, jeans, white shirt, and sheepskin vest. His turquoise belt buckle gleamed, and he wore his hair pulled back. With his vision focused on something in the distance, he presented a profile the world knew well: the Indian warrior come to rescue the white world from its nether self. The reporter, in a voice edged with awe and what Cole suspected to be lust, explained that Alex Yazzie, a Native American professor and martial arts expert, had taken it upon himself to trap the killer, dressing as a woman and hitchhiking with the daughter of another Native American faculty member. The camera cut to Abby, so darkly beautiful that Cole leaned forward in surprise. Then the county sheriff came on the screen to say in a stern and unconvincing voice that such citizen actions were a very bad idea. He went on to praise Doctor Yazzie and Abby McCurtain for their courage, pointing out, however, that but for the fortuitous appearance of Robert Malin things might have turned out tragically.

Robert appeared on the television, looking mysteriously brooding and handsome, his even voice explaining the events that had led him to the scene. Then the reporter took over once more to describe the unearthing of heads in Paul Kantner's yard.

Cole swung around to face Alex, who sat on the floor, his back against the couch. "How in the world did you think of such a brilliant disguise, Doctor Yazzie?"

On the far end of the couch, Luther snorted.

Dressed just as he had been on television, Alex lifted both palms and shrugged. "Jim Chee tribal investigator correspondence school."

On the couch behind Alex, her legs folded beneath her, Abby rested a hand on his shoulder. "I can't help wondering," she said. "Robert didn't have to shoot him."

"Robert didn't know," Alex responded. "I must have been in the way, so that he couldn't see you holding the gun."

"But Paul was just sitting there."

"There wasn't much light. All Robert knew was that Paul Kantner wanted to kill us."

"But . . ."

"Something is outside," Luther said abruptly.

"The whole world's outside," Hoey replied from his end of the couch.

"He is outside," Onatima said from beside Hoey.

The bear shuffled out of the trees, sniffing the air with its nose held high. It paused and sat back on its great haunches and then slowly rose until it stood on two legs. The massive dished head swiveled to take in the expanse of grass and the lighted house. A current of air flowed up from the sea and spilled over the ridge, and the stars were distant and cold. Far below, the water seemed touched by fire. Wind

223

bent upon the redwoods and they groaned against one another. For a long moment the bear stood there, and the world was irrevocably strange and void.

Onatima held her head high, as if listening.

"It's gone now." She leaned back in the chair, looking suddenly delicate and fragile.

"What?" Cole said.

"We'll find some of them tracks tomorrow," Luther replied. He settled more deeply into the couch. "It happened so quick with these Indians here, not like with us where it took three hundred years. It's very sad. One minute these people was living like they always did, and the next minute everything was gone. They seen their children die. They seen their whole world die. And they remembered. When I go to bed in this house, I hear all that out there. Now they woke this gambler up, and he wants his world back."

"Is it true you've all dreamed about him?" Abby asked. "Even in Mississippi?"

Onatima nodded. "Dreams come to us in different ways, Abby. Some people, those with power, can send dreams." She paused, appearing to consider her words carefully. "Spirits can send dreams, too. But this one isn't like anything Luther and I have experienced before."

Abby's face had grown more animated. "Maybe that explains Paul Kantner. Maybe the dreams made him crazy."

Cole shook his head. "I don't think so. For Kantner it seemed like some kind of psycho-sexual thing with women. He told me his mother talked all the time but wouldn't say anything to him. The news said he cut out her larynx after he killed her."

"My God, Dad."

"I'm sorry, Abby." Cole turned toward his father. "You and Uncle Luther never did tell us why it took you so long to get here."

Hoey watched the television, where a man was talking about rain. "You might say Uncle Luther got us sidetracked."

"Hoey didn't have no jack in his truck."

"Jobe stole my jack," Hoey said. "Probably traded it for a pint." He scratched his neck and looked at Luther before he said, "First we had a flat and no jack. Then we had to save a woman from what Uncle Luther called witches and take her way to hell and gone in the middle of the Navajo reservation. It's twenty-five-thousand square miles, and we drove through the whole damned thing. But before that we had to take an old man named Robert Jim home. He was hitchhiking and was the one told us to look for the witches. So we had to spend a night in Gallup."

"Them Navajos got a lot of witches," Luther said, "and powerful medicine. We had to take some of the witches back, too. Those Indians got round houses, lots of skinny horses, and more sheep than you could shake a stick at. They got dogs everywhere out there."

Onatima snorted. "This old man's so full of hog talk it just doesn't pay to listen to him." She turned to Hoey. "After that drive, you're obviously as full of it as he is. I imagine he corrupted you right to the core."

Fifty-Eight

"So he wants his world back, but his world's gone?" Cole lifted the pot from the stove and poured more coffee into his brown mug.

Luther held a scrap of toast in the egg yolk on his plate and looked up, as if trying to remember the conversation from the night before. "It's good to be awake for sunrise, ain't it?"

"Your braid's in your coffee, Uncle Luther."

Luther glanced at the cup, where the end of one braid soaked. "That's a old Indian trick, Grandson, and I'm a old Indian. Us Choctaws always did that for the warpath, you see, when we might not get coffee for a long time. We'd go along sucking on braids. That's why we all got that black hair, too. We used to all be blond-headed Indians, but good coffee wicks right to the roots." He laid the toast down and lifted the braid from the cup, carefully drying it with a napkin.

"It's wonderful hearing the traditional stories of my ancestors," Cole added. "I suppose that's why most Choctaws today keep their hair short."

"Ain't you glad I made you get up from that floor now, Grandson? How else would you be so cheerful so early in the day? Which reminds me. How come you ain't wrote no more of them books? You used to write good stories."

They sat on opposite sides of the little table. Through the window above the kitchen sink, Cole could see dawn spreading gradually along the ridge, the light coming pale and late through a fine drizzle. In the living room his down sleeping bag was bunched on the floor, and his father lay under a comforter on the couch, snoring evenly.

"Not much of a sunrise, but it doesn't take much to get me off that floor," Cole said. "I don't know. Maybe I've been resting up."

Luther nodded approvingly. "They got too many stories about us. We need to write books about them now. Get even." He blew on the coffee and sipped it experimentally. "This gambler's world is gone all right, just like for the rest of us. But I know plenty of people that that didn't stop 'em none from wanting it all back. Some of the ones that don't even know what it was still want it back. It's natural for a ghost, but not the ones still living." Luther sopped the remaining yolk and folded the toast into his mouth, chewing in a rolling motion. "When I was a boy, those teachers used to take a belt to us if we talked Indian in school. They thought that'd make us forget, and sometimes I suppose it worked."

Cole sipped the coffee and made a face. "Your coffee, Uncle Luther, would take the bristles off a pig." He reached for the carton of half-and-half. "Alex gave me a copy of an 1877 interview with an Indian named Lorenzo Asisara, the son of one of the men who killed the priest. His parents were Venancio and Manuela Asisara."

He tested the coffee again. "That's the name I woke up with, Venancio Asisara. I think Venancio is the painted gambler. The interviewer referred to Venancio as *indio*—Indian—but he said Lorenzo Asisara was *color quebrado*. It's a term the Spanish used for mixedbloods. It means 'softened color.'" Cole held out his arm and raised his eyebrows. "The interviewer also noted that Lorenzo had green eyes."

"Breed eyes." Luther looked into Cole's green eyes, and Cole could see the gummed toast through the old man's missing teeth. "You said his name."

Through the kitchen window, Cole could see a line of low clouds or fog along the ridge, graying the morning. "How do you think the son ended up with green eyes?"

Fifty-Nine

By evening the drizzle had passed inland, leaving a heavy dampness behind. The old couple, wearing identical wire-rimmed glasses, were on the couch, where Luther was looking intently at a clear plastic box of trout flies and Onatima read a *Time* magazine.

"What's this one supposed to be?" Luther asked, lifting a tiny, outlandish-looking blur of hair and hackle.

Cole walked close and bent to look at the number sixteen fly. "That's a Parachute Grizzly Wulff," he said.

"What kind of bug is it supposed to be?" Hoey asked, rising from his chair to look.

Cole shrugged. "I don't know. I just followed a pattern in the book."

"What's this one?" Luther held up a fly with a black and gold striped tail, furry black body, and white and brown hackle.

"I don't know," Cole answered. "I guess I'd have to look it up."

"You made all these?" Hoey asked, poking his finger around in the box, where blue and red and gold and white hair and hackle covered miniscule hooks.

"Yeah. Abby badgered me about tying the same thing all the time, so I branched out. We're planning a trip to the Golden Trout Wilderness next summer, before we move back."

"I like chicken liver," Hoey said. "Leave it out a couple days and those mudcats go crazy for it. Before he quit fishing, Columbus Bailey caught a forty-pound channel cat on a whole duck once. His brother America run over the duck."

"Where is Abby?" Onatima asked, looking up from the magazine and removing her glasses.

"She's coming home with Alex," Cole answered. He looked at the wall clock. "They should have been here half an hour ago."

The old couple looked at one another, and Luther removed his glasses and laid them on the coffee table.

The phone rang in the kitchen, and Cole answered it. For several minutes he listened, murmuring occasionally, and then he hung up and walked back to the others.

"That was the Santa Cruz police."

Luther set the box of flies on the coffee table, and Onatima lowered the magazine. Hoey turned from where he had been looking out the big window.

"They matched the bullet that killed Paul Kantner with bullets from several of the other murders."

Onatima stood up. "Robert killed those people."

"They searched his cabin and found notebooks filled with writing about us, mainly about Abby."

"Robert's that other painted one," Luther said wonderingly. "How come we didn't know that, old lady?" He turned to stare at Onatima.

"Robert has a lot of power," she said, the idea obviously taking her by surprise.

Cole started for the door and then stopped. "I'm going to go look for Alex and Abby. Uncle Luther, you'd better stay here with Onatima. There's a shotgun in my closet."

"We'll take my truck," Hoey said, following Cole out the door.

Sixty

The dining room was warm with color, from the rich mahogany of the table to the creamy carpet and the brown Mexican tile that lead to the kitchen. The family sat at the table, and he watched them, his presence everything they had feared all of their lives. He knew he was what they had come together to deny, but he was there at the window nonetheless, a fraction of a transparent inch from being inside with them. He could shatter the window with a touch and come in, and there wasn't a thing they could do about it. He had always been there, and they had desired him, inviting him to build his little house as if surrounded by the movement of water he would be rendered safe. It was as though there were a window in their lives at every single moment of every day and he had always been there, looking in, painted and naked and near to exploding their world, separated by a mere breath of space. He wanted to move, to touch the glass, to smile death at them so they would have to see, for their recognition would be an invitation. But he did not, for he would return that night and visit his dreams upon them. Instead he turned back, moving across the black stream and finding the trail in the dark, his feet familiar and sure.

The gambler's song covered the whole forest, faint and wavering, as though it might be only a movement in the high branches, and he half ran, filled with the power of the song.

Sixty-One

He felt the night part for him. When the car appeared, stumbling in the deep ruts, he stepped into the middle of the road and stood unmoving. The headlights were blinding, a tunnel of fire, and he held his hands out, fists closed, knowing his own image.

"What's that?" As Alex spoke, he stomped on the brake pedal.

The Volvo skidded and spun, thrown into and out of the ruts, and Abby's head snapped sideways, striking the car window. Alex bounced forward, braced against the steering wheel and held suspended by the seat belt.

When the movement had stopped, Abby reached one hand to her cheek. The hand came away covered with blood, but she felt no pain. Beside her, Alex held his side and whispered, "Christ!"

Abby watched as the painted figure that had stood outside her window walked toward them. The car sat at an awkward diagonal across the road, and the headlights, angling up at forty-five degrees, brushed the moving nightmare with peripheral light. She could see vaguely the lines of division between white and black. The night was cold, yet the figure was naked.

Alex put the car in low gear and gunned the engine, but the wheels spun uselessly, the rear end suspended off the road berm.

"Lock your door," he said finally. He opened the other door and stepped out, pushing the lock down behind himself.

She watched him move around the front of the car, one hand holding his side. The painted man walked evenly, neither increasing nor decreasing his pace, until he was less than two yards from Alex.

For the second time, she watched as Alex shifted into his martial stance, knees and arms bent, feet spread and hands raised. She saw the other step back, and then she heard a small popping sound. She screamed and heard two more shots as Alex fell.

She was still screaming as she tore the door open and ran to where Alex had fallen. The front of his shirt and the edges of his sheepskin vest were already soaked with blood. She knelt and lifted his head, feeling for a pulse, and blood flowed over her hands and breasts.

"I really didn't want to do that. I liked Professor Yazzie."

She looked up. The face was divided between white and black, the sockets of the eyes deep and heavily coated, the hair pulled back tightly.

"You shot Alex?" she said. She cradled Alex's head and bent her own over it. "Oh, my God," she repeated.

"Do what I say, or I'll have to kill you, too."

She heard a strange sound, like eddying water, and real-

231

ized it was her own breath, and then the voice of the nightmare was familiar. She raised her head. The gun looked preposterously small, a toylike, silver twenty-two.

"Robert?" she said. "Robert? It's you?"

He gestured with the gun. "The most effective sacrifices are those things we value most. Maybe one will be enough this time. Maybe you and I can get away now. Jonah ran to the sea, where God could just look and find him. There's no place to hide unless you go beneath the surface, and even there he'll find you. He couldn't hide so the men on the boat sacrificed him, and that saved them. But he had only the sea, and we have the forest. It's dark, like the belly of the whale, and I know places."

She bent again, lifting Alex's face to her own. "He's still alive," she said.

"Quick. We have to hurry." He gestured with the gun. "Get up now, or I'll have to kill you, too, and all the others. Your father, the old ones, all of them."

"No," she said. "He's alive. We have to help him."

Robert grasped her upper arm, and she felt the gun shoved into her side.

"I hope you believe I'm sorry, but we're almost out of time." His voice took on a pleading quality. "Alex is dead. Now it's time." The hand lifted her and dragged her backwards, so that Alex's head fell to the road. With astonishing strength, Robert spun her, shoving her toward the side of the road. "Come with me or I'll have to kill all of you," he said flatly, as though he were giving an assignment in class. "Your father and grandfather and Luther and Onatima, too. Just like him."

Abby pressed a hand to her bleeding cheek, which had begun to throb, and she looked over her shoulder to see Alex's body illuminated at the edge of the headlights. She heard herself sobbing, as though the sound came from far away.

Her foot caught and she tumbled into the maple thicket, grabbing at the brushy trunks. Instantly the hand had the back of her shirt, lifting her to her feet and shoving her forward. The sobbing stopped as she tried to connect the strength in the arm that controlled her with Robert Malin.

"There." He shoved her again, and she found herself through the thicket and inside a clearing between the trunks of trees. The smell of Alex's blood surrounded her, and she felt the weight of it in her soaked shirt and pants. The hand steered her across the dark clearing and pushed her into the blackness beyond.

Sixty-Two

The first thing they saw was the headlights angling into the trees. Then they saw the object outlined in the dim lights of the old truck. By the time Cole had the pickup stopped and the ignition off, Hoey was out and bending over the body.

"It's Alex," Hoey said over his shoulder. "He's shot." He moved at once toward the car.

Cole knelt beside his friend, lifting Alex's head with one hand and searching for a pulse with the other. He raised his eyes toward the trees beside the road, feeling the darkness moving over him like the sea.

"It's like Attis again," he said.

Hoey turned around. "Don't do that. That won't do no good."

"He's alive," Cole shouted. "He's breathing."

"Abby's not in the car, and there's track's going in the brush here," Hoey said from beside the Volvo. He returned to where Cole knelt.

233

"Help me get him in the truck." As Cole spoke, Hoey bent and took Alex's feet, and together they lifted the body into the back of the pickup. Hoey wrapped the wool blanket from the pickup seat over and under the body, taking off his coat and folding it beneath the head. Then he reached behind the seat and pulled out the big deer rifle. "I'll get him to the hospital. There's four shots in that rifle."

Cole took the gun and turned toward the brush.

"Wait a minute." Hoey reached inside the pickup and then shone a big flashlight on the bushes beside the Volvo. "Look."

Cole reached for a shiny leaf, and his hand came away sticky. He held the hand under the flashlight and then looked at the opening in the brush. "Abby," he said. "He's got Abby."

"They took that deer trail," Hoey said.

Cole jerked the light away from his father. "Take care of Alex," he said, before he began to run.

"Don't use that light if you can help it," Hoey shouted after him.

Sixty-Three

For half an hour she stumbled through the forest ahead of him, feeling his hand on her shoulder or arm when she slowed or tripped. The smell of Alex's blood choked her, causing her to gasp for breath. At one point Robert stopped her with a hard grip on her shoulder and gestured with the gun. Through the trees and brush she saw a distant, warm light.

"That's your home," he said. "It looks secure, doesn't it? That's what everyone does. They build homes, communities, towns, and they think walls will protect them from their own guilt, their past, that they won't have to pay what they owe. They think they can do all those terrible things and then go home to their families and lock their doors and everything will be all right. Or they think that just because they didn't personally do those things, they're innocent. They don't understand that somebody has to accept responsibility, somebody has to finally say no and do something about it. It just can't go on forever that way. You have such a wonderful family. They love you very, very much. But everyone is responsible, Abby." He shoved her forward.

"Why?" she panted, holding branches away from her face. "Alex liked you. He hurt no one."

Behind her he said, "No, he liked you, not me. He loved you. I could see it when he looked at you. But that doesn't matter anyway, because I didn't have any choice. No one really has any choice." His hand was in the small of her back again. "I'd have dreams, and I'd get so angry. It was like there was a voice telling me what I had to do, but it wasn't really a voice because there weren't any words. You probably can't understand that, but I knew it was all true. The Bible is full of voices that speak to people—small, still voices, or voices from whirlwinds. It was like I knew all these things that I had to do, and I'd paint myself and do them. I can't explain it. It's like dreams when I'm awake. But in the end it's just our responsibility and things we have to do."

"You don't have to," she said over her shoulder, between hard breaths. "I'll just go back and help Alex. Please, Robert. I won't tell them where you are. I promise."

"I believe you," he answered, his mouth close to her ear. "I know you couldn't lie. But Doctor Yazzie is dead, and none of that matters any longer."

They reached a circular clearing with a huge, fire-blackened redwood stump in the middle.

235

"Sit there," he said, gesturing with the gun toward the base of the stump. "Don't try to run. I'm a very good shot."

She sat, feeling tears running down her face, the salt burning her cut cheek, and she wondered why she couldn't hear herself cry any longer. Her chest and shoulders jerked spasmodically, and that, too, she thought, must be crying. But there was no sound.

Robert shuffled in the damp leaves and moved a layering of fresh redwood fronds to disclose a stack of dry twigs and branches. Abby shivered and watched him lift a coffee can from beside the piled wood. From the can he extracted a folded square of newspaper and a plastic lighter. Glancing at her every few seconds, he carried a double handful of twigs to a stone fire ring a few feet from the stump. At once he had a small fire burning and had begun to lay larger sticks on the fire, leaning them into one another pyramid-style until the blaze leapt a foot from the ground, sending shadows dancing up the stump and splashing light around the little clearing. He laid bigger pieces on until she could feel the flaring heat and see the lines between white and black very clearly on his skin. As he crouched close to the flames, looking back at her frequently, she could see that the paint extended even to his penis and scrotum, half-black and half-white.

He stood upright and stepped back from the fire, the gun held down at his side. "On the edge of darkness," he said. "There is light. But nobody will see a fire this far into the forest. No one but me ever comes here." She could see the leaping flames in his eyes.

"What will you do?" she asked, feeling a hopeless exhaustion overwhelming her.

He walked to the back of the stump, returning with two large coffee cans which he set close to the fire. "We live in the Ring of Fire, you know. The great half-circle from New Zealand in the southwest to Cape Horn in the southeast, north to Japan and Alaska. Do you realize that eighty percent of the earthquakes in the world occur in that ring? She tries and tries to tell us, but we don't listen. Somehow we have to communicate, though. Don't we? And we've always really known how. All peoples everywhere have always known; that's what your father lectures about. That awful daring he talks about, the awful sacrifice and agony." He cocked his head as though waiting for an answer, his eyes like caves. "That which is most valuable, most precious, most perfect. The agony in stony places."

Abby hunched against the dampness of the stump, her arms folded around her knees. The spasms had stopped, and she felt intensely cold. "Why?" she said. "Why did you . . ?"

When he spoke, his voice was the same one she'd heard him use in her father's class. "Edgar Cayce said that there are conditions in the activity of individuals, in line of thought and endeavor, that often keep many a city and many a land intact through their application of the spiritual laws in their association with individuals. Don't you see what he meant? Keep in mind that from the North Star's viewpoint, the earth travels around the sun in a counter-clockwise motion. Do you see *my* line of thought and endeavor? If I had not sacrificed thirteen times, we all would have tumbled into the trenches of the molten sea, like Lemuria, the lost continent. It is our responsibility. You're part Native American; you should know that in at least part of your soul. Your father will understand what I've done. What I'm doing. There is a very special family. Closer to me than my own. Children so beautiful you can't imagine. It's so hard to sacrifice the things we most value, isn't it, the things we love? That's how she tests us, and she feels the pain, too, all the way through her. We try to cheat by making substitutions, but that doesn't work. Voices come in dreams."

He felt the side of one of the cans. "It should be warm enough," he said. "Stand up and take off your clothes."

She tried to speak, to say "No," but no sound came out. She shook her head and clutched her arms more firmly around her knees.

"I never knew what to do with my freedom," he said. "Until the dreams came. Now I've killed thirteen times, fourteen, and more won't matter. But that's not what I want for you. It just isn't necessary. I worried they would think I was doing those other sick things, raping and cutting people up—always young women. That was revolting, disgusting, incredibly sick. I wouldn't do something like that. I never wanted to hurt anyone."

Holding the gun in his left hand, he grabbed her arm with his right hand and jerked her to her feet. Again, she was shocked at the strength that seemed beyond him.

"Take off your clothes or I will have to kill you now." He raised the gun.

Silently, her breath so thin and cold that it seemed to cut through her chest, she began to unbutton her shirt. He watched with a dispassionate expression until her clothes were piled beside the stump.

"Now," he said. "Native Americans know that the world is precariously balanced between good and evil, light and dark, black and white. It is up to us to maintain that balance. Mother Earth gives us life and asks that we give something in return. One man consenting to be murdered can protect the millions of other human beings living in the cataclysmic earthquake/tidal area." He bent and reached a hand into one of the cans. When he straightened, she could see something dark on his fingers.

He began with her forehead, carefully smoothing the black paint from a precise line in the center to one side, down from the temple, delicately edging the cut cheek, and covering her neck, continuing down one arm to the tips of her fingers.

"It's harder with one hand," he said as he rubbed the paint evenly up and down the arm and onto the shoulder. "I wish you understood, so that I could trust you. It requires a lot of paint." Reaching for another handful, he streaked it down over her throat and across one breast and onto her belly. Then he repeated the procedure of smoothing, spread-

238

ing it evenly with the soft palm of his hand, using a finger to round and cover the nipple and four fingers together under the cup of the breast. Methodically, he continued down one half of her body, spreading the thick paint across her belly and pubic hair, being careful to edge one side of the labia before moving down the leg.

"Turn," he said, and when she had turned, he did the same with her back.

When he had covered the other half with a thick, white paint, he stood back and scrutinized her, letting his eyes travel slowly from hair to toes. She could feel her nipples standing hard and erect from the cold, and she clenched her eyes against tears. She heard him move closer, and felt the tip of his erect penis touch her leg.

"Lie down," he said.

Her mind rushed in search of escape, and she thought of the Indian song her father loved so much. *I had been looking far, sending my spirit north, south, east, and west, but I could find nothing, no way of escape.*

"Don't kill me," she said, and she sat and then lay on her back.

He knelt at her feet and she felt the barrel of the gun touch the painted skin of her belly.

"You can't tell anyone," he said. "If you tell them, they might misconstrue it and think that I raped you, that I was some kind of sexual deviant like him."

He laid himself over her, his hands on either side of her head, the pistol forgotten. "They wouldn't understand anything I've done," he said between breaths. "Sex has nothing to do with it."

Her breath was choked, and she reached to dig her fingernails into the thick earth. She stiffened, and then her grasping fingers touched something hard and metallic. Her hand groped and found the handle of the gun.

So close, the sound of the twenty-two was deafening. As if her vision were magnified, she saw his head jerk with the impact of the first bullet, and she pulled the trigger again.

239

With the second shot, his arms folded and he collapsed. Blood washed over her face, salt-tasting and hot, and she shoved with both hands, rolling him to the earth beside her.

The heat of the fire was searing one of her legs, and the damp cold of the forest floor radiated up through the rest of her body. She pulled herself to a sitting position, drawing away from the fire, and looked at Robert. The paint was smeared across his stomach, groin, and thighs, the black and white blurred into a mottled gray. Blood ran from wounds in the side and back of his head, thickening in the painted hair and spreading darkly on the leaves.

Cole saw the light through a tangle of branches seconds before the two shots cracked the night. He lunged toward the sound, bursting into the clearing. A fire lifted bladelike shadows across a large stump, and beside the fire a sitting figure, painted like the gambler from his dreams, resolved itself into the image of his daughter. He stood still, opening his mouth to shout her name but hearing only silence. On the ground beside her lay another painted form, a body bent at odd angles to the earth.

With her head turned from her father, Abby used one hand to push against the stump and rise to her feet. The silver pistol dangled from the other hand, glinting red and orange in the shifting fire. Cole could see the paint smeared down her breasts and stomach, and a coating of leaves and redwood fronds on her side and legs. As he started forward, the rifle held loosely at his side, he saw the other one step into the ring of light on the far edge of the clearing.

The paint was the same, but the lines were clear and distinct. A cape of shining black feathers covered the shoulders.

Cole watched the gambler move toward Abby, who raised the gun and began backing away.

The gambler stopped and squatted between the body and the fire. With his eyes fixed on nothing, he held out both hands toward her, fists closed, and began to move them slowly in a rhythmic motion. He started to sing, and the

240

motion of the hands increased to match the increasing tempo of song.

Abby knelt, setting the gun on the ground, and watched the dance of the painted man's hands.

The hands stopped, and Cole saw that for the first time the gambler was looking directly at his daughter.

Abby pointed at one of the dark fists, and slowly, a fraction of an inch at a time, the hand opened. In the pulsing light of the fire, Cole saw the painted bone.

"Abby!" he shouted. "No!"

At the eruption of sound, the gambler's fist closed. He rose and turned toward where Cole stood fifteen feet away.

"Venancio Asisara." Cole spoke the name clearly, as he had heard it in his dream.

A smile spread across the gambler's face. *"Eran muy crueles,"* he said. For a long moment he looked at Cole, and then he turned and walked slowly away toward the trees.

At the edge of the forest he was a shadow, and then the shadow bent, seemed to stumble. The bear paused and looked back, once, before it was gone.

Sixty-Four

Along the mountains to the west, the red New Mexico sunset was stitched by a ragged line of forest, and as he leaned against the deck railing Cole watched four nighthawks swerving erratically in the dry creekbed. An afternoon thunderstorm, mixing wet spring snow and freezing rain, had briefly rocked the high country and moved on to the east, chilling the air and leaving a cold electricity in its

241

wake. On the other side of the house, the first coyote began singing on the slopes of the Ortiz Range, a tentative cry that hung in the air for seconds before vanishing. Cole looked toward the twisting lines of a juniper across the creekbed, seeing even from two hundred yards the silver-gray pattern of the trunk. A clutter of wet snow hung on the ends of piñon and juniper branches and melted darkly into the wood of the deck. He longed to drive up to the Sandia Crest, where the quick storm would have left an inch or two of snow, and sit with his legs over the five-thousand-foot drop to watch the rain that would still be hanging over Indian country in the west.

"You could just stay," he said. "We have enough room for everyone. It would make us very happy."

"We have to go home, Grandson, we've been gone far too long. My trailer will be overgrown. As soon as Luther and your father and Alex return, we'll go back. You have a houseful with Abby and Alex."

Onatima reclined in a deck chair, a blue and green Pendleton star blanket wrapped around her and clutched to her chin. In the transitional light of evening, the old lady seemed about to disappear, and once again he had the illusion that her thin face was translucent. Beside her, Abby sat in an identical chair also wrapped in a blanket.

"Please, Grandmother?" Abby said.

Onatima smiled. "We have our own worlds, Granddaughter. We carried our people's bones a thousand days just to find a home. When so many were removed, we stayed behind. So how could we leave now? Who would talk to them out there at night if I never went home? And how would I find the path so far away? Who would tell them of their granddaughter in these strange, lightning-struck mountains?" She shook her head again. "Luther and I have our tasks back there, and your father's father has found his world there. He pretends he doesn't understand, but when the time comes he will surpass all of us. Luther has always known that. Hoey is *hoyo*, the hunter, the searcher, the one who seeks and finds." She seemed to shiver and pull the blanket still tighter, so that her face was disembodied above the green wool. "So the crux of the matter is that we have to go home."

"We'll be lost without you."

"You will do fine, Abby. You can all come and visit us." Onatima shifted her attention to Cole. "How about you, Grandson. How will you do?"

He turned around and looked first at the sky and then at the old lady. "I keep thinking about him," he said.

"Yes," she replied. "It was a brave thing saying his name like that."

He was silent for a moment, and then he shook his head. "No. It was what he wanted all the time."

Abby rose and went to stand beside her father. "They've been gone a week, so they should be nome soon. It seems like a miracle that Alex is alive."

"He'll be well soon," Onatima said. "Robert Jim told them the ceremony for Alex would take nine days. I think Hoey went because he was curious, but Luther just wanted to visit somebody who hasn't heard all his lies. Those Navajos have probably thrown that old man out by now."

Onatima stopped speaking and pointed toward the west.

Below the mountains, a broad gust of wind had lifted a layer of mist from the treetops, sending it across the valley. Against the last light of sunset, the vapor looked like a cloud of yellow-orange pollen that spread until it covered everything they could see.

It is a world so like his own, of black streams and changeless skies. His shadow falls across the town and bay, undulating with the slow waves. *Eran muy crueles.*